FINAL

HOUR

ALSO BY CARLA KOVACH

The Next Girl

HER FINAL HOUR

CARLA KOVACH

bookouture

Published by Bookouture in 2018

An imprint of StoryFire Ltd.

Carmelite House
50 Victoria Embankment
London EC4Y 0DZ

www.bookouture.com

ISBN: 978-1-78681-519-4
eBook ISBN: 978-1-78681-518-7

This book is dedicated to all those who are struggling with daily inner battles and are striving to overcome them. Whether it be anxiety, depression or addiction, don't give up the fight. X

PROLOGUE

Saturday, 14 August 1993

It had been a sticky night – so sticky, she had constantly been wiping a drizzle of sweat from her brow. She inhaled the smell of beer mixed with body odour and smiled. Turning eighteen had been brilliant, better than she'd ever imagined it would be. She went out to a pub or club most weekends and this weekend it was the Angel Arms in her hometown of Cleevesford in Warwickshire. Her friend Sarah had left her alone after pulling Jake, the boy Sarah had been after for months. No doubt they were down some alley, making out.

As last orders were called, *he* walked over to her, insisting on paying for her last drink, a pint of lager. The disco was still going through the decades and had just about reached the nineties. She'd intended to leave after the eighties had played. Jake would probably walk Sarah home after finishing up in the alley and she hadn't wanted to hang out alone for too much longer.

'Don't think because you paid for the drink it means anything,' she said. The man laughed. There was something striking about him. His piercing blue eyes felt like they were already stripping her naked. 'I mean it.'

He laughed and passed her the beer. 'It's just a beer. The rest would be up to you.'

'There is no rest,' she said as she took a swig and almost fell off the stool. She'd already had far too many and would never hear the end of it from her dad when she returned home drunk. 'Can you watch my drink while I go for a piss?'

'Of course,' he replied.

On her return she smiled and took a large swig of the pint, reaching the halfway mark. She'd show him she could handle her drink. 'What do you do?'

'I'm studying accountancy in London. I'm just back for the summer,' he replied.

She looked up, almost falling as the room took a quick turn sideways. The room hadn't moved, she'd just had too much to drink. 'Aren't you a bit old to be a student?' she slurred.

Then his sickly grin turned into a predatory look as the sound of 'All That She Wants' by Ace of Base played.

The music was quieter as he escorted her away from the pub, into the darkness of the car park. 'Get in the car, I'll drive you home,' he said in a robotic voice, or did he say that? She hadn't told him where she lived. As she stared up at the stars, she lost her balance and stumbled. It was okay, the man from the bar had her and he was taking her home. As her limbs deadened, she gave up and nestled into his neck as he took her weight.

She opened her eyes and a shot of pain flashed through her head. Birds sang and the rising sun caused her to squint. The sour taste in her mouth almost made her gag as she realised she was lying next to a pool of sick in the car park. The intense headache made her flinch.

A scruffy collie scurried towards her and began licking her face, soon followed by its owner. 'Stupid slut,' the middle-aged woman said as she put the dog on a lead and pulled it away.

Ace of Base, the robotic voice, the beer, the blue-eyed man – her mind filled with everything that had led up to her being in the pub car park, looking worse for wear. But the man was taking her home. That much she remembered. Her heart quickened. She reached down, her skirt was on but her knickers felt damp and cold. She'd urinated, or had she? Why couldn't she remember leaving the pub? Her cheeks burned. What had the woman with the dog thought? Had she had sex with the blue-eyed man in the car park of a pub? The smell of oil came back to her as she tried to stand. She remembered the creaking back and forth. Where had she been? What had he done to her? What had she done? Why couldn't she remember anything that had happened after she left the pub? She flinched, feeling a deep throbbing pain below as she got to her feet. She wanted to cry with each step. She'd never have agreed to doing that – never. What had he done to her and why had her mind gone blank?

As she stumbled towards the path home, tears fell down her cheeks. She couldn't hold them in any longer. She tried to think back, bridge the gap between her memories of being in the pub to ending up on the pavement. Her memories were gone, nothing. A car drove past, blasting out 'All That She Wants'. All that she wanted was to remember what had happened. Who was the man? She was going to find out.

CHAPTER ONE

Thursday, 12 April 2018

Melissa grappled with the duvet until she poked her head out, reaching the cool air of the bedroom. She gasped as she rode the strengthening palpitations, fighting the waves of nausea back with a few deep breaths. The wine had gone down far too well and now it was getting its revenge. She should have stopped at one glass. Staring into the darkness of her bedroom, she rubbed her sticky, sleep-filled eyes. Same story, different day. Her relationship with Darrel was slowly killing her. She needed out.

They had a lovely house in an exclusive part of the Warwickshire countryside, savings, and an investment portfolio – whatever that consisted of. She could get her divorce settlement and make a new start with their two-year-old, Mia. She could go back to working as a customer service agent in insurance, earning a living, something Darrel had never approved of in their six years of marriage, even though they'd met when she started working for his company. He'd never approve of her lover Jimmy, either, if he ever found out, but that was another story. Things were getting harder; Jimmy wanted her all to himself. Why had he complicated what they had? She checked her phone, making sure all Jimmy's messages were deleted and, as always, they were. Even after hitting the wine, she always tried her best to delete any traces of what she was up to. She tucked the phone away in its secret place. Darrel could never know.

During their marriage she knew there had been others in his life. He was forever in the pub, or attending courses and conferences that needed overnight stays. Then there was his insatiable sexual appetite, to which she knew full well she wasn't attending. Credit card receipts showed meals for two in cosy restaurants. He certainly wasn't taking the staff to those types of places. He'd never even taken her to those types of places since they'd married.

Dating had been different and so had their four years premarriage. He'd given her everything, taken her on last minute romantic escapes and bought her flowers. He'd been perfect in every way. Handsome, intelligent, successful and considerate. What happened? That was the only question she'd been unable to answer. After their wedding, their relationship declined. She thought that having Mia would bring him back to her but it had driven him further away. Her needs and wants were no longer a part of his reckoning.

She stared at the fluorescent clock. It was only nine thirty but the quietness of the house made it feel like the middle of the night. The television had been on when she'd gone to sleep. It had obviously turned itself off due to inactivity. The other side of the bed was empty and the house was silent. Darrel probably wouldn't come home until closing time at the Angel Arms. He'd taken everything he'd needed from her earlier that day and, after, he'd gone to the pub without so much as a kiss goodbye, leaving her alone, tending to the pain while looking after their child. She clenched her thighs together and wiped a tear away.

She'd originally gone along with all the things he wanted to do, hoping the fad would pass. He'd hurt her, but it had also been over quickly – and, quite often, he wouldn't bother her again for a few days. Maybe she hadn't been enough. It certainly felt that way. She'd wanted nothing more than to keep him happy. Having an affair hadn't been part of her plans. A solid marriage, a child and a nice house were all she'd originally craved. She hoped that when he was happy, he'd then think of her and her needs, but that never happened. He blamed her for not making an effort. Maybe she just didn't want to make an effort with him – maybe that was it. She brushed her fingers over her nipples and winced.

She flicked the lamp switch on and ran her fingers through her matted hair. The taste of sour wine reached the back of her dry throat. She rolled her tongue around her furry teeth. Why had she drunk the whole bottle again? It was so easy to have a couple, put Mia in her cot and finish the rest – far too easy.

She flinched as she got out of bed. Reaching between her legs, she dabbed the torn skin, almost bringing tears to her eyes. Pulling on her dressing gown, she padded down the stairs in need of a tall glass of cold cola – the only thing that helped quench her thirst after being dehydrated from wine. The wine had soothed away the pain he'd left her in but its soothing properties had soon worn off, leaving her with a sandpaper throat, a deep ache inside and a thirst for cold pop. As she reached the hallway of their large, four bedroomed, detached house she heard a chair scraping behind the kitchen door.

'Hello.' She paused and listened – silence. 'Darrel, is that you?' Her quivering fingers gripped the door handle. A shuffling noise startled her. Darrel didn't normally come in through the back door when he returned home. She went to call his name again and hesitated. Her heart began to hammer against her ribcage. If it was Darrel, he would have answered. It might not have been the most welcoming answer; it never was when he'd come home from the pub. They'd argued a lot lately, not today, but most days they argued.

The silence was broken by Mia's cries. She had to get her child and get out. Her mobile phone was in the bedroom. She ran back towards the stairs, fighting the light-headedness that threatened to knock her off balance. If she could get her phone and run to Mia's room, she could shut them both in. She could push a chest of drawers against the door and call 999.

Footsteps thundered behind her and the sound of her beating heart whooshed through her head. As she stumbled forward, the well-built intruder shoved her face into the stair carpet with ease. She went to scream but a blow to her head rendered her world dark. As she drifted into unconsciousness, the only thing she heard was her daughter's cries.

She awoke to the sounds of her little girl screaming, woozy from the blow to her head. The chair she was sitting on was being scraped across the kitchen floor. The pain to the right side of her head flashed through her neck, then finally calmed to a dull ache. The light from the cooker hood was all that illuminated the room. As the masked intruder dragged the chair again, it screeched across the floor until it stopped in front of the cooker hood. She tried to reach out but her wrists were bound to each armrest of the carver chair. She could feel the binds that tied her feet together as they rubbed the skin on her bare ankles. She tried to yell but the cloth in her mouth just shifted further back. Her heartbeat revved up, almost making her gag as she gasped for air through the fibres. *Breathe through the nose*, she told herself.

A large figure stepped into the shaft of light in front of her, casting a long shadow across the stone kitchen floor. Tears slipped from her eyes. There was no way she was going to be able to get out of the binds. All she could see was a thin gauze covering the man's eyes. She couldn't see him but he could see her perfectly. The man stood tall and broad, his red mask reminding her of the devil. Covered from head to foot in a white crime scene suit, she knew he wasn't planning on leaving any evidence behind. As her heart battered her chest, sweat began to trickle from her brow. The figure moved closer. She flinched as his gloved hand reached forward and slapped her across the face. He was so close, she could smell a hint of his musky aftershave.

'Please,' she tried to yell through the gag. She wanted to be able to speak, to reason with the intruder. Why? What had she done? Who was he? What was he going to do with her? He stared as she wriggled in the chair. She bowed to the side as he struck her again. A flash of pain shot through her head. Blood trickled past her ear. She trembled as it dripped into her lap, dotting her pale green dressing gown. His gaze moved from hers, to the top of her head and beyond. She wriggled, fighting the binds. She needed to stand, to fight back but the cord around her waist snatched her back. A flood of tears streamed down her face as her daughter's distressed cries filled the house. Was there another intruder up there with her daughter? Would they hurt Mia? Forcing her weight forward and back, she managed to build up to a rocking motion. She had to free herself, get Mia and run. The man grabbed the chair and firmly held it.

'You're finished,' he said as he held his fist to his heart before nodding. She tried turning, but it was no use. It was as if her neck was locked into place. She swallowed down the nausea as her head flashed with pain once again. As the room started to sway another pair of gloved hands brought a cord down, laying it gently under her chin. She trembled, writhed and wriggled. Panicking, she almost choked on the rag in her mouth as she inhaled it further. Tears dripped off her chin and mingled with the blood in her lap. Mia – what would happen to Mia? Her body trembled as the intruder standing behind her wrenched the cord.

As her body jerked in its confines she thought of Mia, her little brown-haired girl and the love of her life. She tried to inhale and to butt her head back. The man before her remained still as he watched her struggling for her life. She could sense his grin under the red mask as her vision became peppered. After no more than a few seconds, the world went black to the sound of Mia's cries. A final tear rolled down Melissa's cheek as the cord's pressure continued to constrict her arteries until she reached her end.

CHAPTER TWO

Darrel stopped at a lamp post and almost wanted to fling his body around it and attempt a tap dance like Gene Kelly did in *Singin' in the Rain*, but he stopped. There was no rain, there were no puddles to splash into. He could also feel the ale swishing in his stomach. It didn't stop the tune from playing out in his mind as he did a little skip off the kerb then back onto it as a car passed. His night out with his friend, Rob, had been another good one and the new barmaid, she was hot. He almost envied Rob for his way with women. He had a wife who doted on him and did everything for him and he'd had extra marital relationships, which his wife had discretely overlooked.

He hurried along the roadside and out of the town until he finally reached the house he shared with his wife, Melissa. As usual it was in darkness. He let out a laugh as he put his key in the lock and turned. 'Melissa,' he called. The only sound was his feet echoing in the hallway as he felt for the light switch. Then the silence was broken by little Mia's piercing cry.

As his eyes adjusted, he noticed the streak of blood along the hallway. His heart began to pound as he crept towards the kitchen, stepping to the side of the blood. Mia's screeches turned into a whimper. 'Melissa?' He placed his ear against the door. The only sound coming from the kitchen was the humming of the fridge. He gently opened it and his knees buckled as he saw his wife tied to one of their carver chairs under the light of the cooker hood. A piece of blue cord was looped under her chin and the raw marks around her neck told him exactly what had happened. He gazed around the room. There was no one there and the back door was closed.

When he reached his wife, he felt her wrist for a pulse but there was no heartbeat to be found. He stepped back as he stared at her expressionless face. Almost stumbling, he grabbed the worktop to steady himself as the kitchen began to sway. He'd never seen a dead person before, let alone someone so close to him.

Mia's cries filled the house. He almost fell as he ran out of the kitchen and up the stairs, passing another pool of blood. He flung open Mia's bedroom door and saw the screaming toddler standing in the middle of the room, hair soaked from all the tears. Her usual auburn wispy curls were stuck to her sweaty forehead. He scooped her up and ran downstairs and out of the house. His daughter began to shiver as he held her in the cool night air. Opening the car door, he bundled her in. With shaking hands, he grabbed his phone from his pocket and called the police.

'Emergency, which service?'

CHAPTER THREE

Gina tipped the taxi driver and dragged her case along the damp path. The security light lit up the path ahead. Ebony ran around the side of the house and began rubbing her head against Gina's legs. She'd only had a long weekend away in Mallorca. Anyone would think she'd been gone a month. 'I suppose you're sick of dried food, Puss,' she said as she put the key in the lock and entered her cold lounge. A relaxing three-day bargain break, to think and rest, was what she'd truly needed.

She thought back to the last conversation she'd had with Chris or DCI Briggs, as she'd now address him, seeing as their five-month long, casual relationship was over. Keeping it a secret from her team had been tough. She'd made him believe it was the secretive nature of their relationship that had ended things. He'd kept pressing her to talk about her past and it had seemed easier to cool things down. Discussing her relationship with her late husband Terry wasn't something she really wanted to do. Although he had seemed understanding, there are some things a person of his position would not understand. Her secrets were her secrets. They were nibbling through her flesh like worms trying to eat their way out of an apple, but, as far as she was concerned, the apple could rot and take her with it. Terry and all her tainted memories would never leave. That was her burden to bear.

As she walked over to turn the gas fire on, she yawned. She needed to sleep. She squeezed a pouch of meat into the cat's bowl and left Ebony chewing in the dark kitchen.

The flight hadn't been a long one but the wait at the airport had seemed like forever, especially after the delay. The unpacking could wait until she finished work the following day. She turned off the main light and closed the curtains before slumping on the sofa. Grabbing the snuggle blanket that was folded up on the footstool, she dragged it over her tired body. Having three days off had been wonderful, something she hadn't experienced for a while given the fact that they had been so underfunded and understaffed for such a long time. That short break had been much needed. She hadn't fully recovered from the last major case she'd worked on over the Christmas period. The break had given her time to reflect on what had happened and move forward.

She stared at the flickering flames that were slowly trying to draw her into a hypnotic trance. Through sleepy eyes, she checked her messages. Nothing from Hannah yet, but then she wouldn't expect her daughter to call at this time as her little granddaughter Gracie would be in bed, and the young mother would no doubt be exhausted. Mind you, her daughter could be in any number of moods. She expected nothing. Her finger brushed past the last message that Briggs had sent.

I miss you and I really thought we had something good. I won't message you again but I wanted you to know, I'd love it if we could talk. I need closure, need to know what I did wrong. X.

She wouldn't know where to begin. Had he done anything wrong? How would she start to explain? *Yes, when policing was only a pipe dream, my ex-husband would beat and rape me. Yes, he died after falling down the stairs one night after drinking too much – oh and I helped him on his way.* It was easier to say that the relationship wasn't working because it was unprofessional, her being a DI and seeing her DCI. Besides, if the powers above found out, one of them would most likely be transferred. Her job in the little town of Cleevesford meant more to her than any relationship, especially one that she was never going to give her all to.

Her head nestled into the cushion and her focus moved back to the flickering flames. As her breathing deepened and the fire's warmth flooded through her body, she sank into a restful slumber.

She stirred and opened her eyes as the phone rang. Maybe Hannah was in one of her good moods after all. 'Hi, love,' she said as she closed her eyes and held her phone to her ear, not wanting to fully wake up.

'Hi, love to you too, guv. Holiday's over,' Detective Sergeant Jacob Driscoll said. 'Welcome back.'

She opened her eyes and sat up. 'Sorry, I'm half asleep. I thought you were Hannah. I've only just walked through the door and I'm still on holiday until seven in the morning.'

'Sorry to bear this news. Briggs has called in all units, as there's been a major incident. Wyre and O'Connor have been called to the scene too. Did you have a nice time by the way? Dancing, cocktails?'

Gina checked her watch. It was just gone eleven. 'I got some sleep if that counts as nice. What's happened?'

'A woman, Melissa Sanderson, thirty-five years old, has been found dead in her home on the outskirts of Cleevesford. The call was made by the woman's husband, Darrel Sanderson. He called 999 about twenty minutes ago. He'd just got in from the pub. Crime Scene Investigators are on the way too. I'll meet you there.'

'Bloody hell. I'll head straight over. Message me the address and postcode.' She rubbed her eyes and stared ahead. The holiday was well and truly over and it was back to work.

'Get this, guv. It looks like strangulation from what's been reported so far. She's been tied to a chair in the kitchen. I'll send you that message now. On my way. See you there.'

Gina went through to the kitchen and downed a glass of water. She patted the feeding cat's head, grabbed her car keys and ran out of the front door. As she thought of the scene she'd be entering, she shivered. Strangulation, tied to a chair – a brutal murder.

CHAPTER FOUR

Selina heard her husband, Rob, slipping in through the utility room, almost silently removing his shoes and overcoat before entering the kitchen. He crept past their American style fridge freezer and skirted around the large island, being careful not to tap any of the stools. Selina continued straightening up her dress and buttoning up her fine knit cardigan. She always wanted to look her best for when Rob returned. He placed his arms around her waist. 'You made me jump,' she lied as she turned and stood on her tiptoes to receive his kiss. She inhaled the rosy perfume that followed him as he continued kissing her. It definitely wasn't her scent. Feeling him harden beneath his jeans, she glanced into his blue eyes before turning away. 'Your dinner's almost done and you have guests in the drawing room. Do you want to eat now or later?' Sometimes he wanted to eat, other times he didn't, but she always had a meal waiting for him.

He shrugged. She gazed up at him with her large hazel eyes. She knew he'd like to take her there and then, while thoughts of another woman were still fresh in his mind. She needed to let him. She needed to banish thoughts of other women from his mind, make sure all he thought about was her. She lifted the hem of her dress, bit her bottom lip and bent over the worktop. She still had it. He needed her and she knew it – guests or no guests. She'd never stopped him before and she knew he would be quick and quiet. As she turned, her mouth opened, inviting his tongue to find hers. He slipped down her lacy pants and unzipped his jeans. Within moments, he'd closed his eyes as he took her against the worktop. Always with closed eyes. She wanted him to look at her while they were making love. As he reached his end, she wanted to cry. Instead, she made a discreet moan in his ear. That was all he needed. She kissed him on the head and quickly moved aside, patting her hair back down. She would be the only woman in his mind now and that's all that mattered.

'Your friends are waiting. What did you say about dinner?' she asked as she forced a smile and pulled her pants up.

'I'll have it when they're gone,' he said.

Although she wished he only ever thought of her, she continued smiling as she arranged the cupcakes on the platter. All the effort she made was for him and she wished he'd show a little more appreciation. She hoped he'd like the blend of lavender colour she'd managed to mix, and how it perfectly complemented the yellow flowers she'd moulded out of icing. She wanted him to appreciate the pie she'd made just for him, and the work that had gone into perfecting her pastry skills. Their house always looked like a show home. Some recognition would be welcome.

Voices came from the lounge. He poked his head around the corner and came back. 'Selina? What have you not done that you should've done?'

Her gaze travelled from her clothes, to the worktop, to his almost-made dinner. The Jersey Royals were nearly cooked and she'd planned to finish them as soon as he declared it to be food time. The home-made steak pie was on a low heat in the oven, ready to ramp up at the same time the potatoes went on. Timing was everything. The carrot batons she'd so expertly prepared were all the same length and were parboiled. Ten minutes would be all it took from his request for dinner, to dinner being plated and on the table. As she passed the bi-fold doors, she checked her appearance in the reflection. The dress she'd changed into just before the guests had arrived was one of Rob's favourites.

He always said baby blue suited her. Her travelling gaze met his. 'Is my make-up smudged? You want the poker table setting up?'

'Guests?' She placed her hand over her mouth. He slapped her bottom as she jogged past him, her glossy hair swinging as she sashayed out of the kitchen and along the corridor of their mock Georgian mansion, before entering the drawing room. She'd play the good hostess as she always did.

'What can I get you all to drink?'

'I think we should crack open the brandy,' Dan replied as he smoothed his comb-over.

'Brandy on ice coming up,' she said with a smile. 'How are we all tonight?'

Lee nodded and Ben smiled. 'We're all good, Selina,' Dan replied. 'Better for having seen you. It's always a pleasure.'

She smiled and blushed, enjoying the compliment. Since her two children had grown up and left home, she'd felt a little lost. They'd always appreciated everything she'd done for them. She just wished her husband did too; and that he wouldn't come home smelling of another woman's perfume. She always tried her best to be his all. She didn't need a fancy job, a degree or the opportunity to go out and play at being a ladette. She just wanted to be a good wife and mother. He was her life. She made the home the beating heart of their lives. She kept him happy. And he'd wanted her as soon as he came home. That said a lot. If he'd been with another woman, he wouldn't have wanted her – would he? Doubts flashed through her mind as she thought of the Viagra he kept in his wallet. He must have taken a pill recently to have been so quickly aroused by her when he arrived home. Had he taken the pill to screw someone else, then got turned down? Was she his second choice? It wouldn't be the first time. Thoughts dashed through her mind. Was it someone he'd met at the pub? Someone who worked for him? She'd find out who he was trying so hard to impress. He wasn't fooling her. The weight loss, the extra hours in their home gym, the new fitted shirts. It all led to one conclusion.

Re-entering the kitchen, she grabbed the brandy from the drinks cabinet and poured a perfectly matched measure into four glasses.

'My little perfectionist,' Rob said as he leaned against the worktop, smoking a cigar.

She added two lumps of ice to each glass and put them onto a tray along with the cupcakes. She passed him a brandy and wandered back to the drawing room.

'Thanks, Selina. Beautiful cakes,' Lee said as he took a glass from the tray. She beamed a smile at him. The other two took a drink and the group continued talking. 'Is Rob around?'

'Of course I am.' He entered the large room. The huge swags of curtains reached the floor and shut out the rest of the world. Selina stood back as they all clinked glasses. 'Selina, would you leave us be? We need to talk.'

She brushed her hair behind her tiny ears and smiled as she left. Closing the door, she placed her ear against the grain, listening from the hallway. All she heard was muffled voices. She hated it when he shut her out like that. They were meant to be partners in everything and it felt as if she was slowly losing him.

Her heartbeat quickened as the doorbell rang. She almost skidded along the hallway, reaching the kitchen as Rob stepped out of the room, and opened the front door. 'Come through,' he called. Her husband led someone into the drawing room. As he closed the door, she crept back and resumed her position.

Startled by a loud bang, she jumped. It sounded like someone slamming a drink down. She hoped it wasn't on the antique sideboard that had been in her family for three generations and she hoped whatever had been slammed had missed her Tiffany lamp.

She moved her hair from her face and leaned in again, her ear almost sucking the door. After a few muffled words, the sound of their laughter filled the hallway. 'Selina,' Rob called. Her heart skipped a beat. She combed her hair with her fingers and counted to five before opening the door.

He called her over and whispered in her ear. 'You can go and clean yourself up and I'll have dinner in a short while.' She knew full well what a short while meant, but she'd wait for him, as she always did.

She gazed at the furniture, looking for damage. Only one thing was out of place. She snatched her paperweight and returned it to its usual place. It belonged next to her Tiffany lamp. It couldn't be out of place – nothing could. Everything had a home. She gazed at the sideboard, looking for any evidence of damage. She breathed a sigh of relief, it was all intact.

'Oh, get our guest a drink. Bring him a brandy will you?'

'Will do.' Her gaze met the new man's blue eyes.

CHAPTER FIVE

Gina could see all the commotion from afar. Portable lights shone through the trees that lined the driveway. A small forensics team had gathered outside the house as they waited for further instruction. Police were applying an outer cordon to keep the public from entering the scene, not that there were any members of the public hanging around in the quiet rural location. The most attention they'd attract in these parts would be late night drivers' rubbernecking as they passed.

Gina watched as the man sitting in the back of PC Smith's car cradled a toddler. He looked awkward as he tried to position the fidgeting child. Smith passed him a blanket. It was all happening. She pulled up alongside DS Jacob Driscoll's car and stepped out into the cool night.

'That's your holiday cut short, guv.' Jacob rubbed his eyes as he approached her.

'Aren't they all? I must say, this was a bit of a shocker. I'd only just walked through my door as you called. Anyway, no rest for the wicked, as they say. When you called me you told me that the husband was first on the scene,' Gina said.

'Yes. Darrel Sanderson. He's sitting in Smith's car at the moment, with his daughter. He arrived home just after ten thirty. He'd been out to the Angel Arms. Smith was the first officer on the scene. The ambulance beat him by a couple of minutes and the paramedic confirmed that Mrs Sanderson was indeed dead. Smith then called Crime Scene Investigation and here we all are now.'

'Who's the Crime Scene Manager?'

'Bernard Small. Here he comes now. Crime Scene Investigator Keith Freeman is working the scene too.'

Bernard stepped around the side of the building as he zipped up his protective suit. He moved his beard cover aside and waved Gina over.

'Bernard, DI Gina Harte. We've met before. Is there anything you can tell me so far?' she asked as she walked towards him.

He straightened his back and towered over her with his wiry physique. His unkempt grey beard was half tucked under the top of his forensics suit. 'We haven't been here long but I'll give you what we have so far. I haven't entered the kitchen, we were waiting for you to arrive but I have looked through the kitchen window and lighting has been rigged up in the back garden. The victim, whom we believe to be Mrs Melissa Sanderson, is tied to a kitchen chair. Her feet are bound to the chair legs and her arms are bound to the chair arms. She is also tied around the waist to the back of the chair. I suggest that we all tread the route we've been taking, just follow everyone else.'

Keith and a couple of Bernard's team passed them, following the route, and waited on the back patio, all dressed to investigate. Another member of the team met them with a couple of cameras. One for the photos and one for the video log.

'Can we get the stepping plates put in place?' Gina asked.

'I'll hurry them along.' Bernard waved his arm, ordering one of the crime scene assistants to follow his instruction. The suited assistant nodded as she passed, then headed back to the van. Gina turned to PC Smith who was standing, making notes by the hedge.

'Smith, are you running the scene log? Take a note of everyone's name, shoe size etcetera and we need to organise elimination prints for Mr Sanderson. You know the drill. Is there someone monitoring the cordon?'

'Yes, ma'am. There are a couple of officers heading there now.' Smith walked towards Gina, frowning as he approached the scene.

'Will you organise someone from your team to collect witness statements from neighbours? I know the houses are spread apart but someone may have seen something.'

'Certainly will,' he replied as he left.

Bernard handed Gina a forensic suit, along with boot covers and a mask. She began pulling the suit over her jeans as she approached the back door and looked through the window. Gina could see that there was blood surrounding a wound on the right hand side of the woman's head, and it was matted into her hair.

She opened the back door. Her heart began to pound as she stared at the body that was clearly lit by the bright cooker hood and the light seeping in from the half-closed door to the hallway. She'd seen many crime scenes but each and every one still had an impact. To see the aftermath of human suffering was never easy. The dead woman was bound to the chair and was slightly slumped to the left. A strip of blue washing line cord was loosely looped around her neck. Gina stepped as close to the back worktop in the large kitchen as she could, trying to avoid contaminating the scene. Bernard followed her close behind, carrying a torch.

'Bernard, could you please step through into the lounge, dining room and hall and tell me what you see?'

Bernard and one of the assistants carefully continued around the body, then through to the lounge and back through the hallway, flashing the torch into all angles of the rooms as they passed through.

'There is blood and hair on the stairs and a few trail marks of blood along the hallway. Apart from that there is nothing out of place. The front door is closed. I don't want to tread the stairs until we've taken samples and thoroughly searched this area.'

Bernard came back to the kitchen, followed by his assistant.

'So she possibly received the blow to the head on the stairs and was dragged to the kitchen, where she was bound to a kitchen chair?'

'I can only report what I see. There is a blood trail.'

'Any ideas on cause of death as yet?'

'Not confirmed until we do the post-mortem. As you can see, there is a piece of blue washing line around her neck and ligature marks on her neck. We haven't as yet found any evidence of forced entry either but the back door was unlocked. My team will need to go through everything. We will get you more information as soon as we've had a chance to process the scene.'

'Time of death?'

'The paramedic said the body was still warm. Given the temperature in here and the temperature taken on arrival, we estimate time of death to be within the past two hours.'

'Thank you. Appreciate what you've given me so far. I'll be back in a short while.' She stepped into the garden and took a deep breath. Gina walked on the freshly laid out stepping plates until she reached the edge of the cordon on the front drive. She watched as Smith continued logging notes while directing another officer to set up an inner cordon. Wyre pulled up and entered the scene. Gina nodded in her direction before turning her attention to the man sitting in the back of the police car.

Jacob walked over. 'Just to update you, Mr Sanderson called us at twenty-two forty. When Smith arrived, he was apparently cradling his crying child in his car. That is where he waited until Smith and the officers arrived.'

'We'll need him to come in for a formal interview. Did the paramedics check him over?'

'Yes. He's in shock but he is responding. His child is fine, doesn't realise what's happened, the poor thing.'

'I'll have a quick word then we should get back to the station. I want him interviewed and we need to check out all alibis and witnesses that have seen him tonight.'

Gina headed towards the police car and opened the back door. 'Mr Sanderson, I'm Detective Inspector Gina Harte. Can I have a quick word?'

'My wife, she's gone. Who did this to her?' he cried as a tear rolled down his cheek.

'That's what we're trying to find out. We will need you to come to the station and give a formal statement.'

'Do I have to do that now?' The little girl began to bawl and the man held her in his arms and stroked her soft brown hair. 'My daughter's only two and she knows something is wrong.'

Gina spotted a red scratch on the little girl's arm. She reached over and pointed to the scratch. 'Are you hurt?' she asked the child. The little girl lifted her arm up further and Gina noticed some bruising just above the scratch.

'When I went up to her, she was crying. She'd climbed over her bed guard and was banging on the bedroom door. She's fine apart from she's scratched and bruised her arm climbing out of bed and it's a little sore, isn't it, Mia? She does that quite a lot.' He stroked the child's damp fringe and kissed her forehead.

People walked back and forth between the house, the vans and the back garden.

'Do you have anyone who's able to look after her while you come to the station?'

'My brother Alan is on his way. He lives in Redditch so he won't be long.' As he finished his sentence a man in his early fifties, wearing an outdoor leisure jacket was trying to climb under the outer cordon. Gina left Mr Sanderson and ran over to the man who was talking with a PC.

'Sorry, sir, you must stay behind the cordon.'

'So I've just been told. That's my brother and little niece in the car. I can't believe what's happened,' he said as a tear seeped from the corner of his eye. 'Is Mia okay?'

'The little one is fine. I'm so sorry for what's happened to your family, I really am. We need to take your brother to Cleevesford Police Station to give a statement. Would you be able to come along and take care of your niece?'

'Of course. He's not under arrest, is he?'

'No. We need to formally interview him, that's all. I'm going to head there now. Can you follow us there, Mr Sanderson?'

The man choked on his words as he fought the urge to sob. Gina pulled a pack of tissues from her pocket and passed one to him. 'Thanks.' He wiped his wet face and blew his nose. As she waited for the man to compose himself, she heard footsteps approaching from behind. She turned and saw Darrel carrying his daughter.

'Can I go to the station with my brother?' he asked.

'Of course.'

She watched as Darrel handed Mia to his brother and went to his car to get her car seat. Alan hugged the little girl as Darrel fastened the car seat in the back of his brother's car. Shedding more tears, Alan strapped Mia in and closed the door.

'Are we heading back to the station?' Jacob asked as he neared her.

Gina ignored him, her focus remaining on Darrel Sanderson as he got into the car. 'Where did you say the husband was tonight?'

Jacob pulled his notebook from his pocket. 'Angel Arms, with his friend, Robert Dixon. He was there all evening but we still need to verify that.'

'Wyre, can you tell O'Connor to meet you at the Angel now and report back as soon as you've verified Mr Sanderson's where-abouts? We need to check out his alibi. I want it verified sooner rather than later and double check everything. I want the CCTV checked. If he so much as stepped outside for a cigarette or went for a slash, I want it noted and I want to know for how long.'

'On it, guv. I'll meet you back at the station when I'm done.'

Gina stared into the darkness as Alan Sanderson's car disappeared into the distance. She checked her watch. She didn't have much time to speak with Bernard and Keith but she needed whatever information they had to offer. She hurried around to the back of the house, knowing that Darrel Sanderson would be waiting for her at the station.

CHAPTER SIX

Gina flung her coat over the back of a chair and darted across her office to grab the ringing phone. She placed the unappealing machine coffee on her desk and picked up.

'Harte. I'm putting you in charge of tonight's incident. You're the SIO. I want to know what's happening as always, but it's your show.'

She could barely reply. Briggs was making her Senior Investigating Officer. Her stomach fluttered. Had he chosen her because they had been in a relationship? If so, she didn't want it. As with all her progressions in the police, she wanted to know that she had truly earned them. 'It's not because—'

'It's because you're a great detective and you're more than ready for this. Don't insult me by saying another word.' He hung up, leaving her standing there holding the receiver with her mouth open.

She stared out of the window. Squad cars were lined up against the back wall, ready to be called out for action. She bit her bottom lip as she replayed Briggs's last few words. She had insulted him. Reality suddenly hit her. She was SIO. This was a huge step in her career. She'd be managing her own budget, leading the investigation and having the final say on everything to do with the case.

Within three hours, she had stepped off the plane, been home, attended a crime scene and ended up back at the station to find out she was SIO on a major crime. She said the words *Senior*

Investigating Officer again in her head and smiled. Briggs had always declared himself SIO when it came to major crime. This was a big extension of his trust in her.

Apart from tonight's incident, the station had seemed oddly quiet. The past few weeks had been mostly filled with volume crimes, such as break-ins, car damage and a handful of minor assaults that had been easy to solve, but this, this was big. On first instance it appeared that Melissa Sanderson had been found in her home by her husband, and she'd been bound and strangled following an already violent attack.

Why would anyone want to harm Mrs Sanderson? Find the motive and that leads to the killer. Gina shivered as she thought of the perpetrator's knuckles brushing Mrs Sanderson's neck as they pulled the cord.

Were they looking for someone without a conscience or was Mrs Sanderson constantly in their thoughts? Gina thought back to the look in her ex-husband Terry's eyes as he reached for her when he was tumbling down the stairs to his death. Her mouth went dry. She wasn't letting Terry into her thoughts tonight. She had a conscience, not like some of the people she'd dealt with.

Time of death. Between eight thirty and ten thirty, give or take. Could the injuries have occurred before Mr Sanderson left for the pub? Why Mrs Sanderson? And what did the perpetrator assault her with? She quickly submitted a form to the coroner and placed her computer into sleep mode.

Gina grabbed her drink and headed straight towards the interview room, almost colliding with Jacob as she turned a corner.

'We're ready, guv,' Jacob said.

'Where's Sanderson's brother and daughter?'

'We put them in a room at the end of the corridor for now. One of Smith's team is seeing to their needs.'

Gina looked past him. The door to the interview room was closed and she knew Darrel Sanderson would be nervously awaiting her arrival. 'Great. I want his drinking buddy, Robert Dixon, checked out too. We need to confirm that he was with Darrel Sanderson tonight. Then we need to crossmatch any information that Wyre and O'Connor come back with after speaking to the landlord at the Angel, our friend Samuel Avery.'

'I'll get Dixon's number from Darrel Sanderson and I'll be right with you. We'll contact Mr Dixon.'

Gina opened the door to the sparsely furnished room and placed her notebook on the desk, taking a seat opposite Darrel Sanderson. There was a coldness about him. Not a muscle in his face moved. He twiddled his fingers and stared into his lap. As he looked up, he wiped his eye. She couldn't tell if his eye had been wet but he looked tired. She noted down his full name and personal details on the witness statement form while she waited for Jacob to return. 'We'll just wait for DS Driscoll, then we'll get started.'

'I can't believe this has happened. What happens next?' he asked as he fidgeted in the plastic chair. The overweight man sat in a hunched position, forcing his stomach to fall over the top of his trousers. She could tell from the tightness of his jacket that he wasn't comfortable. He pulled his chair closer to the table, awaiting her questions.

'Well, the crime scene investigators are at your home and they will work through everything, hopefully finding forensic evidence as to who murdered your wife.' Gina grabbed a leaflet from the shelf to her left and handed it to Sanderson. 'I thoroughly recommend you contact Victim Support. You don't have to go through this on your own,' she said as she analysed his reaction. He stared at the text on the front of the pamphlet.

'I have family. I don't need it.' He placed the pamphlet on the table.

Jacob entered and sat beside Gina.

'Mr Sanderson, this is DS Jacob Driscoll and I'm DI Gina Harte. We'll try to make this as brief as possible as we know you need to be with your brother and daughter at a time like this. From the initial call that you made, we know you were the first witness on the scene. Please tell us what happened, as it happened, and in your own words,' Gina said. She leaned back and watched as Jacob took the form from her and sat poised with a pen in hand.

'I'd been out since about seven. I meet up with my mate Rob quite often and mostly at the Angel Arms as it's fairly local for both of us. It's a bit of a walk but we don't need taxis. We talked and had a few pints, then I left just after ten. It takes me about twenty minutes to walk home. I followed the High Street through Cleevesford until I reached the edge of town. The path ends there and I began walking on the road alongside the woodland. I remember getting nearer to the house and all seemed as it normally did. The house was in darkness. My wife hasn't been too well lately, I suspected she was in bed.'

'What was wrong with her?'

Darrel unzipped the jacket he was wearing and let out a deep breath. 'She wasn't physically ill.'

'Go on.' Gina waited for the man to begin speaking again.

He hesitated and looked at Gina. 'She'd been drinking a bit more than usual. I think she was depressed. I tried to talk to her about it but she never wanted to talk. She always jumped down my throat. Things were getting bad.' He paused and looked to the side. 'I also think she'd been seeing someone else. I wanted to save our marriage. I tried my best, you know, well I did everything a man can do. She was never happy, but I never hurt her – never.' For the first time she saw what she perceived to be genuine emotion in Darrel's face. He began picking his thumbnail and biting the skin around the edge.

'Do you know who she was seeing?'

Darrel stared at the wall and shook his head. 'I wish I had known. The only clue I found were a pack of unused condoms in her bag. We don't need condoms.' He cleared his throat and ran his fingers through his thin, greying hair. 'I had a vasectomy after Mia was born. Melissa had suffered with the most horrendous post-natal depression and we said we'd never have another child.' Darrel's face had turned a crimson colour as he spoke about his suspicions.

'Going back to when you arrived home, tell me what happened?'

He bit his thumbnail and flicked it on the floor, before rubbing his eyes. Gina spotted a bead of sweat forming just under his hairline. 'As I approached the door, I heard Mia crying. That in itself was nothing unusual, she wakes up a lot during the night, never been a good sleeper. I used my key to open the front door and turned the hall light on as I always do. It was then I noticed a streak of red across the hall floor, leading through to the kitchen. I continued walking in silence. I called her name. I thought, maybe she'd had a bit too much to drink, fallen over and hurt herself. It wouldn't be the first time. I was almost angry with her for leaving our daughter crying and all the drinking she does – did.' A stream of tears began to fall down his cheeks and land on the desk.

'I know this is hard, Mr Sanderson. What has happened to your wife is truly awful and we need to catch who did this. What do you remember after that?'

The man wiped the tears with the sleeve of his jacket and looked directly at Gina. 'I opened the kitchen door and she was…' He began to sob.

Gina slid a box of tissues across the table. Maybe she'd wrongly judged him about being cold. She'd seen the way shock developed in some people. In her experience, sometimes people blocked things out for a while but when realisation hit, they let it all go. 'This is really helping us, Mr Sanderson.'

'I saw her under the light of the cooker hood. She was positioned in one of our carver chairs. Bound with something on her wrists and feet. A blue cord, like washing line, was loosely drooped around her neck and her head was covered in blood. It was at that point, I panicked. I ran over and checked her pulse but felt nothing. I had to get my daughter out of the house. I remember feeling like I was going to pass out. My beating heart felt as though it were coming out of my mouth. I was scared, so scared. I thought the person who did this to my wife might still be in the house. I ran up the stairs, grabbed Mia from her bed and left. I couldn't think of where to go. Mia was cold in just her pyjamas, so I sat in the car and called the police.' The man broke down and placed his head and hands on the desk as he sobbed.

'Mr Sanderson, I'm just a bit confused as to what you just said.' Jacob looked at her inquisitively. The man lifted his head and looked up with red-rimmed eyes. 'When you spoke to me in the police car, back at the house, you said that Mia had scratched and bruised her arm by climbing out of her bed, and she'd been banging on her bedroom door. Just now, you said you grabbed her out of her bed.'

'Are you accusing me of something, Inspector?'

'Of course not, Mr Sanderson. You are a witness. I'm just trying to establish what happened, that's all.'

The man stopped sobbing and wiped his eyes. The veins in his neck began to protrude. 'I was out all evening, I didn't do this. The truth is I can't remember, it all happened so fast. I think I grabbed her from the floor by her cot. It's all such a blur. Mia climbs over her bed guard quite often. Sometimes she does, sometimes she doesn't. I ran down the stairs and burst through the front door while holding her in my arms, after just seeing my wife like that in the kitchen. I was running for my life and hers. I would never hurt my daughter. Now, do your job and find my wife's murderer.'

Gina watched as Jacob made copious notes. Had he been lying or had his answer reflected that of a confused mind that had been through a horrific night? Had he wanted his cheating wife dead?

'When you left earlier that night, how did your wife seem?'

He took a deep breath and continued. 'She was tired. She was lying in bed and Mia was asleep. She said she was going to have a bath and watch TV in bed. That's what she normally did when I went to the pub.' The man paused. 'I want to go now. I need to be with my daughter. I have to tell the rest of the family what's happened. As you can appreciate, I have a long night ahead of me. There's nothing more I can tell you.' He zipped his jacket up and stood.

'Do you know of anyone who would want to hurt your wife, Mr Sanderson?'

'No, not at all, but as I said, I think she was seeing someone. You should try him.'

'When did she see him?'

'Look. I need to be with my daughter.'

'Please sit down and answer the question, Mr Sanderson.' He stared at her as he slumped back into the chair. There was something about his reddened face, his stare and his demeanour that wasn't sitting well with Gina. He didn't like being told what to do.

'She quite often drops Mia off at her friend Su's house and who knows where she went then. I only started suspecting when I found the condoms. This could've been going on for ages. Her full name is Suzanne Barker. Try contacting her, she might know who killed my wife. Ask her,' he said as he slammed his fist onto the table. 'That's all I'm saying. Unless I'm under arrest, I want to be with my daughter.'

Jacob noted Suzanne Barker's name down and placed lines through the empty space at the bottom of the interview notes and pushed the statement across the table towards Mr Sanderson. 'Can you please read and sign the statement.' The man scanned the three pages before him and signed at the bottom of the page.

'If there's anything else you can think of, please let me know. Any little thing that will help us to catch your wife's killer is important, anything.' Gina passed him one of her cards and smiled. 'Jacob will reunite you with your brother and daughter now. We'll be in touch. Will you be staying with your brother, Alan Sanderson?' The man nodded as he stood. 'We'll need to take his address before you go, to keep you informed of any updates, and we'll need Suzanne Barker's too.'

Jacob led him out and Darrel slammed the door as he left. Gina grabbed the notes and headed back to her office, ready to enter them onto the system. She remembered Bernard saying that the body was still warm. They needed to confirm when Darrel had arrived at the pub. Had it been just after seven? Or was it a little later? Could he have had the opportunity to kill Melissa before he went out?

She needed O'Connor and Wyre back with information on his whereabouts. She needed the Angel Arms landlord, Samuel Avery's statement and that of Darrel's friend, Robert Dixon. And was his daughter in her bed when he went up those stairs or was she out of her bed and banging on the door?

CHAPTER SEVEN

Friday, 13 April 2018

'As you know, I'm Senior Investigating Officer on this case and I need everyone focused. Mrs Sanderson was murdered in her own home and I want whoever did this caught quickly.' Gina grabbed a biscuit from DC Harry O'Connor's cluttered desk and swigged her coffee.

He ran his hands over his shiny head and sat up. 'Congratulations, guv. Hear, hear.'

Gina smiled and continued. 'Thank you. Right, I know it's the middle of the night but there's no time to waste. As we know these hours are crucial. The victim is a Mrs Melissa Elizabeth Sanderson, thirty-five years old. Full-time mum to two-year-old Mia. I've just come off the phone to Bernard, who is the Crime Scene Manager, and who's still managing the scene. Their preliminary findings show there is a small pool of blood on the stairs – starting on the tenth step to be precise. A thin blood trail leads down the stairs, along the hallway and into the kitchen. It is highly likely that this is Mrs Sanderson's blood but we don't have the results to confirm this as yet. Bernard called me to confirm that she had been hit on the right side of her head with a blunt object. This object has not been found at the scene yet, but Bernard's team are still searching.'

Wyre looked up. 'How was she found?'

'Coming onto the body. She was positioned upright in a chair, in the kitchen. Her wrists and ankles were bound by cord to the chair legs and arms. She had the same cord around her waist and around her neck. At first glance it appears to be washing line cord. We can confirm that there are ligature marks around her neck too. All I have is in this report to date, including the interview with Darrel Sanderson. I have entered this information into the system so you can all access it. Here's a printout too.' She handed each of the detectives a bound file. 'Wyre, O'Connor, did you manage to verify the whereabouts of Darrel Sanderson this evening?'

'Yes, guv. We've just got back. We went to the Angel Arms and spoke to Jill Keller and Charlene Lynch – the bar staff – and Samuel Avery – the landlord,' Wyre answered for her and her colleague.

'That lecherous slimeball still makes my skin crawl. I wouldn't trust anything he says after the last case. He enjoys playing the police,' Gina said.

'You're right about him being lecherous,' Paula Wyre replied. 'I caught him looking me up and down at one point. Anyway, both Charlene and Samuel state without any doubt that Darrel Sanderson and Robert Dixon met in the pub about twenty past seven. Sanderson stayed until a few minutes past ten and Dixon left about twenty minutes later. I also checked the CCTV and can confirm that they never left the building during those times. Neither smoke so they stayed inside all evening until they left to go home.'

Gina looked down. It was a long shot thinking he could've sneaked out to commit such a crime and got back without being noticed. He'd been in the pub all evening.

'Did you speak to Dixon?'

'Yes.' Wyre smoothed down her black trousers. 'We called at his house after we'd been to the Angel and he was in with his wife, Selina Dixon. He was just finishing a meal when we arrived, which was a bit odd as we were so late. I'll update the system in a moment but, in a nutshell, he confirmed that he too was in the Angel Arms all evening with Mr Sanderson. They had a couple of drinks, did a lot of talking and apparently talked business too. Mr Sanderson runs a business called, Cleevesford Insurance Company, and has a shop just off the High Street, employing the best part of thirty people. Dixon was looking to get his insurance renewed for his electrical parts company, and they were talking shop for a while too.'

'Did he mention any of their personal conversation?' She wanted to know more about Sanderson, drill a little deeper into his life.

'Not really. He said they normally just talked about work and sometimes they had a game of darts when they met at the pub – but not that evening. They talked about football as they were both fans of Aston Villa.' Wyre looked up as she finished relaying her notes.

As Smith entered the room he rubbed his tired eyes.

'You're back,' Gina said. 'Any news from the door to door?'

'Apart from everyone being scared witless, no. It wasn't so much door to door, but street to street. How the other half live. Anyway, no one saw a thing. Most people were in with their curtains closed, watching TV. Not a thing came out of our investigations.'

'Thank you.'

'I'll grab a coffee and then I'll be with you.' Smith removed his hat and headed towards the kitchenette.

'So we have no witnesses then. On the suspect front, we need to find out if Mrs Sanderson was seeing someone and who this person is. We need to speak to her friend Suzanne Barker.' Gina looked up. 'Could Mr Sanderson have got someone else to do his dirty work? Have a look at the interview notes and let's look into everyone he knows, his friends, acquaintances, neighbours, everyone.' She finished the last of the biscuit and walked over to the window. 'I'll get started on prepping the incident room. There will be no sleep for a while. Grab some coffee and get started.'

O'Connor and Wyre turned their chairs and faced their computers.

Jacob followed Gina to the incident room. She inhaled the damp musty air. A streaky brown patch led from ceiling to floor, a reminder of a small leak that developed in January and had never been painted over since the roof had been fixed. 'It stinks in here, guv.'

She grabbed a can of old air freshener and passed it over. 'This should mask the problem for now.'

She'd give it an hour and chase Bernard for more of his findings. She wrote Melissa Sanderson's name in the centre of the board and jotted down the rest of the information they had so far.

Her stomach turned. Briggs would be in soon to see how things were going. She'd have to face him sooner or later. She just wished she could have had a few more hours to prepare herself.

CHAPTER EIGHT

The early morning sun's rays splayed across the far wall of the incident room. Bernard had emailed her some of the crime scene photos and they'd also sent a photo they'd found of Mrs Sanderson before her attack. She stuck the photo to the incident board just above the case notes.

The dawn chorus filled the room through the open window. Briggs entered and dropped the blind, shutting out most of the fresh air and light. It wouldn't be long before the stale smell returned.

Her grumbling stomach flipped. She was still fully aware she had hurt him and there was nothing she could say to make things better.

'Any more news?'

'Only what we've reported so far, sir. I'm awaiting further information from Bernard. It's been a long night for them and us. O'Connor, could you give him a call, see if there's any further updates?'

O'Connor nodded as he picked up the phone.

Gina turned away and yawned. A couple of times in the night, she'd fallen asleep at her desk. She watched as Briggs walked past her and began looking at the photos pinned up on the incident board. His hair looked more unkempt than usual, almost like it needed a trim or just a good comb. He rubbed his stubbly chin as his gaze fell onto the photo of Mrs Sanderson. His creased suit jacket showed her all she needed to know about how he was coping with their breakup.

'I'm back.' Wyre entered, having popped home for a shower and freshen up. Her crisp white shirt with starched collar and cuffs made everyone else look like they'd been on a heavy night out.

Gina stared down at her dark jeans and the crumpled pale blue T-shirt that she'd been wearing on the plane under her comfy zip-up sweater. The grey suit jacket she always kept at work now replaced the zip-up sweater, making her feel a little more professional. She lifted her arm up and the smell of sweat hit her. She needed to pop home for a shower soon.

O'Connor placed the receiver down. 'Bernard's calling me back in a moment. He's just in the middle of something.' His phone beeped and he left the room.

Gina looked up, trying to catch Briggs's attention. She needed to know that he didn't hate her after she'd ignored his message. As he turned, her heart sank. Did she care for him? Did she ever love him? She swallowed and looked away. Images of Terry flashed through her mind. He'd never let her go. Moving on would mean creating more lies to live with. One big lie was enough.

Briggs looked back, catching her stare. Her heart pounded as she cleared her throat and turned away. Things weren't going to be easy. Wyre looked up. Had she noticed? Gina felt a stickiness developing in her armpits. She wanted to scratch them and wipe them clean. Her body was giving away all her secrets. She undid the button of her jacket and took a deep breath. Wyre was looking back at her screen. They hadn't been rumbled.

She turned back to face him. 'Sir, would you send some basic information to the press? They are used to dealing with you. We need to warn the general public to remain vigilant, keep their doors locked, come forward if they've seen—'

'I know what to say, I've been doing this for many years now.'

'Sorry, sir, I know you have.'

Briggs nodded as he left the room and headed towards his office.

Wyre swivelled around in her chair, swinging her neatly clipped up ponytail as she did. 'He seems a bit tetchy. Everything okay?'

'Yes. I think we're all a bit tetchy. A killer on the loose, no sleep. He's also relinquished responsibility of the case to me, which is a first.' Gina stared in the direction in which he'd left.

'Are you okay, guv?'

'I really need to go home and change. I stink. I'm still wearing the same clothes I wore on the plane and I'm starving.'

A sympathetic look washed over Wyre's face. 'I feel a bit better after a shower. You should go home and do the same. I'm sure Jacob will be back any minute too.'

'Breakfast is in the building!' O'Connor announced as he walked across the incident room with a tray. The buttery aroma of a fresh bake followed him to the table, masking the damp air. 'Mrs O just delivered a batch of her croissants. Said she's been working on the recipe and wanted us to taste test them, so if you eat one, feedback is a must. She also knows something big has happened and she thought we could do with breakfast.'

'Tell Mrs O she is our saviour once again. Coffee and a croissant – yes, please.' Gina took a pastry from the tray and bit into it. PC Smith followed the scent and sat at a spare desk. 'Tell her from me, they are delicious – and thank her too. She really is a key member of our team. Just to update you, Briggs is heading up the official press release. A woman found strangled in her home, this is going to send the good people of Warwickshire into panic mode. Best thing people can do is make sure their doors are locked and their security systems are functioning.'

O'Connor moved the mouse until the computer screen lit up. The case notes appeared before him. Wyre began to pin a map onto the corkboard in the corner of the room. The overpowering smell of damp almost put Gina off taking another bite of the croissant. She reopened the blind, letting the sun and fresh air back in.

Wyre squirted a blast of lily-of-the-valley air freshener into the damp corner. 'I suppose we need to get used to this stench,' she said as she placed the can back onto the window ledge.

Gina took another bite of the croissant and washed it down with a swig of cold coffee. She walked over to the map and placed pins into the Sanderson residence, Robert Dixon's residence and the Angel Arms. After the last major case she'd worked on, she'd hoped not to have to deal with Samuel Avery at the Angel any time soon, but circumstances had put the pub on the map again.

O'Connor grabbed his phone as it rang. 'Bernard?'

Gina turned to face him as O'Connor nodded, made the odd sound and listened. 'What is it?' she mouthed.

He held up his hand as he continued to process what Bernard was telling him. 'Thanks, Bernard,' he said as he placed the receiver down. 'He just wanted to update us with what he has so far. The blood sample taken from the stairs and the trail in the hallway matches that of Mrs Sanderson. He also found two traces of material at the scene. The one was denim, the other was white, highly dense polyethylene. That's the same material forensic suits are made of. Whoever did this to Mrs Sanderson knew exactly what they were doing.'

CHAPTER NINE

As soon as Gina entered her house, the wall of heat hit her. She'd left her fire on all night. The cat lazily slid off the sofa and headed towards her. She ignored the cat and turned the gas fire off. It was nine in the morning and it had been a long night. She had a couple of hours before she needed to be back at the station. A nap in the bath was calling.

As she walked up the stairs she thought of the last message Briggs had sent to her. He was missing her but he wouldn't message her again. She ran the bath and swallowed the lump in her throat. The past few months had been some of the best she'd experienced. Briggs had been an excellent companion, a passionate lover, exciting, slightly dangerous in that they might get caught, but she'd allowed her past to warn her off. He'd wanted to get too close to her, asked too many questions about her past. Their relationship was unprofessional, she'd told him. Damn it, she hated Terry and all the Terry baggage she still carried around. She swiped the toiletries off the window ledge in the bathroom and stared at the dripping condensation on the frosted glass.

Steam filled the room. She kicked all the toiletries under the washbasin. The clock was ticking and before she knew it, the steaming hot bath would be as frosty as her love life. She turned on the radio, threw her sweaty clothes onto the landing and dipped her toe into the hot water before getting fully in and letting the soothing properties of her orange-scented bath bomb kick in.

She opened Facebook on her phone and smiled at the photo that Hannah had posted of Gracie wearing a new dress. Maybe thing weren't quite so bad. She smiled even more when she saw the dog in the background. Rosie the black spaniel had been rescued from her last case. She'd returned to the rescue centre a few days later and picked the dog up. Hannah had fallen in love with it and offered the little dog a home.

Trying to rebuild her relationship with her daughter had been tough. Hannah had been too young to see the abuse Gina suffered at the hands of Terry. Gina had finally told Hannah about the past and they were now repairing their relationship slowly. She placed the phone on the floor and closed her eyes, her mind flashed to Mrs Sanderson. She envisaged the young woman, scared for her life as she ran up the stairs, only to be struck with a blunt instrument on the right side of her head. Had she been dazed or unconscious at that point? As she'd run, had she been trying to save her crying child who was still in her cot – or was the little girl banging on the door after climbing over her bed guard? She tried to imagine the woman's panic as she ran to save her child. Her attacker caught up with her and she knew first hand that there was no other feeling in the world like it. When the life you are responsible for is in danger, you will do anything to protect that life. She would have panicked, fought and struggled. A tear ran down her cheek as she remembered the time Terry was kicking her in the kitchen. She'd been cocooning baby Hannah. She rubbed her head, remembering the one kick that had almost rendered her unconscious. She wiped her eyes and shook her head.

She forced her mind to focus back on Mrs Sanderson. What next? The attacker dragged Mrs Sanderson down the stairs and along the hallway, leaving a trail of blood. What was her attacker thinking? Why Mrs Sanderson? Mother of one, nice house, quiet area, husband with an alibi, no money worries. But there was more to Mrs Sanderson – she possibly had a lover. Who was her mystery man?

Gina's mind flashed back to the body. Her attacker hadn't even disguised what they'd done, like they were proud to show all – all except their identity. They hadn't even made it look like a robbery. The perpetrator went in with intent and Melissa Sanderson was a very specific target. Had she looked into her attacker's eyes as the cord tightened around her neck? And where had that cord come from?

O'Connor's last words before she'd left the station left her wide-eyed in the bath. There was no chance of grabbing a short sleep with her mind whirring at one hundred miles an hour. The perp knew exactly what they were doing. The forensic suit they'd been wearing would almost certainly have stopped fibres belonging to them dropping onto the crime scene. If they were that forensically aware, had they also been wearing boot covers, gloves, hair covers and masks? Bernard had the elimination prints and hadn't reported any further prints at the scene.

There was only one thing the killer hadn't banked on: slightly tearing the forensics suit and their jeans on the splintered leg of the carver chair, leaving a couple of shreds of material behind. It was the only clue so far as to who killed Mrs Melissa Sanderson.

Her heart hummed and she couldn't help but focus on it. Her mind flashed back to how she imagined Melissa to be in her final moments. Her body would be jerking violently as the life was squeezed out of her. She'd never know that her daughter was safe now. As she took her last breaths, she'd have heard the crying coming from upstairs as Mia screamed to no avail.

Gina fully immersed her body into the water, then sat up as she listened to the news come on the radio. The report simply described Mrs Sanderson as a thirty-five-year-old mother, found brutally killed in her home, and urged anyone with any information to come forward. She stepped out of the bath and grabbed a towel.

*

As Gina pulled her coat on, her phone beeped with a message. Her eyes widened. A smile spread across her face as she read the email with Bernard's report attached. At last a break in the case. She snatched her keys from the coffee table and darted out the door without even drying her hair. She needed to get the whole team in straight away.

CHAPTER TEN

Staring through her wild, dirty blonde curls that had flapped over her eyes, Natalie approached the path to the front door carrying the last of the boxes. She turned and stared back at the long drive and the rolling fields in the distance. The world was so big, an everlasting expanse her mind couldn't fathom. She tried to swallow but her mouth was producing no saliva. She tried again and swallowed hard, feeling every motion in her throat, hoping it wouldn't close up on her. As she gasped for breath, her heart raced, she needed to get inside quickly. Bruce grabbed a bag from the boot, failing to notice her distress. She turned to the front door and the path began to very slightly sway, leaving her nauseous. The items in the box clattered as she ran as fast as her thick legs would carry her. Leaning against the door, she closed her eyes, unable to face her surroundings any longer.

For years, they had lived in a row of detached houses in Stratford-upon-Avon, next to a smattering of bed and breakfasts. She'd enjoyed seeing tourists coming and going, but her husband Bruce wanted to live somewhere quieter, so they were moving back to his hometown of Cleevesford, a place she'd never really visited in all their years together. He promised that life in Cleevesford would improve her health. With her anxiety worsening and her memory forever deceiving her, he said she needed to be in a place where her mind could be uncluttered. So, today, they were officially moving in to Rosewood House, the type of house Bruce had dreamed of for so long. The front garden needed a lot of work. When she eventually settled and was feeling better about their new place, she'd get out there and make a start, but it would take time. How much time? She couldn't tell as yet.

The spring shoots had started to work their way through the block paving. This house was going to be a major project, but she knew she'd need something in her life to take her mind off her worries. This new start needed to work, and the countryside location would hopefully help her get a grip of her life once again.

'What if this move doesn't make me any better?' She stood in front of the main door, waiting for Bruce to let her in. With closed eyes, she listened as his heavy footsteps approached the door. She couldn't look out. The swaying trees and the distant hills were just too much. The drive had already caused her enough stress.

'I'm not expecting miracles. You shouldn't either. Come on, open your eyes.' He turned the key and opened the front door, shoving her into the hall as he passed.

She opened her eyes, squinting into the darkness of their new cottage. Placing the box onto the kitchen table, she took a few deep breaths. Resting two fingers on her wrist, she monitored her pulse rate until it calmed down. Every step she took on the flagstone tiled floor echoed through the chilly building. It wasn't yet a home but she'd make it a home, and she'd show Bruce that she could get better. She'd been reading a self-help book on overcoming anxiety, managing attacks and eventually combatting her fears. As one suggested, she'd been keeping a diary of her feelings. She had to remain positive. Last thing she needed was to have a breakdown. She checked her pulse again. It was almost back to normal.

The removal company had been the previous day and early in the morning. They had left all the correct boxes and furniture in the correct rooms. Bruce had spent the day before assisting them with erecting the furniture and he'd returned to their old house in the early hours of the morning. For the past three days they'd been gradually moving their personal belongings, but today was the day where there was no going back. They'd handed in their keys to the estate agent, ready for collection by the new owners.

She stared at her husband. His chiselled jaw, deep blue eyes and determined look had been the thing that had originally attracted her to him. That and his car. All her friends at college had been impressed with his Porsche and he'd also been a qualified accountant. She'd enjoyed being taken out and treated to meals, mini breaks and spa days. She'd been studying floristry when they first met and she had dreamed of one day owning a shop; now, she'd settle for a well-stocked garden and a veggie patch. Soon after meeting they'd had a child and she'd settled into her motherly role with ease. That's when her illness had begun. Severe anxiety the doctor had said.

She opened the kitchen blind and stared out at the huge garden full of bushes, shrubs and trees that were all entwined in weeds. She certainly did have her work cut out, but she could do it – she could make it perfect.

'Where's the coffee?' She stared at her husband, opening and closing her mouth like a solitary goldfish in a bowl, living the most meaningless of existences. 'Coffee. Where did you put the coffee?' Her heart rate began to creep up again. She checked her pulse willing her heart not to start palpitating. She couldn't let him see she was losing her grip.

The stack of boxes marked kitchen were stood in front of the pantry. She began ripping at the tape as he watched her. 'They're in one of these boxes,' she said as she forced a smile. He couldn't see she was jittery, thankfully. The first box came open as her trembling fingers tugged at it. Reaching down, she dislodged the washing-up brush, the tea caddy, the biscuit tin but no coffee. Where had she packed the coffee? She would only have packed the coffee with the tea, sugar and biscuits, wouldn't she?

'Bloody hell,' Bruce said as he grabbed the open box and placed it on the floor. He proceeded with opening the next box marked *under the sink*. 'Why you'd put the coffee in a box with the disinfectant and cleaning products, beats me,' he said, taking the coffee from the box.

She looked up at him, bottom lip quivering as tears streamed down her face. 'I'm sorry. I'm so stupid.'

'You're not stupid. You just need some rest. The move has been stressful. Go up to bed and I'll bring you a drink.'

With each step, she felt the weight of her failure dragging her down. The burden of her illness ever heavier. Bruce had seen her breakdown. So much for the stupid book she'd been reading. There was no help, only acceptance and survival. She turned at the top of the stairs, grabbed the folded-up quilt from a box and climbed into bed. She hadn't even put the cover on their new quilt before she packed it. She'd do it later, when she felt more rested. A wash of exhaustion travelled through her muscles as she relaxed into the bedding.

Within moments Bruce came up with a hot black coffee. 'You need to order some milk.' She needed to order many things – she'd do their online shop later. The bed dipped as he lay down on top of the quilt and stared into her eyes.

'I'm sorry,' she said as she wept into the pillow.

He grabbed her and pulled her close, kissing her as he stroked her hair. 'It's fine. I think this new start will be good for you, for us. What I meant to say is I should've been more understanding back there, with the coffee and all. It's part of your anxiety and I need to be a bit more patient.' He removed a tangled curl from across her face. She leaned in closer to him, enjoying his warmth. He was all she had. Their son, Craig, was at university and never came home to see them. Bruce was always there and always had been. 'Right, I'm popping to the office for a while. I need to catch up with what's been happening in my absence. Will you be okay ordering the shopping?'

'Yes. I love you.'

'I love you too. You know that, don't you? We don't need anyone else, do we?'

'No,' she whispered. She closed her eyes as his warm lips met her forehead before he rolled off the bed. Maybe the diary was worth persevering with. She needed to stop thinking about all the things that were making her anxious and instead think of happy things. She thought of her new garden. She'd start by pulling the weeds up, trimming the hedges and cutting the trees back. She'd properly dig the borders out and get a rotavator on the patch at the back. They both liked organic vegetables with their dinner. She'd like to grow potatoes, onions and leeks. She'd also grow carnations and roses.

'Natalie,' he called. Her heart rate began to quicken again. 'Where did you put my office keys? I gave them to you to hold when we were in the car.'

Her thoughts flashed between the car, the house and walking up the stairs. 'Are you sure?'

'Of course I'm sure. I asked you to hold them while I got the bags out of the boot. You put them in your pocket before I passed you the box.' She listened as he began throwing things out of the boxes and cluttering around the kitchen. He left the house and the central locking of the car beeped, then it beeped again before he stormed back into the house.

Still wearing her light jacket, she checked her pockets. She didn't have the keys any longer.

'Don't you worry about it, princess. Just stay in bed. I suppose I'll have to take a copy of Sylvie's key. Bloody hell,' he shouted as he kicked the kitchen door and slammed the front door as he left. His receptionist would no doubt be tasked to go and get a copy made.

She sobbed into her pillow. Ever the failure. She tried so hard to retrace her steps in her mind. They were in the car. They pulled up on the drive at the end of the path. She remembered looking out and everything seeming so daunting. The hills in the distance had been closing in on her. Her need to get into the house without Bruce noticing her anxiety had been at its greatest. Had he passed her the keys then? Had she grabbed the box and dropped the keys at the same time? Could they be on the drive? She wasn't going out again that day. No way was she checking. Failure – that word obsessively repeated itself in her mind. She dragged the quilt over her head and buried herself in the bed as she cried.

CHAPTER ELEVEN

Gina scraped her damp hair into a ponytail as she entered the station and headed towards the incident room. So much for a restful bath and a couple of hours sleep.

'Feeling better, guv?' Jacob asked, interrupting her from her thoughts.

Gina brushed a scattering of croissant crumbs onto the floor with her sleeve. 'Much, thanks. Bernard has sent me his report from last night. I'm having a quick recap and I want to bring forward the team briefing. Check on all incoming calls as the news is now out. Give me five then pop through.'

She hurried to her office and turned the computer on. 'Come on,' she said as she watched the cursor whirling into action. As soon as she logged in, she clicked straight onto her email and scanned the information in Bernard's report. There had been a drawer in Mrs Sanderson's divan bed containing crotchless leather trousers, ball masks, and nipple tassels. What did that prove? Mr and Mrs Sanderson had interesting sex lives. She continued reading. Mr Sanderson's drawer contained a pair of pliers and a collection of vibrators, ranging in size.

She then reached the really interesting part. They had recovered a pay-as-you-go-phone that had been carefully stashed under the bed, against the wall, on Mrs Sanderson's side. Gina smiled as she read on. The last message came from a contact Mrs Sanderson had named Jimmy in her phone.

I can't stand to see you living the rest of your life with that man!

Her phone vibrated across the desk and then began to ring. 'DI Harte.'

'Have you looked at the email yet?' Bernard asked.

'I'm re-reading it now. Well done on recovering the phone. We'll need to see if we can get a trace on this Jimmy from his number. Any updates on the post-mortem?'

'No, still waiting at the moment but it should be soon. We've had major staffing issues.' Her shoulders slumped. She needed it doing now so she could be fully informed for the investigation.

'Tell me about it.'

'As soon as I get the PM appointment, I'll get straight back to you. You got the blood results, didn't you? We managed to push those through.'

'We did get those. As suspected at the scene, evidence shows that Mrs Sanderson was struck on the stairs and was dragged to the kitchen. Have we come across anything that could have been used as the weapon that struck her?'

She heard Bernard flicking through his notebook. 'Not as yet. We have recovered several items but until we assess the cadaver thoroughly, we won't have anything conclusive for you.'

Gina looked down. 'Can you hurry this up a bit?'

'I wish we could, but we just don't have the resources.'

'A woman has been killed in her home! This has to take priority, surely.'

There was a pause on the phone. 'We're rushing like mad this end. There was a lot to process in the house and the back and front gardens. We've dusted for prints, checked for footprints. Nothing so far on either front. Whoever did this knew what they were doing. Not a jot of anything from which we can obtain DNA from. We've analysed blood spatter. We're still processing more crime scene photos, logging all the evidence, all on a shoestring budget. I will have everything you need, either later today or early tomorrow. I promise, Inspector.' He

placed his receiver down and ended their call.

Someone knocked at her office door.

'Come in.'

'Guv. Coffee?' Jacob placed the cup of hot liquid on her desk. 'It's a shame you had to walk straight into this after your holiday.'

She nodded and smiled. 'So what's new? Have we had anything from the public as yet?'

'Nothing yet.'

Gina scrolled up and down Bernard's report and stopped at the section mentioning Mr and Mrs Sanderson's bed drawers. 'Mr Sanderson kept a pair of pliers with a collection of sex toys in the drawer under his side of the bed. I'd say that was a little unusual.'

Jacob smirked. 'From what we see, nothing is unusual. I wouldn't keep pliers with sex toys though. That is odd. But I wouldn't mind at least having *someone* to share sex toys with.'

Gina took a swig of coffee. 'No luck with the ladies at the moment then?'

'Not a jot. I'm thinking of taking up celibacy.'

'You already are.'

'I mean as a way of life, a philosophy.' Jacob looked at her, she looked back at him and they both laughed. 'Maybe I'll give Tinder a go.'

'Yeah, right,' she replied as she gazed back at the report. 'Mrs Sanderson also kept a collection of black leather crotchless trousers, tasselled nipple accessories – what I'd refer to as kinky sex clothing.'

'It sounds very much like they were into something but then, isn't everyone. Even I've bought an ex-lover a little something kinky that would turn me on. It's not unusual.'

Gina stopped scrolling and stared into space. 'Pliers?'

'Everyone has their oddities.'

'She had a lover called Jimmy, well that's the name she kept in her phone. He sent a message saying that he couldn't stand her being with Mr Sanderson. Would someone so unhappy in her marriage – drinking, depression – be so enthused about nipple tassels and sex toys? Maybe they were from an age long gone, who knows. Maybe they used them in the past and they've just festered in their secret little place under the bed.'

'Maybe, guv.'

Gina gulped the rest of the coffee down in one. 'That's better. I love coffee, almost more than life itself.' She picked up the phone and dialled Wyre's extension. 'I need you and O'Connor to investigate anyone named Jimmy who could be in Mrs Sanderson's life. Check on previous work places, toddler groups, friendship circles, neighbours, friends' partners, even people registered at the same doctor's surgery. If he's called Jimmy, Jim or James, I want him eliminated. Also, the phone has been booked into evidence. I want a record of all calls and a trace put out on the numbers in the phone.' She thanked Wyre and placed the phone down. 'We need to find Jimmy.'

CHAPTER TWELVE

The late morning air whistled through the partly opened window at the back of the bus. It hopped over a speed hump before heading along the main road through Cleevesford.

'Stop the bus,' Ellie called as she ran to the front and pleaded with the driver. Over the past year, her mind had toiled with confronting her past and she'd tried to resist, but sometimes the past just wouldn't go away. It wasn't for the want of trying. She wanted to forget so badly. In her mind she'd denied it had ever happened but denial would only work for so long. On nights when she'd lie awake next to Becky, listening to her gentle breaths as her chest rose and fell, she'd try to remind herself how lucky she was. She had a wonderful partner, soon to be wife; she had an okay job managing a coffee shop, which she loved, and she worked as a part-time artist, taking on portrait commissions. She was living the dream – only the dream was curdled by her past. Once and for all, she needed to confront what had happened, come fully clean to Becky and leave the burden of her past behind.

The driver tutted as he pulled up just past the Angel Arms, flinging Ellie forward as the bus came to a halt. 'Next time, ring the bell, love.'

'Next time don't drive so fast, and don't call me love. Jerk,' she said as she stepped off the bus. An elderly lady sitting at the front grinned as she looked back. Ellie returned her smile. Love – who did he think she was? She wasn't his love. He didn't even know her.

She straightened her cropped jacket and ran her fingers through her shoulder-length, dark hair, and headed towards the pub.

As she reached the car park, she stopped. A tear rolled down her cheek. She rubbed it away. Why had she shed a tear? That bastard didn't deserve any of her tears. That summer had been long – longer than any other she'd experienced. She'd been eighteen, just out of art college, and had been looking forward to a future studying fine art at Edinburgh University, but she hadn't stayed long. Every time she left her shared house, she saw him. He was at the pub, at the shops, in her mind. Every man she passed in the street had been mistaken for him at some point. She'd done a term at university, but the drink had assisted her failure. No longer able to function through the addiction, she came home to Cleevesford, having given up on her dreams of becoming a professional artist.

Years had passed and after many a failure, she eventually found him through an article in the local paper. A year ago his firm had received an award and there was a photo of him on the front page, holding the certificate. He had aged but not beyond recognition. As her anger consumed her, she'd made it her mission to find out more, which is why she'd been led back to Cleevesford.

She leaned against the wall at the front of the pub and stared through the windows. A hot looking, auburn-haired woman came out and collected a few glasses. She was followed by a shorter, scruffier woman. 'Charlene.' A voice bellowed from within. The scruffy woman scurried back into the pub leaving the auburn-haired woman alone to clean the exterior.

As she passed the corner of the car park her memories flooded her mind, like they were yesterday. She gasped for breath and a trail of tears forced their way out. She didn't want to cry but her body had other ideas. The smell of beer travelled through the air. She'd kill for a beer. She thought of Becky and all they'd been through with getting her clean, and she began to walk towards the entrance. Just one – one measly little drink. It had been several years, surely she was able to control it now. As she got closer she stopped at the door, sitting on a bench to the left of the entrance. 'Jill,' the slight cockney accented voice bellowed from within.

'Just a minute, Sam,' she replied. 'Morning. We're open in ten minutes. Are you okay?' Jill smiled as she grabbed an empty glass from the floor.

Ellie wiped her eyes and smiled back. The woman stepped into the pub, leaving Ellie alone with her thoughts. Back then, after the attack and her failed stint at university, she'd swiftly moved to Redditch, found a bedsit and started afresh. She'd needed to get away from him but he'd never left her. Becky had been her saviour following a turbulent few years, mostly spent in an alcohol-induced trance, sketching caricatures for pennies on the streets. Her wonderful wife to be had helped her to get clean and find gainful employment. So far, they'd had a wonderful eight years together and life had been treating them well.

Becky never pressured her for answers or reasons, always just citing that she was always there. Ellie had recently opened up about the attack but she'd not filled her in with the details. She wasn't about to tell Becky that she'd been stalking her attacker. That she knew he'd moved to Cleevesford after flirting with the driver of the removal van on the road outside her attacker's old house. As soon as she'd spotted the new address on his paperwork, she'd dropped him like a stone. The thoughts of his tongue trying to find hers, almost made her want to heave. She'd accomplished her mission though. She couldn't let him move and not know where he was going. Not before she'd confronted him.

With shaking legs, she got up and took one step after another until she reached the corner of the car park. She wiped away the beads of sweat that were dampening her fringe. Ellie gasped as she reached out with trembling fingers, touching the neatly trimmed hedge. It hadn't always been this well trimmed. She kicked the bush over and over again until she'd almost destroyed the corner piece. Exhausted, she slumped onto the floor until the breathlessness passed. Her phone beeped.

Are you nearly home? Xx

Becky was waiting for her. But Ellie was having a drink first. She wiped her eyes and followed the beery scent.

'What can I get you?' Jill asked.

'A pint of IPA.' The woman grabbed a glass and went to pour. 'Wait.' She stopped and looked up. 'It's a bit early, can I just have an orange juice?' She couldn't drink. It wasn't fair on Becky. Her mind toiled with the *just one* scenario. Although she'd had minor relapses, she had been off the booze for too many years.

Jill nodded and went to get a small bottle from the fridge at the other end of the bar. As she bent in her tight jeans, Ellie turned and noticed the other man behind the bar staring at her rear. 'What are you staring at?'

'None of your business, missy,' the scrawny man replied as he took his paper and went to sit by the scruffy server.

'Samuel.' The sound of a male voice bellowed behind her. He was addressing the pervert who had been staring at Jill's behind. Ellie shuddered as he got closer to her. She'd never forget that voice and she'd known that he wouldn't be able to stay away from his own past. He'd come straight to her.

'How you doing, mate? Not seen you in here for donkey's years. Jill, get my old friend here anything he wants. Welcome back, mate.'

She grabbed her glass and took it to the corner of the room. Back then she'd had long blonde hair and was quite the waif. With her fuller figure and short, almost black hair, he'd never recognise her.

She'd taken the bus to Cleevesford to keep him in her sights and he had been so predictable. Clenching her fists under the table, she promised herself that he wasn't going to get away with what he had done.

CHAPTER THIRTEEN

Wyre jogged towards Gina. 'Miss Barker's here. I've put her in interview room one.'

'Great. Come with me.' Gina replied as she passed DC Paula Wyre a pen.

Wyre smiled and followed her along the tired-looking corridor until they reached the interview room.

'Morning, thank you for coming in,' Gina said as she entered and sat opposite the round-faced woman. The woman rubbed her red-rimmed eyes. Her brown roots had reached halfway down her long, fiery red hair. 'Can you just confirm your full name?'

'Yes, it's Suzanne Eleanor Barker.' She pulled a crumpled tissue from the pocket of her denim jacket and wiped her nose. 'I can't believe what's happened. When your officer called me...' The woman let out a little sob. 'She was my friend, my best friend. We met through a meet and play group. My little one, Seth, is three. He's a little older than Mia, but he loved it when Auntie Melissa and little Mia came over to play... She's never coming over again, is she?' The woman wiped away a stream of mucus that reached her top lip.

'I'm really sorry about what happened to Melissa. We need to ask you a few questions as we want to catch the person who did this to her.'

The woman wiped her eyes with the already wet tissue and nodded. 'I'll do everything I can to help.' She pulled a strand of tear-soaked hair from the side of her mouth.

'When did you last see Melissa Sanderson?'

'This Wednesday, the eleventh. She came over with Mia.'

'About what time?' Gina watched as the woman's brow crumpled as she tried to think back.

'She arrived just before ten in the morning. We had a coffee and she said she wanted to pop out if I'd mind Mia. I never mind looking after Mia. She left about ten thirty.'

'Where was she going?' Gina asked as Wyre took notes. The woman looked down and scratched the back of her hand. 'Miss Barker, Suzanne, where did Melissa go?'

Suzanne began to sob as she spoke. 'I promised I wouldn't say anything…'

'Suzanne, Melissa is dead. The information you have may help us to catch your friend Melissa's killer.'

As she tried to open her mouth, loud gasping sobs blurted out. 'She was seeing someone. She went to see him.'

Gina leaned forward over the table. 'Who was she going to see at ten thirty in the morning on the eleventh of April?' The woman sobbed into the back of her hand. 'Suzanne, it's important that you tell me.'

'Jimmy Phipps. His name is Jimmy. They used to be an item back in high school. She's only been meeting up with him for a couple of months. He's recently moved back into the area after trying to make it in London as a theatre director. I think the money ran out along with the work so he came back to Cleevesford. As far as I'm aware, he's a teaching assistant or theatre technician at a school in Redditch.'

Gina glanced at the woman who now appeared to be concentrating.

'Was it him? Did he do this to her?' Suzanna blurted out.

'We're just gathering witness statements at the moment.' Suzanna looked up at her. She could tell the woman was sure in her mind that her friend's killer was Jimmy Phipps. She fumbled with a piece of straggly hair, tucking it behind her ear, revealing several piercings.

'How long was she gone?'

'About two hours, all together. She then came back to mine about twelve thirty, got Mia and left. She looked upset.'

'In what way?'

'I think she'd been crying. She was blowing her nose and her eyes were a little puffy. It looked like she'd just reapplied her eyeliner as she'd made the wing in the corner of one eye a bit longer than the other. I asked her what the matter was and she just shrugged it off. Said it didn't matter. She kept checking her phone and scrolling back and forth. I didn't leave it there. I nagged her until she gave in. She told me Jimmy wanted her to leave Darrel. He wanted to take her away, take Mia too. He'd been angry with her for stringing him along. I knew she wouldn't ever leave Darrel. They had too much together, had built a life and had a child. She said she'd ended it with Jimmy and told him to leave her alone and not contact her again. That was all really.'

'Did she ever mention her husband, Darrel Sanderson?'

'On occasion. I don't think things were going that well. She said whenever they went out he'd always look at other women. They didn't spend much time together – he'd just go to the pub with his mates and leave her at home. She was always in a rush to prepare his dinner and make things just as he liked them, even though they were distant. I think she was fighting to keep a failing marriage together. I think her thing with Jimmy had been more about revenge.'

'Do you know where Jimmy Phipps lives?'

'Salt Lane. His block of flats is the first block you see when you pull into the road. His is the top flat on the right. I don't know the number. I only know where it is as I dropped Mia to her a couple of weeks ago so she could make it back before Darrel arrived home. He'd called her to say he was finishing work early.

When I turned up in the close, she saw me pull into the parking space and waved out of his flat window. That's all I know. She kept the rest to herself. You have to catch whoever did this. She was such a lovely person, she didn't deserve this.' Suzanne began to weep again.

'Did you ever see Jimmy Phipps? Could you give us a description?'

'I couldn't see much. All I know is he's just a little taller than her and she was about my height, five eight, so he must be about five ten. His hair was dark and he had a full head of it. I couldn't see any of his features from where I was.'

'Do you know anyone who had it in for Melissa, anyone who could've hurt her?'

'She didn't know anyone else. She was quite a timid person. I think I was her only friend. Apart from her husband and Jimmy, I can't think that she even knew anyone else. Her mother lives in Birmingham, somewhere. I don't think they were that close and she never mentioned her father. She took Mia to see her mother occasionally, but that was it.'

'Thank you, Suzanne. You've been really helpful.'

Wyre passed the statement across the table for the woman to read and asked her to sign.

'If you think of anything else that might help us in the meantime, please call me.' Gina handed the woman a card and Wyre stood to see her out.

'Will do,' she replied as she left the room.

As the door closed, Gina could now envisage a fuller picture of Melissa. Melissa was probably lonely, not feeling valued at home and had fallen for Jimmy, an old flame, when he'd returned from London. She thought of Melissa spending most of her time alone in the big house that she and Darrel had shared, pining for the odd hour with Jimmy. She pictured Melissa toiling with her emotions over one too many glasses of wine, wondering if she should leave Darrel and run off with Jimmy, or make her life with Darrel work. They had everything. He had a successful business that allowed her to be kept in the life of luxury. If she was happy, why had she been drinking? She made a note to ask if there was alcohol present in Melissa's blood.

Wyre knocked and entered. 'You still here, guv?'

'I need this Jimmy Phipps contacted immediately. We need him interviewed.'

CHAPTER FOURTEEN

The lunchtime rush had passed and a few drinkers were dotted around the pub. Ellie's stomach turned every time he spoke or laughed. The scrawny man in his fifties, wearing jeans that made his legs look too thin, she now knew to be called Samuel. He'd been laughing and joking about a woman he'd pulled as he laid a hand on the man's shoulder. She watched as he swigged the rest of his pint and began doing his jacket up.

'Hopefully we'll see you again soon now you're back,' Samuel called after him.

Don't look up, don't look up, she kept repeating in her mind. She couldn't resist. Just a glance. He caught her eye for a second, maybe not even a second, more like a millisecond. She held her breath as she gripped her glass of orange juice. A small gust of wind caught her hair as he opened the door and left. She peeped out of the window, watching him turn right, leaving on foot, out of the car park. She slammed her drink onto the table and left, hurrying towards the path – she couldn't lose him. She needed to follow him, find out more about his life – finally see his new house.

As she reached the path, she spotted him in the distance. She began following him along the path that led out of town.

*

It felt like she'd been walking for ages and her toe was now poking through a hole in her sock. There was a dampness in the air, despite the bright weather. She zipped up her jacket. Although there was a bit of sun in the sky, it was still early spring and the wetness of the ground had been seeping into her cheap boots. She hobbled along the country lane, trying to ignore the material that was cutting into her big toe. As he reached an opening in the trees, he took a left into the woodland. The sound of her erratic heartbeat filled her head. It definitely wasn't safe to be doing what she was doing, especially as she knew what he was capable of. She slipped on a pile of damp leaves and fell onto a branch. The crunch stood out against the gentle birdsong. She edged towards the trunk of a large oak tree and held her breath.

Should she look? She couldn't lose him but she couldn't risk being caught by him either. She couldn't let him get away. Exhaling gently, she leaned forward and glanced in his direction. He'd stopped and was checking his phone.

He held his phone to his ear. 'Natalie, have you found my keys yet?' He paused as the other person on the call replied. 'That's good. You just keep looking.' He grinned as he dangled a set of keys in front of his eyes. He turned, facing the tree she was tucked behind. Her heart raced and she couldn't move. She wanted to run, escape in the direction they'd come, but part of her hoped he'd turn around and keep walking. She remained still, unable to look away. A squirrel darted from the other side of the tree and disappeared into the distance. He grinned and continued through the foliage. 'Bloody squirrels,' he muttered.

Tears fell down her face. He hadn't seen her, he'd spotted the squirrel. She stood, continuing to follow him, but keeping further back. What would Becky say if she knew what she was doing? She knew exactly what Becky would say. She'd be angry. There's no way she'd want her to be playing vigilante. Then again, she hadn't told Becky much about what had happened to her. She hadn't shared the contents of her nightmares with Becky. All that would change soon. She was going to tell Becky everything. Maybe then, Becky would understand her better, understand what had pushed her to drink all those years ago. In her opinion, there was nothing like blanked out memories to make a person feel as though they were losing their mind. This new start, her upcoming wedding and today, was all about confronting what had happened. No more denial. She was going to confront him.

They'd been walking in the woodland for the best part of ten minutes when she saw a house in the distance. The large country house stood alone amongst the trees. When growing up in Cleevesford, her mother had never allowed her to come this far to play as a young child. She could hear a road close by. The country road that led all the way to a little village called Wixford, fronted the house. Becky had driven her along it when they'd gone for a day out and they'd spent a balmy summer's day sitting on a riverbank with a picnic.

She held back as she watched him stop outside a back gate. He pulled his phone out of his pocket and held it to his ear once again. 'I'm nearly home. Maybe we should have some *us* time. I love you, my darling.' He put his phone away and began peeping through a tiny gap in the fence.

Opening the gate, he walked down the path. She listened as the back door opened and closed. She ran along the side of the house, wedged her body through the dense hedge and looked through the large bay window. He wasn't stalking anyone, he was home. She flinched as he placed his arm round his wife who was sitting in a chair. He grabbed both of her breasts from behind and began kissing her neck. She watched how the woman's expression didn't change. It wasn't an expression of pleasure or disgust. The woman looked vacant. Ellie knew that look. That's the look she'd given when her relationships had become sexual. She'd managed to force her nightmares to the back of her mind and function for the sake of her relationship with Becky. Becky was different though. Becky cared.

A tear ran down her face. Now wasn't a good time to be here. She had all these dreams of confronting him but it never happened. What did she think she was going to do? Knock on the front door and blurt everything out to his wife. She'd keep him in her sights while she thought about it.

She started the long walk back to Cleevesford, where she would get on the bus and go home. She didn't have a plan, or know how to avenge her younger self, but she'd be back soon, she knew that for sure.

CHAPTER FIFTEEN

'You look how I feel,' Jacob said as he entered Gina's office. Darkness had begun to fall as the day progressed and a rain shower was brewing in the air. The weather had been so changeable lately.

'Believe me, I can see exactly how you feel,' she said with a smile. His tie was pulled into a loose knot, his shirt was crumpled and he had bags under his eyes. His tall figure looked like it needed feeding up as it always did. 'I'm heading home soon. I'm dead on my feet. You should go too. We need to be back here tomorrow with our brains in gear. Any news on Jimmy yet?'

'No. We checked with his school. He left work at five following a play rehearsal and hasn't been seen since.'

'I want someone watching his flat for when he arrives home. Then I want him picked up immediately before he gets a chance to go in and tamper with anything.'

'Do we have enough to bring him in?'

'He's a witness. Ask him to come in voluntarily. If he refuses, we may need to interview him under caution. Melissa's husband has an alibi and we can't risk James Phipps going home and destroying any evidence. We need the phone Melissa was sending the texts to. We need to know why she went back to Suzanne Barker's house looking upset, and if Melissa had given her friend the full story.'

'Smith is going to be pleased. I've already pre-warned him of the likelihood of him being on stakeout duty. We've also put a call out. Officers on patrol will be looking out for Phipps's car. We'll put an ANPR out too.'

'Great. Anyway, Smith enjoys working with us. Get him down there. In the meantime, I'm going home to sleep. If we get Phipps, call me immediately and I'll be back. I want to be the one to interview him.'

Jacob nodded. 'See you tomorrow then, guv.' He smiled and closed her office door as he left.

As she went to yawn, her office phone went. 'Bernard. Tell me you have something good for me.'

'We're conducting the post-mortem first thing. I've emailed you the details. See you there.'

CHAPTER SIXTEEN

Saturday, 14 April 2018

Gina glanced at her watch, it was nine forty in the morning and she'd been in the station three hours already. She'd come straight in the moment she'd got the call to tell her that they'd picked Phipps up at six o'clock outside his flat. Jacob caught her up as she was about to enter the interview room.

'I've just had a call from Smith's team. Not one of Phipps's neighbours can give him an alibi for the night of Melissa's murder. No one can verify whether his car was there, his light was on or that he was in his flat.'

'Thanks for that. Let's go.' Gina led the way in, passing Phipps as she took a seat opposite and Jacob sat beside her.

'James Anthony Phipps.' Gina continued for the tape. Jacob sat beside her in the sparse interview room, taking notes. 'You've been brought here today for questioning about your whereabouts during the murder of Mrs Melissa Sanderson on Thursday the twelfth of April 2018. The interview will be conducted under caution and will be recorded. You have attended voluntarily.'

'I haven't done anything. I loved her,' he yelled as he placed his head in his hands and wiped his eyes. Gina pushed a box of tissues towards the man.

'We're just here to establish what happened, Mr Phipps. Please tell me where you were on the evening of the twelfth of April.'

'I was at home in my flat.' His thick dark hair flopped over his eyes.

'Can anyone corroborate your whereabouts?'

'No,' he replied as he sucked in air and began to hyperventilate. 'I didn't do this.'

'Mr Phipps, we are just trying to establish your whereabouts and your relationship with the late, Mrs Sanderson. You are not under arrest.'

'Does that mean I can go, just walk out,' he said as he stood. Stubble covered his chin and his eyes looked heavy.

'It does, but as you can't corroborate your whereabouts on the evening of Mrs Sanderson's murder, I can arrange a warrant for your arrest and then you'd be straight back. We'd really appreciate your help and cooperation.'

The man sat back down. 'Do I need a solicitor?'

'Do you want one? You are not under arrest but I can call a duty solicitor or your solicitor if you'd prefer to have one present,' Jacob said as he looked at the man, then looked back at Gina.

'I don't know. No. I just want to get out of here.'

Gina kept her gaze on him. 'Tell me everything in your own words.'

Jimmy leaned back in the chair and ran his shaking fingers through his mop of dark wavy hair. 'She told me she wouldn't leave him, her husband that is. She came over on Wednesday morning.' Gina made a note. His information tied in with what Suzanna Barker had said. 'We argued and not for the first time. I wanted her to leave him and be with me. But I couldn't give her half the things he could. He's a successful businessman, me, I'm a teaching assistant.' The man paused.

'Tell me about the argument,' Gina continued.

'She said she needed to try and make it work with her husband and that she couldn't end up with nothing. I kept trying to tell her she wouldn't end up with nothing but if she did, it wouldn't matter; we could make it work because I loved her. She wasn't happy at home. That husband of hers didn't treat her like a husband should. It's him you should be looking at.'

'Can you elaborate on that point?'

'He failed to make her happy any more, which is where I came in. I made her happy.' Gina made a note. It looked like Mr and Mrs Sanderson were leading very separate lives. She was getting a good glimpse into Mrs Sanderson, now she needed to know more about Jimmy Phipps and Mr Sanderson. 'He went out a lot leaving her alone. I wanted to give her so much more!'

'Do you know where he went?'

'She went on about him spending time with his friends. She talked about Dan, Rob… err, Lee, I think, and I'm sure she mentioned the name Ben. She spoke about them a lot, actually. She didn't like them. I was glad though, it meant I had her. Anyway, had he been a brilliant husband, she wouldn't have been seeing me. She said his friends were all basically a bunch of slimeballs but she didn't go into detail.'

Gina noted the names down. Was the Rob he referred to Darrel's alibi at the Angel Arms, Robert Dixon? 'Can you tell us any more, their surnames, anything about them?'

'That really is all I have. I didn't press her, I just let her speak freely and she enjoyed talking. If I asked her too much though, she'd clam up.'

Gina cleared her throat. She knew that feeling all too well. Her mind whirred. What didn't Melissa Sanderson want to talk about?

'Going back to Thursday. Tell me what you did all evening?'

'I got home from work about five. I had dinner, a microwave meal for one, lasagne. The box will still be in my bin if you want to check.' He paused. 'I ate my food then took a bath. I was in the bath until about seven then I got out. I sat in my living room, read and did some work.'

'Did you have the TV on?'

'No. I was working on the school play, *The Importance of Being Earnest*. I had to prepare a rehearsal schedule for the pupils, note down the technical requirements, lighting, sound effects and break down the scenes. That took me most of the evening. After that, I afforded myself a few glasses of wine. I won't lie to you, I tried to call Melissa but her phone was turned off. I bought her a phone so we could just use it for each other. I always made sure mine was turned on but I also understood that she didn't always have hers on.'

'And you were happy with this arrangement?'

'No. I was distraught. I've been around, believe me. Working in London, directing theatre, I had no shortage of interest but Melissa was different. We had history. When you fall for someone that hard for a second time, you don't think about others. I wasn't going to let her go again.' The man sat on the edge of the plastic chair, leaned his elbow on the table and placed his head in his hands.

'Let her go?'

'You know. Do my best to keep her, not physically restrain her. You're not going to pin this one on me!'

The man began to fidget in his chair.

'Tell me about your history with Melissa?' Gina asked him.

'We met in high school. We were both in a school pantomime. She was just in the chorus, I played the giant in *Jack and the Beanstalk*. Fifteen we were. That's how it began. We hung out for the best part of a year and then I braved asking her out. It was a tough one as I didn't want to ruin our friendship but it turned out she was thinking the same. We soon became an item. When we finished our A levels, she went on to get a job in admin and I went down to London to study theatre and drama. Soon after, I heard she'd met another boy and we were over. I won't lie, I was gutted. I begged her to come to London, live with me and get a job in the city but she turned me down. She never replied.

Then I friended her through Facebook about three months ago. I didn't care that she was married, I just knew she was the one, and I wanted her.'

'So you pursued her?'

He moved from the table and leaned back a little. 'I loved her, I still love her. I'm devastated. I would've done anything to be with her.'

'Anything?'

He slammed his fist on the table. 'How dare you! I don't know any more. I've told you where I was and all I know. If you need to arrest me for being a loner and staying in with a ready meal, then go ahead, but I don't know anything else.'

'Over to last night. Why didn't you come home?'

'I'd heard about the murder on the radio. When I drove past Melissa's house, I saw the police tape outside. I struggled through work and went to the pub to get hammered. I'm the other man. No one cares about my feelings.' He paused and wiped his wet eyes. 'I drove into Redditch, went to a small pub in Crabbs Cross called The Eagle. I stayed there until close, you can check.'

'The Eagle, you say?'

He nodded. 'I left about twelve, realised I was pissed and didn't have enough cash for a taxi home. I slept in the back of my car on the main road running through Crabbs Cross. I drove home about half five this morning and you lot brought me here.'

'Interview terminated at nine fifty-one,' Gina said into the recorder.

'Can I go now?'

Gina watched as he began to do his jacket up. She wasn't going to allow him to leave and potentially destroy any evidence. He had a motive, they'd argued. He had no alibi for the evening of Melissa's murder and, in his own words, he wasn't going to let her go again.

'No. Mr Phipps, I'm arresting you on suspicion of the murder of Mrs Melissa Sanderson on Thursday the twelfth of April 2018.

You do not have to say anything, but it may harm your defence if you do not mention when questioned something which you later rely on in court. Anything you do say may be given in evidence,' Gina said as Jacob closed his notebook. Gina leaned back in her chair.

'What does that mean?' he cried as she stood.

'Please sit, Mr Phipps. It means that we have the power to detain you for twenty-four hours while we conduct our investigations. We will also be taking a DNA sample from you.'

'I want a solicitor. You're not getting any more from me.'

Jacob led him out of the interview room. Gina checked her watch. The post-mortem had started without her.

Wyre entered. 'Can you get O'Connor to check when Phipps left school and when he arrived at The Eagle pub in Redditch? See if he can pick up any CCTV that shows our suspect sleeping in his car. I just want to verify what he's been up to. While he's doing that, can you look into the names Dan, Ben, Lee and Rob? Phipps mentioned them during interview. See if you can find out who they are. I suspect the Rob he's referring to may be Robert Dixon. I need an urgent sample of Phipps's DNA too, and fast track it – I don't care about the cost. Right, I have a post-mortem to attend.'

CHAPTER SEVENTEEN

The pathologist had already started when Gina and Jacob arrived. They were shown into a small room with a glass divide, where they could hear and watch the pathologist and crime scene investigators working. One of them placed the camera on the stainless steel side and began adding Gina and Jacob's names to the log. He picked up the camera and began taking photos, from all angles, of Melissa Sanderson's body.

Melissa looked so small without her clothes on. She had quite a tiny frame, almost bony. Gina's gaze focused on Melissa's nipples. They looked almost scarred, deformed. Her chest seemed to look a little different on both sides, a little uneven where her ribs were. Gina knew from looking that the woman had broken a couple of ribs in the past. She knew exactly what broken ribs felt like.

Gina watched as they went about their business. Only a couple of days ago, Melissa was a healthy young mother with her whole life ahead of her. She had a little girl who would've depended on her.

Whenever she saw bodies laid out in the clinical environment of an autopsy room, she always tried to remain connected to who they were. Melissa's nightdress and dressing gown had been bagged. She watched as they measured her, checked everything they needed to check and made recordings of the results. They took the many samples required – hair, and swabs from every orifice. She listened as the pathologist called out measurements from behind his mask. The other CSI made notes and took samples from him, cataloguing each item of evidence as it was passed over.

The camera focused on the blow to the head. 'The right side of the corona capitis appears to have been hit with a spherical object of approximately five inches in diameter, causing a slight crack on the skull,' the pathologist called out. The clean CSI came in close with the camera, refocusing on the wound. 'Spherical object, like a ball.' As far as she could remember from the files, there had been no spherical objects of that size logged into evidence that could've caused that kind of injury. 'And the blue cord recovered at the crime scene matches the dimensions of ligature mark on the neck.' The same cord found at the scene was the same used for the strangulation.

The pathologist continued until he reached the woman's breasts. 'Looks like a clamping device used on many occasions has caused a build-up of scarring.' Gina's mind flashed back to the pliers in Mr Sanderson's bottom drawer. Had he been abusing her over and over again? She stared at the scarring. The skin looked thick, almost like it had healed on several occasions. The pathologist continued. 'Vaginal scarring, including more recent trauma, possibly caused by aggressive insertion of a large instrument.' Gina flinched and looked away. Anger built up inside her. No one should have to suffer the indignity and pain that Mrs Sanderson had suffered in the past. 'Four previously broken ribs,' the pathologist said. Gina struggled to swallow as she thought of all Melissa had been enduring. Her body was a mess.

'Something bad has been going on for a long time. Phipps or the husband?' Jacob asked as the pathologist continued.

'Who knows? Phipps was under the impression that she and Darrel weren't having sex any more but she wouldn't tell him if they were. Besides, does what Mrs Sanderson has been going through look like sex that anyone would consent to?'

Gina looked just above the cadaver as he went to make an incision, a perfect Y. It was something she'd seen before on several occasions, but she'd never been able to look directly at what was happening when the pathologist made the cut. She looked at her watch. With them being late, the autopsy had been going on for two hours. She turned to look at Jacob. He slouched with his arms folded in front of his chest as he watched.

Again, the pathologist shouted out the weights of the organs as they were weighed in turn, before returning them and sewing up the body. Gina turned to face the door. The pathologist began scrubbing down.

'Well between that and arresting James Phipps, it has been an eventful day so far,' Jacob said.

Gina looked at her watch. It was past lunchtime but she didn't fancy a thing. She felt dirty from hearing of Mrs Sanderson's sufferings. She wanted to go home and shower. The pathologist entered their area.

'Can you summarise that for me? Cause of death?' Gina asked.

'Asphyxiation. The blow to the head would've stunned Mrs Sanderson, may even have rendered her momentarily unconscious but it was the strangulation by cord that caused her death.'

'With all the information you already have, can you give us a more precise time of death?'

'With all the information we have now, it would have been between twenty-one hundred and twenty-two hundred, on the evening of Thursday the twelfth of April.'

'Is there anything else you can tell us?'

'We found semen present. She'd had sex that day. You already know the blood samples from the stairs and in the hall match up to Mrs Sanderson's. We don't know who the semen belongs to but if you can obtain suspect swabs, we can crossmatch them. Also, the pliers that were booked into evidence look to be a match for the injuries caused to Mrs Sanderson's nipples. We should have all the samples processed by early tonight. I will call with further findings as we get them.'

'Thank you,' Gina called as the pathologist made his way towards the changing area. 'We best go and tell the rest of the team – make sure Bernard attends the next briefing. We'll need his input. I'd hoped they'd find more though. Last night when I looked over the case notes there were still no fingerprints except for the householders', no footprints, no tyre tracks leading up to the house, nothing except what they wanted us to see. The spherical object, what could that have been? Maybe a stone, a cricket ball, something ornamental? There was nothing like that in evidence. This person is a ghost. Does Jimmy seem like he could be that good?'

'They are never as they seem. Someone certainly knows a lot about concealing their crime. I forgot, just before we left, Darrel called, asking if he could go back to the house.'

'I suppose now that we've seized everything we need we have to hand it back to him. I think we need Mr Sanderson to come back into the station. Will you call him? I'll just give Wyre a call, see how they're getting on.'

'Will do.'

Jacob turned to make the call and Gina took her phone out. 'Any news?'

'Yes. Mr Sanderson is here. Keeps bleating on about getting back into his house. He wants the PC removed from his front door.'

'Keep him there, we're on our way back. I need to speak to Mr Sanderson.'

CHAPTER EIGHTEEN

The tape had been rolling for several minutes and they were getting nowhere. Jacob sat beside Gina, ready to take notes. Darrel Sanderson stared at the wall behind them as he rocked back and forth in the plastic chair with his arms folded. He'd agreed to attend an interview under caution. A grin spread across his face. Gina almost wanted him to rock a little too far back. She didn't like his grin. Seeing him splayed out in discomfort would bring her a small amount of pleasure.

'Answer the question, Mr Sanderson. Did you and Melissa Sanderson have sexual intercourse on the day of her murder?' Gina asked.

'You know. You're sitting here, wasting time on me. It's that lover of hers you should be pursuing. She probably had sex with him.'

'Oh, don't you worry, Mr Sanderson, we'll be asking him too. We have obtained a semen sample. There will be no doubt as to who it belongs to soon. If you and Mrs Sanderson had intercourse, it would be in your best interests to tell me now.' The man stopped rocking on his chair and looked down. 'We are trying to find out who murdered your wife. We need your cooperation. Surely you want to find this person too?' Gina leaned over the desk and looked directly into Darrel Sanderson's eyes.

The man broke her stare. 'Yes, we did. We had consensual sex earlier that day. She was my wife. We did things like that.'

'Like placing her nipples in-between pliers and squeezing, like inserting objects into Mrs Sanderson's vagina that caused some of the most horrendous scarring and damage I've ever come across in my career. She had four broken ribs. Your wife was in a bad way. What do you have to say about that?' The man remained silent. 'Given the extent of injuries to your wife's body, we will be organising a medical examination of your daughter.'

'I love my daughter. I'd never hurt her. How dare you,' he yelled as he stood, knocking his chair over as he pointed at Gina.

Gina thought back to the bruising and cut on the little girl's arm on the night of Mrs Sanderson's murder. Mia had to be checked out. She'd never forgive herself if Mia was being abused and she didn't do anything. She made a note on her pad to call Devina Gupta of Children's Services as soon as the interview was complete. With the little girl already being looked after by Darrel's brother, now was the right time. If her father was harming her, he wouldn't get another chance.

'Sit down, Mr Sanderson.'

The red-faced man sat back in the chair and slammed his fist onto the table. 'Everything my wife and I did was consensual. I have an alibi for the night of her murder. Despite her affair, I loved her and I love my daughter.'

'Mr Sanderson. Tell me about the friends you went out with.' She watched as Darrel shifted in his chair before staring back at her.

'Are you insane? I don't know what this has to do with my wife's murder. I've got nothing more to say. I want a solicitor. I'm not saying any more until I see my solicitor, do you hear me?'

'Interview terminated at fifteen fifteen,' Jacob said as he stopped the tape.

'When do I get to go back to my house? Mia is unsettled, she needs to go home.'

'Your house will be released back to you later today. I will keep you updated.'

She thought of all the evidence they had. They had nothing to formally charge Mr Sanderson with. He was right, he had a watertight alibi for the time of his wife's murder, but there was something about him. Her mind kept bringing forth the extent of Melissa's injuries and scarring. How could that ever be consensual? Having Mia examined was the right thing to do. They couldn't risk any further harm to the little girl if she was being abused. He stared directly at her. The intensity making her want to look away, but she wasn't going to let him win. He eventually looked away.

'Are you okay explaining to Mr Sanderson what happens next?' Gina said to Jacob.

'Yes, guv.'

She needed to get on with the investigation. She'd get Wyre to explain to Mr Sanderson's brother what was going to happen. Whilst Jacob was answering all of Darrel's questions, she'd have everything arranged for his little girl's medical examination. As soon as she closed the interview room door, she pulled her phone from her pocket and pressed Devina's number. They needed little Mia examined immediately. She was not going home with that monster if her suspicions were confirmed.

CHAPTER NINETEEN

Gina grabbed a chocolate bar from her desk drawer and began checking her emails. Bernard had now released the scene and had also confirmed that he was attending their afternoon briefing. He also mentioned that the pathologist had sent a copy of the photos from the post-mortem over. She continued scrolling. Briggs had emailed her to say that Annie from the Corporate Communications Department would be attending the briefing and that she and Briggs would be working closely together on the press statements. The last email was from Devina to say that Darrel Sanderson's brother and daughter were with her, and that a doctor had arrived to complete the medical examination.

She finished chewing on the chocolate bar as she once again read the crime scene notes. Leaving her office, she headed towards the incident room where O'Connor was working away with his earphones on, alongside the team of four that had taken the initial calls. She could see that he was listening to the calls that had been forwarded to him in response to the press release. The new crime scene photos had been added to the boards. Gina shuddered as she stared at the post-mortem photos.

'Thoughts so far,' Briggs asked as he approached her from behind.

'It all seems so straightforward. We have a suspect, her lover Jimmy, who has no alibi. He had just been dumped and couldn't bear to lose her. He seems so obvious. Then, we have Darrel Sanderson.' She walked over to his photo on the board and pointed. 'His wife had been suffering hideous abuse for a long time, way before Phipps came onto the scene. I've never seen anything like it, sir, but he has an alibi. He was in the pub at the time. He couldn't have killed her.'

She looked at the photo on the other side of the board and focused on a close up of Mrs Sanderson's breasts. Scarring over scarring, topped with a fresh wound. 'This had been happening to her for years. Anyone capable of doing this has to be danger-ous. Her husband kept spouting that everything they did was consensual. I reread the crime scene notes that Bernard updated.'

'And?'

'It did appear that she was drinking a lot. Several wine bottles were found in the recycling bin and an empty glass was on the side. They reported a high level of alcohol in her bloodstream on the night of her murder. I guess she was drinking to escape this,' she said as she nodded at the photos.

Briggs stepped a little closer and stood beside her. 'It's nice to catch up with you, even though we are in the middle of such a horrible case.' He smiled.

She watched as he combed his hair with his fingers and adjusted his slightly wonky tie. Seeing him look so unkempt had been a first. 'You look tired, sir.'

'You know how it is when you have personal issues to deal with.'

She cleared her throat and shifted her gaze from Briggs to the board. 'Phipps gave us names of some of Darrel's friends. The only one I have tracked down is his alibi, Robert Dixon. They were both at the pub together on the night of the murder. We'd need to speak to the rest of his friends.'

Briggs paused and looked away. 'Nice holiday?'

'Yes. Thanks for asking, sir.' An air of awkwardness surrounded them. 'We're heading over to Phipps's this afternoon to search the place under a section eighteen.'

Briggs turned to leave the room. 'Keep me updated. I'll see you at the briefing later.'

As she listened to his footsteps disappearing down the corridor, she took a deep breath. He was obviously struggling more than she was to get over what they had. A few months of a secretive, casual relationship was all it was. It was nothing more than a one-night stand that had lasted far too long. She checked her watch and called Devina. She needed to know how the medical examination had gone.

CHAPTER TWENTY

Darrel stood in front of his house, watching the policeman lean against his front wall. How dare they stop him going into his home and make him wait. How dare they ask him about his and Melissa's sex life – just, how dare they. He wanted to go and kick the copper hard in the head. He scrunched his fists into a ball. How dare they take his daughter from him pending further investigation! He had an alibi – for heaven's sake.

A police protection order they called it. He just hoped Mia wouldn't end up with strangers. He'd begged them to place her with Alan and Cerys, his brother and sister-in-law. They'd take care of Mia. His brother was a good candidate for caring for her. At least his brother had lived the life of a saint. He'd had the same job for twenty years, his wife was a nurse and they'd just announced they were expecting their first child after struggling for years to conceive. He was lucky they were well-respected, community-minded people, or he'd have to ask his busybody mother and he didn't want Mia staying in her pokey little retirement unit in the centre of Bromsgrove. At least Alan and Cerys had a nice house.

He watched as the copper grabbed a sandwich from his car before sitting on the wall. His beautiful home, covered in police tape – he wanted to tear it off and barge in.

What would the neighbours think? How long would it be before one of the do-gooders from further down the road popped by, offering prayers and home-made pie? As far as he was concerned they could stick their thoughts, prayers, sympathy, pies, the lot. He wanted none of it. He just wanted it all to go away.

The policeman turned to see him standing there. 'Can I help you?' he shouted across the gardens.

'No, it's my house. I'll come back later,' he replied as got into his hire car. They'd taken his car to investigate, as one of the possible scenes. He should've asked when he'd get that back too. He opened the glovebox and took the burner phone out. He'd missed a call from Rob, which he needed to return.

His heart hummed as he listened to the ringtone. 'Hurry up, Rob, pick up.'

'How are you doing?'

'Bad. Terrible, in fact. They've taken Mia. She's with my brother, Alan, at the moment, but I don't know what will happen to her. For now, I can't stay with him and the bastards won't let me back into my home. They took my daughter. That wasn't meant to happen.'

'And it shouldn't have happened. Did they say why?'

'No.' He stared out of the window, watching the copper outside his house. He knew full well that the astute detective wouldn't ignore the bruising, especially as they'd discovered the injuries to Melissa's body, but he wasn't going to tell Rob about that.

'Well, they can't keep you both apart. You've done nothing wrong, have you?'

Darrel held the phone away from his ear as he felt his body tense. He wanted to kick the hell out of the footwell. He wanted to have a good go at putting his fist through the car window. 'No, I'm sure all will be fine.'

'Who took her?'

'Children's Services. DI Harte, the copper's name was. She ordered it. Bitch.' He toiled over the look she gave him towards the end of the interview, forcing him to break their locked stares.

There was silence on the end of the line. 'Just hold it together. You'll get through this and all will be fine. Keep strong for Mia. Go check yourself into a hotel for the night, have some food and try to keep calm. We'll speak again soon.' Rob ended the call.

Darrel turned the key in the ignition, he couldn't go to his brother's and he didn't want to sit in a pub all day. His only option was a hotel. He headed towards Redditch, maybe he'd just have a coffee before checking in, just in case his house became free. He'd rather be in his own home, sleeping in his own comfortable bed. Rob was right, he just needed to keep calm and then he'd get his daughter back. After all, it was Melissa who had been doing all the drinking. He'd questioned her on many occasions about her temper when she'd aimed it towards their child. He'd tell the police that and he wouldn't get angry at Mia any more without his cheating bitch wife being around.

CHAPTER TWENTY-ONE

Dan fiddled with his thinning, black, greased back hair and took a seat in the bay window opposite Rob.

'Tea?' Selina asked as she approached him. She knew Rob was watching her wiggle as she passed and she'd wiggle away. There was no way on earth he'd have the chance to think about other women. She'd make sure of it. She was everything they all wanted, so pristine, so homely, in good shape and she never let herself go. Her neatly straightened hair fell beautifully over her shoulders. The hair stylist appointments that cost Rob so much were worth every penny. She knew exactly how to keep her man. Whomever he was lusting after didn't have a hope in hell of taking him.

'I'd love a tea, Selina, and one of your lovely cakes.'

'Of course. How are things going at the council?'

'It's a job. Just waiting until I can collect my pension,' Dan replied.

She left and placed her ear against the door. Dan didn't usually turn up like this, in the day. Her heart thumped. Something was up, but her husband wouldn't tell her anything. What else wasn't he telling her?

She dashed out to the kitchen and hurried straight back with a tea tray. 'Sugar?' she asked as she bent down and began pouring the tea from the china pot, watching her husband's every expression. He wasn't giving anything away.

'Yes, please. Two, I like it sweet,' Dan replied.

All she ever wanted to be was a wife with a lovely home and two lovely children. She had been a true success.

'Two it is. Enjoy your teas. I'll be in the sewing room if you need me. Got a bit of work to do.'

Rob sipped from his teacup. 'Thanks, love. We'll be fine for now. You can go.'

She leaned over him and kissed the side of his head before she left. Once again she leaned against the door, listening in. If they wouldn't tell her, she'd have to keep sneaking around.

As she listened to their muffled voices, she could hardly understand a word they were saying, but she definitely heard one name repeated over and over again.

DI Harte. That was who her husband was obsessing about. She heard the sofa creak as Dan rose. Within seconds, she was back in her sewing room, re-hemming one of her dresses.

CHAPTER TWENTY-TWO

Gina placed James Phipps's key in the keyhole and Jacob, O'Connor, Wyre, and two other officers followed her in. 'At least he gave us his door key,' she said as she entered the pitch black hallway and slipped on a pair of blue gloves. She felt along the wall, finding the light switch. A worn brown carpet covered the hallway. Phipps certainly didn't have the money that Darrel Sanderson had. A scratch in the woodchip wallpaper showed that the wall had been painted over several times. A slight bit of blue came through, then a speck of peach before the magnolia that covered the walls at present. She pushed the first door open. It led to a small store cupboard containing the boiler, an ironing board and a vacuum.

She continued, opening the door to the next room. 'We have the bedroom,' she said as she entered.

'We'll take a look in the other rooms,' Jacob said as some of the team followed him. Wyre remained behind Gina.

The bedroom was sparse. A double bed and two bedside tables were all that filled the room. To their left was a built in double wardrobe. The large window was covered in condensation and mildew. She tried to imagine what Melissa had been thinking. Maybe she was fond of him but maybe there is no way she could've existed in these conditions. Melissa had been used to a life of money, one of luxury. Her house had four bedrooms and three bathrooms. Jimmy could only offer her a one bedroomed, mildew filled flat, with draughty window frames. She listened as the gentle breeze whistled through the broken air vent in the corner of the bedroom. He had no curtains and while his cream quilt cover had a freshly washed fragrance, it was crumpled and ill fitted. His mattress protector had come away from the mattress. She stared at the bed. He'd arranged a row of pillows on one side of the bed. Had he slept at night, imagining that the pillow wall beside him was Melissa?

Taking a step forward, she unravelled a screwed up photo that had been discarded on his bedside table. A close up of Melissa brandishing a slight smile with a healthy glow to her face, brushing her fingers through one side of her hair. She looked content lying in his bed. Gina imagined it to be the photo he'd see every night as he closed his eyes and thought of her at home, in bed, next to her husband. Had it all got too much for him? Knowing she was still with her husband at night, while he festered here alone.

'That's a rather intimate photo, guv,' Wyre said as she stood next to Gina.

'It is, and she once looked so happy to be in this confined, damp room. That was the look she was giving at some point while lying beside him, in this bed. She's clothed too.' Gina took a closer look at the photo, searching for something in the background, that wasn't there now. The same magnolia woodchip that continued from the hall was all she could see. The crumpled cream quilt cover was the same, but Melissa was not like she'd last seen her, insides out, during the autopsy. A flash of Melissa's body, tied to a chair in the kitchen, the life removed from her, with a blue cord looped around her body, sped through Gina's thoughts. 'We're looking for blue cord, denim or jeans, especially ripped ones, anything that suggest he's forensically aware – forensic suits, gloves, hair covers, boot covers, his phone.' As she poked around the drawer, she found his phone on top of a packet of open condoms. She grabbed it, dropped it into an evidence bag and sealed it up along with the charger.

She walked around to the other bedside drawer, the one that sat next to the pillow mountain in the bed, while Wyre began bagging as many pairs of Jimmy's jeans as she could find. 'I can't see tears in any of these,' she called back.

'Keep looking, it could be tiny. Bag them all anyway.'

As she opened the drawer, she spotted a couple of boxes and a little teddy bear with *I love you* sewn onto its belly. The boxes contained a gold necklace, a pair of earrings and a bracelet. 'She could never take his gifts home. She left them safely in Jimmy's bedside drawer. Could you bag and tag these when you're done over there?'

'Will do, guv. He has lots of denim. Six pairs and I've barely touched the surface.'

Gina kneeled on the floor and looked underneath the bed. Nothing. It was as tidy and sparse as the rest of his bedroom. She headed out of the room and into his lounge-come-kitchen. This small flat was his world. A worn but comfy looking two-seater sofa almost filled the lounge area. The one wall was covered in posters from his past theatrical productions. *Waiting for Godot*, *A Midsummer Night's Dream*, *Pygmalion*, *Talking Heads*, and many more. He'd had a steady career in the big smoke. Why had he come back to rural Warwickshire after spending so long building a career in London? Had he come back to search for Melissa? Had he come back to stalk Melissa after reconnecting with her on Facebook? Had he been a poor artist, struggling to survive and starving between each job? He'd spent over twenty years there and one day decided he was moving back to little old Cleevesford. He'd be lucky to even find an am-dram group to involve himself with in this town. Maybe he sought change and teaching provided another challenge in life. Maybe he sought closeness to Melissa, knowing she would never leave her husband unless he was around to influence her. She refused to leave Darrel Sanderson. Had that tipped him over the edge?

His coffee table was marked with coffee rings and his small television was a little dusty, but apart from that, the rest of the room was fairly clean. Basic, but clean. She watched as O'Connor rooted through his cupboards that were filled with the most basic of plates and food stuffs. He had a few tins, and few cup noodle meals. She walked over to his drop leaf table and spotted the script and production plans that he'd mentioned to them in interview, the production plans he'd supposedly been working on during the night of Melissa's murder.

She flicked through the pages and spotted Melissa's name written over and over again, then scribbled over. She turned the page. He'd scribbled so hard, the pen had gone through four sheets of paper, damaging the table underneath. Had he left his flat, watched until Melissa's husband had left for the pub? Had his hands been shaking with jealousy as he was about to bring his plan of killing her to fruition? After all, they had argued the day before. He also knew a lot about creating a scene. He lived for drama. Did that need for drama spill over into his personal life?

'Bag this,' she said as she pointed to the paperwork. Had Jimmy hidden a forensics suit and the washing line cord in his car? Maybe they'd had more arguments and he'd planned this to happen all along if she were ever to declare that she no longer wanted to be with him. So many thoughts ran through her mind. She reminded herself that Phipps had a motive, he had the opportunity, he was clever – he'd probably researched many roles in his career, maybe he'd written his own script, thinking of himself as the actor when he came into the station and gave a statement. There was no evidence as yet of a spherical object, washing line cord, forensic suits or torn jeans, but he was clever. He wouldn't screw up on continuity.

Smith entered. 'Anything in his car?' Gina asked.

'Nothing out of place.'

She held up the bagged phone. 'I need this analysed as soon as possible,' she said, passing it to O'Connor. They only had until nine the next morning to keep Jimmy, without asking Briggs to contact the Superintendent for a twelve-hour extension. She wanted to have the case nailed before then.

'Guv, I found another pair of jeans in the corner of the airing cupboard. There's a tear in them.'

Gina's heartbeat quickened as she glanced at the jeans that Wyre held up, a smile almost emerging. 'Prioritise them. Bag them and get them across to Keith immediately. They could well be a match to the sample we found close to Melissa's body.'

CHAPTER TWENTY-THREE

After Gina finished relaying everything she knew to the team, Briggs nodded to Annie from Corporate Communications, as she made a note. He even smiled as he whispered something to her. Briggs almost looked happy and Gina was almost pleased for him. Annie was everything she wasn't. She looked glossy, fit and was always well turned out. Her light brown hair was shiny and fell with a wave over her shoulders. Gina's mop of unloved hair had never been shiny. She didn't have time to style and straighten every day. Annie's make-up took a few years off her, giving her a fresh look.

She glanced at the email that came through on her phone. It was Devina Gupta. Darrel Sanderson's little girl had been placed into the care of his brother, Alan, and his wife, Cerys, while further investigations took place.

As Annie spoke, she commanded the room. She had decided that it was in the public interest to release a further statement to the press as they'd made an arrest. At this point, she knew if Jimmy's name got out and there wasn't enough evidence to convict him or if it began to look like he hadn't done it, his name would forever be tarred but the press were hungry for further information, badgering them for more news of the arrest. A murder was huge news in Cleevesford.

'Bernard, where are we with the evidence processed from the house?'

'The washing line is a common type. It is found in just about every hardware store, supermarket and market stall in the country.

It is mass-produced and repackaged to suit the retailer. As for the small sample of material that matches that of a forensic suit, again, these things can be purchased from many online retailers.'

'But, finding a suspect with a history of that purchase on their computer or indeed the rest of the damaged suit would help pin a suspect down. We failed to find the object that Mrs Sanderson was initially struck with too,' Gina added.

Bernard hunched over as he glanced through his notes, his grey beard dangling on the desk. 'No fingerprints were found, no footprints, no palm prints.'

Gina's shoulders slumped. She'd hoped for more. 'So, the person who did this was more than prepared. They only have to watch an episode of any detective series on the TV to know what to do. We're up against educated people. Anything else?'

He leaned back and coiled the end of his beard around his index finger. 'We removed a laptop and a personal computer. Both have been sent away for analysis. I know it's costly but I've put a fast track on them with this being a murder and all. Be good to know what the Sandersons had been up to online, maybe what they'd been buying. The contents of their bed drawers were booked in and forwarded onto pathology. They've since been bagged and filed in evidence. As we already know, we have confirmed that the pliers were used to assault Mrs Sanderson. Alcohol was detected in Mrs Sanderson's blood too, suggesting that she probably wasn't on full form on the night of the attack. The semen samples have come back and there is no match to James Phipps from his DNA sample that we also fast tracked earlier.'

'Mr Sanderson said in his statement that he and his wife had sex earlier that day. We have yet to take a DNA sample from him,' Gina said.

She listened as Bernard continued relaying what he knew. Wyre then spoke about her visit to the Angel Arms. There was no doubt that Mr Sanderson had been in the pub all night with his friend Rob – the CCTV had confirmed that as fact. It was also confirmed that Jimmy had slept in his car outside The Eagle on Crabbs Cross throughout the night of Friday the thirteenth of April. It had shown him staggering to his car late that night and remaining there until early morning. He still didn't have an alibi for the night of Melissa's murder.

'Do we have Jimmy's phone analysis back?'

'We do, guv,' Wyre replied. 'On the Thursday evening he left a few missed calls, then messaged her. They started around nineteen hundred hours. The full transcript is on the system but I'll read the last one. He wrote, "*I can't stand to see you living the rest of your life with that man!*" That was the last one. He sent a couple more messages earlier that day that were similar in content. When we cross-checked Mrs Sanderson's secret phone we couldn't find them. She must have deleted them after she had read them.'

'I'll read the full transcript when I get home. Thanks for gathering that information. Anything else to add for now?'

O Connor looked up. 'Only that Mr Sanderson has called another three times. He wants to go back to his house and we can't do much more to keep him away.'

'Are you sure we have all we need, Bernard?'

'Yes. All the samples have been taken to the lab and all the exhibits have been filed in evidence.'

'We'll have to allow him access. Smith, will you call off whoever's on sentry duty at the moment and let Mr Sanderson know he can have access to his house?' Smith nodded. 'Now keep going over things. O'Connor, Wyre, I want you both to interview Jimmy again. Question him on the messages to Melissa. Take the rehearsal schedule with her name written all over it, press him further. If it was him, he went through a great deal of planning.'

'Yes, ma'am,' Wyre replied.

The level of chatter increased in the incident room as everyone continued with their tasks. Briggs stood and led Annie out.

She wondered if they were going to discuss the media, and then maybe have a drink or two. But it was no longer any of her business. She needed to go back to her office and delve into Melissa's past.

CHAPTER TWENTY-FOUR

Ellie zipped her coat up and pulled her black beanie hat just above her eyeline. It was going to be a long night. She darted across the back of the garden and slipped behind the tree at the back. Snuggling into a recess in the hedge, she tucked her body in and shivered. Although the sun had been warm during the day, the nights were chilly and damp. She gazed up at the stars and spotted the plough. It was the only constellation she knew. Becky had pointed it out to her when they were on holiday in Combe Martin a few months ago. At night, they walked to the top of the Hangman Hills so that Becky could take a time-lapse photo of the stars. She remembered shivering away, hoping she'd hurry. She had wanted to go back to the caravan they'd rented and warm up with a cup of hot chocolate.

The living room light was switched on. A small tremble passed through her body as she watched him enter the room and sit in a chair, facing the television. Luckily for Ellie, the curtains were left open. She supposed he didn't see the need to close them. His house was well secluded, surrounded by trees. The neighbours weren't too close by and woodland covered the back of the house. She eyed the house in awe. He'd done well for himself over the years, not like her. Would she have done better in life had it not been for him? If she'd finished university, would people in the art world have taken her more seriously? Would she have got higher value commissions? Instead of pursuing her goals, she'd wallowed, trying to piece together the flashbacks and, after that, trying to get blind drunk to blot them out.

Shivering, she edged forward so she could get a closer look. His wife walked into the room and sat opposite him. He beckoned her over. Her eyes were red, she'd been crying.

Her phone vibrated as a call came through. She snatched her phone from her pocket. It was Becky. She ended the call and sent a text.

I'll be back soon. Just a little hold up. I'll explain later. Xx

She had to tell Becky that she'd found him. That she'd followed him home from the pub and knew exactly where he lived. Becky had been suspicious yesterday when she'd arrived home late but Ellie hadn't found the courage to tell her what had happened. Becky could tell she was being evasive but she couldn't tell her, not yet.

His wife left, then came back with a shot of something in a glass. Ellie's mouth watered. What she'd do for a shot of anything. The thought of something warm and strong sliding down her throat, relaxing her body as she slumped into a comfortable settee with Becky's arms around her, was a vivid thought. Then she'd have another. One wouldn't be enough. Then the staggered jigsaw pieces that were her memories would come back to confuse her further, until she needed another drink to blot them out. What had started off as an attempt to heal was now further opening the wounds. It wasn't just opening them, it was prodding at the throbbing flesh, digging it away, until she could no longer take the pain.

As her attacker turned around, she took a few steps further forward. The main advantage of having no neighbours close by was that she had no worries about being spotted. All she needed to do was remain hidden from him. She moved a little closer, watching as his wife tried to lean into him for some affection. He brushed her out of the way. As Ellie took another step, a bright security light came on, illuminating her as she stood in the middle of the lawn.

She darted to the side of the building and doubled over as she gasped for breath. Blood whooshed around her body, pounding through her head. She was trapped between the front and the back garden. If she went back the way she had come, he would definitely see her. If she continued into the back garden, she could escape out of the gate and into the woods where she could run and run until she got away. Tears escaped from her eyes and dripped in abundance off her chin as she swallowed what she thought was her heart trying to make its escape through her mouth. A sickness washed over her and she fell to the ground, legs buckling under the stress of a panic attack that wasn't easing away. She needed to get to the back garden – she had to make a dash for it.

Leaning on the wall, she pulled her body to a standing position and took one step, then another. She couldn't hear her surroundings as her heartbeat was so erratic. Pain flashed through her chest. The pain was back. Was she having a heart attack? She took a deep breath. She'd had this pain a lot in the past, when she'd packed up drinking. At the time, drinking was the only thing that both caused it and eased it. *Take a deep breath*, she told herself, *and get a move on – quick.*

As she ran from the side of the house, she spotted the back gate. Now! She stumbled forward as she sprinted over the back garden, treading on a weed filled flowerbed. Her right ankle turned slightly as the back security light came on. Ignoring the pain, she darted to the back gate. Her hand searched for the lock. It was a slide across.

'What are you doing in my garden?' the voice boomed out as the back door was flung open. She slid the lock and opened the gate, hobbling into the darkness.

His footsteps crunched on undergrowth as he caught up quicker than she would have expected. Her only option was to hide out until he'd gone.

'Where are you?' he sang in a taunting way. His taunts turned into laughter. 'I saw you hobbling. I know you can't be too far away. Why were you at my house? Come out, come out.'

The sound of his voice took her straight back to that night. He'd seemed like just a normal guy in a bar. She'd trusted him when she'd taken the drink. Tears continued to fall as she shuffled closer to a tree stump, hoping he wouldn't spot her. All those fragmented dreams that she'd had over the years came flooding back as she heard his voice. A memory of being in the back of a car crossed her mind, him looking down at her, shouting at her, then forcing her to turn over in the confined space. Tears fell. She let out a sob.

'I'm getting closer. I wonder who you are. Do you like playing hide and seek? I do. I love hide and seek.'

She held her breath as he began to walk away in the opposite direction. Her phone beeped as a message came through. Becky.

Give me a call. I'm worried about you.

He ran towards her in a flash. She stood and hopped along, trying to escape his grasp, but he was closing in on her. She gasped for breath and held her pounding chest. She loved Becky so much, she just wanted to be home in their cosy little flat, in Becky's arms, talking about their future – instead, the man who'd haunted her for years was now upon her.

'Get away from me,' she yelled as she continued to jog and hop, fighting the pain in her ankle.

'I win.' He grabbed her hood, yanking her back.

'No!' He dragged her towards the house. 'Help,' she yelled as she caught sight of the plough through a break in the trees.

'No one's listening,' he shouted. Then, a flash of pain radiated from her nose as she took her first blow. The woods went black as she took her second.

CHAPTER TWENTY-FIVE

Sunday, 15 April 2018

Gina sat eating a flapjack as she brought up Melissa's file on her computer screen. There was a tap at her office door and Jacob entered.

'Did I miss out?' Jacob asked.

'No. O'Connor's wife hasn't been baking anything today. I grabbed this for breakfast, on the way in.' She took another bite as she scrolled down the file. 'Want a bite?' she asked as she held the flapjack towards Jacob.

'No, guv. I'm trying to cut down on eating so much sugary shit but this place isn't helping.'

Gina laughed as she finished the last bite, rolled up the wrapper and flung it in the bin. 'Me too. My good intentions only normally last until the next morning, when Mrs O sends O'Connor to work with a batch of fresh bakes. I could do with cutting down, losing a few pounds and all that,' she replied as she fidgeted in her chair. That was a lie. Since her split with Briggs she was barely eating at home and had been struggling to maintain her calorific intake. Even her all-inclusive break away hadn't been enough to entice her to put her weight back on.

'If you don't mind me saying, boss, you've been a bit quiet the past few days. Is everything all right?'

'It's all tickety-boo. Right, where was I? We were going to take a look into Melissa's life outside the home.' She continued reading Melissa's information, while avoiding eye contact from her concerned colleague. 'Oh, tell me the extension came through to keep Jimmy for another twelve hours.'

'That's why I came. The Supers agreed that there's enough to keep him on. I saw Briggs in the incident room and he told me. We have until nine this evening to keep him.'

'Good, he's still our most viable suspect at this stage.' Gina kept scrolling down. 'Damn. We best get a move on.' She squinted as she leaned in to read further. 'I see Wyre has updated Melissa Sanderson's records. Looks like her mother only lives in Kings Norton. We should speak to her, get to know Melissa a little better. Maybe she opened up to her, confided in her. Will you call her? If she's in, I'll pay a visit.'

'Will do. I was going to work with O'Connor on looking into Darrel's friends, the ones mentioned by Phipps.'

'That's great. We need to know what's been going on between them. I'll take Wyre with me to visit Annabelle Hewson. See if she can shed any light on who might have wanted to hurt her daughter.'

'And I'll keep digging this end into Phipps' information and let you know if I come across anything.' Jacob smiled as he left her office.

Apart from spending time with Suzanna Barker, Jimmy Phipps and her husband Darrel, Melissa didn't seem to mix much. Hopefully her mother could provide them with the information they so desperately needed.

Gina's phone began to ring. 'DI Harte.'

'DI Harte, can you tell me if James Phipps is being further detained for questioning on the murder of Melissa Sanderson?'

She leaned forward in her chair. 'Who is this?'

'Lyndsey Saunders, *Warwickshire Herald*. The public have a right to know if they are in danger and we have a duty to spread the news, especially if the community are at risk.'

'This number is used for police investigation work. You've mistaken me for the Corporate Communications Department and you know full well they are who you're meant to speak with. Please don't call again as you are hindering the investigation by tying up this line.' She slammed the phone down.

Wyre knocked and entered. 'Jacob mentioned a visit to Melissa's mother's.'

'Yes. Grab your coat. We're off to Birmingham.'

CHAPTER TWENTY-SIX

Gina drove to Kings Norton in Birmingham. Wyre gazed out of the window in a world of her own as they spotted the skyscraper. 'When did you speak to Annabelle Hewson?'

'Yesterday. Mr Sanderson had already called her. The woman was distraught and didn't really want to say much. She did ask when the funeral would be. I explained that we were still conducting investigations and, due to the nature of Melissa's death, her body wasn't ready for release as yet. She wasn't taking any of it in though. Poor woman.'

Gina stopped at a junction and watched as a mother with three young children crossed the road. 'Poor woman, indeed. Is there a Mr Hewson or a father in the picture?'

'No, and Miss Hewson never married. Mr Sanderson said that Melissa's father deserted her and her mother. I don't know what happened there. Maybe Miss Hewson will give us more information.'

Paula Wyre looked out of the window again.

'How's things with you?' Gina asked.

'Much the same,' Wyre replied. 'I visit my father still on occasion. He's the same bigoted bastard he always was, but now he's started being more active, attending English Defence League marches and taking part in their campaigns. I keep away from him.'

'Sounds like a nightmare. There's no harm in putting yourself first and you should. How are things going with George?'

'He's great. George and I have been seeing each other for three months now. He keeps asking why I haven't introduced him to my family. We are always around his. His mother's lovely, we go there for dinner. His nephews and nieces love me. They think I'm a really cool detective. We play cops and robbers and have great fun.' She paused and began biting the nail of her little finger. Gina had never seen a nervous side to Paula. 'I'm thinking of cutting ties with him.'

'Your dad?' Gina asked as she continued driving. It made a change to think about someone else's problems for a change and she and Paula had become fairly good friends since the last case they'd worked on.

'Yes. I don't like him and I feel bad saying that. My dad's just a low life and he'd never accept George or any of my other friends that weren't white and straight. He also thinks my career is ruining my prospects of fulfilling my so-called womanly duties of repopulating the planet. For heaven's sake. What century are we in? I don't even know if I want to add to the population, ever. There are too many people in the world and we're all ruining the planet.' She paused. 'I think I love him.'

Gina smiled as she searched for a space to park. 'Then he certainly sounds like a keeper. Stuff your dad. Your own happiness is more important.' She gripped the steering wheel as she thought about Wyre's comments. Her father couldn't see the remarkable professional that was sitting beside her.

'Thanks, guv. What about your mystery man?'

She pulled into a space outside the skyscraper where Miss Hewson lived. 'He's no more. I suppose I'm just not in the market for an intense relationship and it was getting too serious. Maybe one day. Right. Time to see if Miss Hewson can shed some light on Melissa's killer.'

CHAPTER TWENTY-SEVEN

A few beads of sweat began to form along Gina's hairline. 'That's me done in for the day. I hope they fix the lift soon. I feel sorry for the people who live here, having to do this every time they come and go,' she said as they reached the twelfth floor by foot.

'You should join me at the gym one evening.' Wyre's voice echoed through the stone corridor. It hadn't been the first time Wyre had invited her along.

'Never.' Gina laughed.

The door to Annabelle Hewson's flat had once been green, it was now a dull grey with patches of green where the paint hadn't worn off. Gina shivered as she tapped on the door. A damp chill filled the building.

'Who's there?'

'Miss Hewson. It's DI Gina Harte and DC Paula Wyre. We spoke on the phone a short while ago.'

The woman slid the chain and opened the front door, exposing the dark flat. Her almost white, straggly hair covered her mascara-stained face. All the doors off the hall were open but each room appeared to be in darkness. The woman let the door fall open and padded across the fraying carpet towards the far room. Gina swallowed as the smell of ammonia caught the back of her throat. As they followed the woman, Gina spotted the cracked toilet leaking onto what was once a pink mat. All the curtains in the flat were closed. She could see that Miss Hewson had her problems.

'I haven't got up properly for a couple of days. It's like everything has come to a standstill,' the woman said in a thick Brummie accent as she led them to the lounge and offered them a seat. 'Can I get you both a drink? I only have tea.'

Gina shook her head. 'Thank you for speaking to us, Miss Hewson. We really just wanted to have a chat about your daughter, Melissa Sanderson. First of all, let us offer our sincerest condolences.'

'It makes me shudder to hear that name, Sanderson. She's a Hewson.'

'Why is that?' Gina asked.

Wyre took a notebook from her pocket and began heading up the page.

'I always wanted better for my girl. It was just me and her until he came along with all his money. He seemed charming, to her at least. From the moment she met him, she was with him every minute, even followed him to London for a while. He only came here once.' She paused. 'I know what you're thinking. You're thinking, I can see why she wouldn't bring a nice young man to a shithole like this, but it wasn't always this way. I tried so hard. I kept two jobs down, kept the place half decent with the money I had, which was never much. I gave that girl everything. Worked myself to death and in return I've rarely seen my granddaughter. Now look at me. This whole flat is the product of what I've become. I'm just another nobody and my daughter is gone.' The woman pulled a can of super strength lager from beside the sofa chair and took a sip.

Gina sank into the settee. 'When was the last time you saw your daughter?'

'She visited at Christmas. Brought me a card and these slippers,' she replied as she pointed to the filthy slippers she was wearing. They looked like they had once been a shade of lilac.

'Had you heard from her since?'

'She called me about once a fortnight, maybe once every three weeks. Mostly just checking to see if I was still alive. I never thought I'd have to worry about her life though. I can't believe what happened to her.' The woman burst into tears and swigged from the can.

'Can I get you a cup of tea, Miss Hewson?' Wyre asked, standing up.

'No. I don't need tea. I need answers. Was it him?'

'Who are you referring to Miss Hewson?' Gina asked as Wyre say back down.

'Her husband. The man who controlled her every move. I'm convinced it's his fault she never came to visit. You should've seen her at Christmas. Constantly checking her watch and fidgeting in the exact same seat you're sitting on. She was here fifteen minutes until she dashed off. Whenever she called it was like she was always in a hurry, like she couldn't speak. I knew he wasn't with her but she doesn't… didn't want me to ask her any questions. We did have a row a month ago.' The woman wiped her damp eyes on the sleeve of her oversized jumper.

'What was the row about?'

'I told her she could have her life, her freedom and that she could leave him. I told her she'd be entitled to some money from the house and she could start a new life. I'd been telling her this for years, but I think she'd finally grown a voice and was enjoying using that voice against me, instead of him. She let rip. Told me to stop interfering and that I was a stupid cow who knew nothing.'

Gina shuffled in the seat. 'That sounds harsh. How about her father?'

'She blamed me for never telling her who her father was. I didn't want to tell her he was some deadbeat with whom I'd had a one-nighter with after pulling him in a nightclub in town. He was married. I saw him around a few times after and decided I'd have nothing to do with him.'

Gina glanced over at Wyre. 'Can you tell me his name?'

'Billy Quinton. It's a waste of time looking him up, he passed away over ten years ago. I saw his obituary in the paper. He wasn't all bad. I suppose I should've told him, given him the opportunity to be a father but I didn't and that's just the way life goes. Melissa resented me for keeping her in the dark. She resented me for not liking her husband. She resented me for not having any ambitions, for struggling to hold down all the dead-end jobs I've had, but such is life. I'd do anything to have her back though. I'd make it better. I don't know how, but I really would. I can't say I'm not full of regrets. I should've told Billy he had a daughter, but that's something I've got to live with forever,' the woman said as a tear slipped down her cheek.

'I'm so sorry to ask you all this at such an awful time. Did she ever mention anyone called James Phipps?'

The woman blew her nose and looked up as she shook her head. 'Not that I can remember. She had a boyfriend when she was at school, called James. Whether this is the same person, I have no idea. What's happening with my granddaughter?'

'She's staying with Mr Sanderson's brother at the moment while we investigate further.'

'Who's this Phipps person?'

'He was your daughter's lover. I was hoping she'd said something to you.'

The woman leaned forward. 'She never said a thing. The only difference I noticed was that she seemed to have grown a voice, as I told you, which she'd enjoyed taking out on me, like I already said. She had changed this past couple of months, she was less passive. She'd badgered me for information about her father. She'll never know now, will she?'

'Thank you, Miss Hewson. Here's my number should you think of anything. Also, here's the number of Victim Support. They'll be able to help you. You shouldn't be going through this alone,' Gina said as they all stood. The woman sobbed. She almost stumbled and held onto Gina. Gina placed her arm over the woman's shoulder, allowing her to bury her head in her chest as she cried.

'Thank you, I'll call them. I can't carry on like this, can I?' she said as she held the can up. She broke away from Gina and forced a smile.

'Please do call them and call me if you think of anything. We are going to find the person who did this to your daughter.'

The woman watched as the two detectives left the flat and they heard her slide the chain across as they walked down the stone corridor, back to the steps.

'That was hard, guv,' Wyre said as they began the long journey down.

'It was. Gosh, look at the time. We only have Jimmy until nine tonight. We need to get back quick.'

CHAPTER TWENTY-EIGHT

The throbbing got louder as blood pounded and whooshed through her head. Red, everything was red and dark and ouch – he prodded her. Ellie yelped.

'See, I told you she was alive. Your pills did the trick. I bet she's had a lovely sleep,' her captor said.

Pain flashed from her tailbone to the middle of her back. Her nose. What had happened to her nose? Her head ached like mad. She gazed around the room and then back at their faces. It was morning. As she gazed at the window through blurry eyes, a flash of pain shot through her whole body. The short woman stared, open-mouthed, as if she was about to blurt something out. Her unruly curls looked as if she hadn't tended to them for weeks, one curl matting into the other, forming clumps. In another life, she'd love to have painted her portrait. Her every feature looked pained and bedraggled.

'What have you done? We should have called the police last night.' The woman kept repeating as her trembling hands spilled the glass of squash she was trying to sip.

Ellie wriggled out of the way to avoid the splashing liquid, but the cord that bound her arms and legs thwarted her attempt. She tried to lean up but the back of his hand came down on her already tender nose. Blood seeped down the back of her throat causing her to splutter as she lay back on the stone kitchen floor.

The man grabbed her bound arms and dragged her along the hallway, through to the living room, stopping at the settee. 'Don't just stand there watching. Grab her legs,' he yelled.

The blubbering woman crept towards her and reached down for her legs. 'Don't make me do this. I'm sorry, I truly am.' Her face came out in hives as her red-eyed gaze met Ellie's.

'What? For heaven's sake. Pull yourself together. Just lift when I say. Now.' The woman failed to respond. 'I said now. Just do it.' The crying woman did exactly what she was ordered to do.

'Let me go. Help me. I know you don't want to hurt me.' Ellie knew her best chance of escape was to appeal to the woman. The back of her jacket and jumper had lifted up and she'd felt the rug burning her flesh as they half lifted and half dragged her unresponsive body through the hall, into a small snug room. Although a snug, the room was far from cosy. It barely looked lived in. There were no pictures on the walls, no ornaments on the fireplace, no books or magazines. She leaned to the right to allow her nose to trickle and spotted a neat pile of boxes marked 'lounge two'. They had just moved in.

'Grab a rag, will you? Did you hear me? Stop staring and help me.'

Ellie yelped as he lifted her and dropped her onto the sofa. Her raw nose stung every time she breathed in. As she breathed out, a bubble of blood formed and burst, trickling down her face.

'Look. The stupid cow is about to ruin the new settee.'

'She's bleeding. What the hell did you do to her?'

'What makes you think I did this? She fell. She's an intruder. She was in our garden, looking through our windows, probably waiting for us to go to bed so that she could rob us or attack us. I like the way you blame me when it is the fault of this piece of shit. Hurry up and get that rag before she bleeds all over the settee. You don't want that, do you? Bleeding all over the settee would make me a very angry man.'

The woman shook her head as her gaze met Ellie's. 'We should call the police. It's not too late. We were just defending ourselves, that's all.'

'Look at her. We can't call the police. We don't need the police. I'm sure we can all deal with this in a civilised manner.'

'Please let me go,' Ellie said. 'Call the police, please.'

The woman began to sob again then she broke eye contact with Ellie and ran out to the kitchen, sobbing.

He'd got her exactly where he wanted and she knew it. She'd made it easy for him all those years ago when she accepted the drink in her usual trusting manner. He'd taken *carefree* from her. He'd taken a lot from her but she had no idea what he intended to take from her this time.

'I know you from somewhere.' He glared at her, lifting her hair and turning her face to the side. 'So you came back for more?' he whispered, as he sat beside her and stroked her forehead. 'You've changed. What happened to your beautiful hair?' She flinched as he stroked her neck and began undoing the zip on her jacket. 'Don't worry, you've let yourself go since the last time we were acquainted.'

He remembered her. 'Let me go.'

'And why would I do that? So you can go running to the police and say I hurt you. They wouldn't believe you anyway.'

She knew he was right. It was far too long ago to prove anything but she'd seen, with a lot of the historic abuse cases that were surfacing in the news lately, if one person came forward, others might. She might not have been the only person he'd raped and attacked. People like him were predators and she knew it. She'd spent years reading about his type and now it all fitted. He had a grandiose style and a strong sense of entitlement when it came to women. People like him don't stop at one.

'When I saw you in the Angel, sitting in the corner, I recognised you straight away. You may have cut your hair off and put a bit of weight on, but I'd recognise you anywhere. I knew we'd become acquainted once again and look, I was right. Here we are now.' He'd known she was there. She'd been so sure he hadn't recognised her. 'Come back to see me, did you? I was that good, was I?'

She leaned forward and spat a mouthful of blood and saliva at his face, catching the corner of his eye. He wiped the mess away with the back of his hand. 'Something like that,' she replied. He may be holding her captive but he wasn't going to break her.

He grabbed her sweaty hair and slapped her face with his other hand. As he leaned in closer, she almost heaved as she inhaled the smell of stale coffee and whisky on his breath. 'Do that again and we'll certainly have a lot of fun reliving that summer night. Twenty-five years is a long time to wait to see you again.'

'What summer? What are you talking about?' Natalie asked as she entered the room with a tea towel and passed it to Bruce.

'Tell her,' Ellie shouted, as another streak of blood slipped from her nose.

'Yes, tell me.'

'Honey. Go and have a lie down, I can see you're getting anxious. When I've dealt with her, I'll be up in a minute with a chamomile tea.'

'I'm not tired.'

'You're not well. This is no good for you.'

'I want to know what happened when I was carrying the baby we lost, twenty-five years ago. I miscarried our little girl that summer and you deserted me, left me alone in London without a word. I didn't know anyone there. You were—'

Ellie began to wriggle, trying to break free from the binds. 'He raped me. It was the fourteenth of August, 1993. He's a revolting evil rapist. Where were you? At home, upset about your loss, while he was out at the Angel, drugging and raping me. A student based in London you said you were. Just home for the summer.'

Natalie began to sob again. 'Is this true?'

He leaned down over Ellie. 'Lies will get you nowhere.' He stood up and held his wife, a hand on each shoulder as he looked into her eyes. 'I didn't do what she's accusing me of doing. Could I rape someone? Have I ever hurt you? I look after you when you're ill. I'm always there for you. This woman is deluded. Look at her. You deserve to know the truth though. Back then, she'd been harassing me and I saw her in the pub the other day, watching me again. I thought when we came back, she'd be gone but she was there, ready to start her stalking escapade once again. I won't let her ruin us or my life, or what we have. I love you, do you hear? And I haven't raped anyone.'

Natalie broke away and wiped her eyes as she took the bloodied towel from his hand. 'I don't know what to believe.'

He leaned forward and gently kissed her. 'You do. You need me. I need you. Go up to bed. I'll deal with this situation and I'll bring you a drink in a bit.'

The woman scrunched her face up as she burst into tears and nodded.

'Don't leave me here with this psychopath,' Ellie shouted, but the woman was already making her way up the stairs.

'She won't listen to you. She needs me. Do you know what it's like to be needed?' He traced her neckline with his index finger until it settled on her necklace. One half of a heart. She wore one, Becky wore the other. 'Pretty. So there is someone out there who needs you. Someone who'll be waiting for your return. Am I right?'

Ellie stared, refusing to give anything away. Her phone began to vibrate. He leaned forward, reaching deep into her pocket, trying to feel her as he grabbed the phone. 'Becky with a heart. You're in love with a Becky. I wonder what Becky's thinking now. Is she the trusting kind? Does she live close by? Where does Becky live? Maybe I'll pop by, see how she is. Is she a looker?'

Another tear dripped down her cheek. She tried to wriggle out of the binds but they were too strong. Hands behind her back. Ankles bound together. Her captor watching her every move. She wasn't going anywhere in a hurry. 'You go near her and I'll—'

'You'll what?' She looked away. 'Thought so.' Her tough exterior, the one most people saw on a daily basis was fast melting.

Panic rose through her body. 'Help. Let me go. Help me.'

'Shut up. You know what happens if you scream and shout.' She opened her mouth to reply but she couldn't. An image flashed through her mind. Creaking, back and forth in a car. She couldn't open her eyes, she could just feel a moving sensation. 'All That She Wants' kept playing in her mind. She remembered not being able to recall the lyrics after line three.

'Help!' She needed to get out, get away from him.

He slapped her. 'No one's coming for you.'

He told her back then that no one was coming for her. It was like it was all happening again. Everything flooded back, as clear as day. They'd been in the back of a car, in the Angel Arms car park. She remembered why she couldn't yell as she spotted other people leaving the pub after closing time. The smell of leather and oil flashed through her mind. He'd gagged her with a piece of leather used to clean car windows. Her heart began to race. She wouldn't yell or scream. She couldn't bear to be gagged again – ever. She was going to find a way out. His wife, Natalie, was her key to escaping. She'd seen an element of compassion in her eyes.

'Please let me call Becky.'

'No deal.' He lifted the phone and opened the message. 'Becky said she loves you and is wondering why you didn't come home. She's begging you to call. I'll answer for you.' He grinned as he read his message back. 'Met an old friend at the pub and had a few. Slept on their sofa. Love you.'

'Please don't send that,' she said as she cried. But it was too late. He'd hit the send button. Now Becky would think she'd gone straight back on the drink.

A message pinged straight back and he read it aloud. 'Please don't tell me you've started drinking again. Tell me where you are. I'm not angry. I'll come and pick you up.' He dropped the phone and stamped on it. 'Bit of a drink problem?'

Ellie sobbed as he left the room. Becky now thought she'd gone on a bender, but Becky also knew she'd still go home. She'd never stayed out the whole night, let alone all the next day. She'd had her relapses but she had always gone home. Becky would know something was majorly wrong.

He returned with two glasses and carried half a bottle of whisky in the other hand. 'Let's celebrate our reunion over a liquid breakfast.'

He poured the rich amber liquid into a glass and held it under Ellie's chin. 'I don't want it,' she cried as he tipped it into her open mouth. The more he poured, the more she wanted it. Soon she was slurping all he'd given her with an open hungry mouth. The last thing she remembered was drifting off into a deep slumber on a comfortable settee, in a warm room, fighting any thought of resistance. She was past working out how she'd explain to Becky that she'd had a drink.

CHAPTER TWENTY-NINE

'You can't keep me here. I haven't done anything,' Jimmy yelled as he leaned forward, scraping the chair on the floor as he did so. Jacob sat back. Phipps's solicitor placed a hand on his client's arm as he whispered in his ear.

Gina threw her pen on the table and leaned forward, her stare meeting his. 'Mr Phipps. Let me lay this out for you. Melissa Sanderson was killed in a most horrific manner. You have no alibi and you have motive and means. We've seen the texts and analysed your phone records. You tried to call Mrs Sanderson several times just before she was killed. She'd told you she was staying with her husband. That must've cut to the core, the woman you love, refusing to leave her husband.'

She watched as beads of sweat slid over his brow and landed on the table. His hands began to tremble. He snatched them away and sat on them. He may be able to hide his trembling hands but he couldn't hide the sweat beads that continued to fall.

'He was everything you weren't, a successful businessman, who provided for her and their child. You couldn't offer her much, not like him. You flew into a jealous rage, couldn't accept her rejection. You waited until he went out. She'd told you in her messages when he was at the pub or out. His routine was exactly that, very routine. She let you in, didn't she, and you were prepared. As their crying child screamed and screamed you watched the life ebb out of her as you throttled her, isn't that right, James?'

He stood and kicked the chair to the floor. 'You have no idea. How dare you make all that up? How very dare you. I didn't do this and you have nothing on me.'

'Sit down, Mr Phipps.'

The man wiped the sweat off his brow and reluctantly sat.

'We took a look around your flat. The work you said you were doing, I believe you. You came to a standstill, didn't you? Couldn't work any longer. She was on your mind.' She pulled the document from the exhibit folder they'd seized from his flat and placed it on the table. 'That certainly came from the mind of an obsessed person. Couldn't get her out of your head. You kept writing her name on your work over and over again until you flipped so bad that the pen you were scribbling with ended up permanently damaging your table.'

'I didn't flip and I didn't leave my flat.' He sucked in a deep breath. 'That's all I'm saying. No comment.'

The suited solicitor peered over his glasses. 'My client has answered all your questions. If you have nothing proving my client murdered Mrs Sanderson, I suggest you release him immediately.'

Gina glanced at Jacob. He glanced back at her. Phipps leaned over the table with his head in his hands. They only had a couple of hours left and unless they could provide evidence that wasn't circumstantial, Phipps was going to walk. What they had so far would never stand with the CPS. She knew it and his solicitor knew it. She checked her watch, the minutes were ticking away.

Had Phipps removed all the evidence and felt secure in the knowledge they wouldn't find anything or did he genuinely have nothing to hide? All the denim found in his flat had been fast tracked for urgent analysis. Keith had called her, confirming that none of it matched the sample found at the Sanderson's house, not even the damaged jeans they found in the airing cupboard.

'I will tell you something,' he said.

Gina straightened her back, waiting for Phipps to continue.

The solicitor whispered into Phipps's ear. 'It's okay.' The solicitor nodded. 'I was worried about her. You should check out her husband.'

'Why's that?'

Phipps grinned and leaned back, enjoying being the person now controlling the interview. Gina had no idea what Melissa had ever seen in him.

Gina watched as Jacob sat poised with his pen in his hand and nodded. 'You should tell us anything you know, Mr Phipps.'

'When we got intimate, she wouldn't take her clothes off. I pulled her jumper up once and she freaked out and went berserk. I never once saw her body at all. I felt it underneath her clothing. Her breasts were all rugged, like scarred. She was hiding something and always refused to talk about it. We tried to have sex a couple of times and she couldn't handle it, said she had medical problems and they caused her too much pain. I'd tried to get her to call the doctors and make an appointment. She dismissed my worries as she always did.'

The scarring he described on her breasts matched up to what they'd seen during the post-mortem. From what the pathologist had said, she was probably in too much discomfort to want sex. 'Did she ever mention much about her home life?'

'I tried to press her for information. I knew something was wrong. He had something to do with it, I know he did. She did say something once, after we'd been seeing each other for about four weeks.' The man stared at the wall behind Gina as he processed his thoughts.

'Go on.'

'Her husband. She said, since having their little one, he'd become more controlling. I know she'd called it off with me, but she hadn't wanted to. She couldn't find the strength to leave him and start again. She loved me. I know she did, and I'd have never given up on her. She was a clever woman, had so much to offer the world but he wanted to keep her at home like all his friends' wives. He was always calling, checking up on her. She said he hadn't always been like that and he'd changed, slowly chipped away at her confidence but he couldn't keep her down.'

'Are these the friends whose names you gave us previously?'

'Yes and that's all I'm saying. No comment.'

The solicitor removed his glasses and wiped his tired eyes before placing them back on. 'Unless you have anything more on my client, I suggest you let him go.'

Gina closed her notebook. 'I'll leave you to finish up here,' she said to Jacob, leaving before she kicked the chair. They were almost out of time and she didn't have anything further to throw at Phipps.

As she left the interview room, she spotted O'Connor walking along the corridor, eating a pie. He gripped the bottom of the pastry so tight with his clumsy fingers, the filling squeezed over the top. O'Connor caught it in his mouth before it fell. His shiny head reflected the flashing strip light. 'Briefing now. We need to talk about Rob Dixon's relationship with Darrel Sanderson.'

As he spoke, he spat out a fleck of pastry. 'Okay, boss.'

She looked at her watch. There was something she really needed to do after the briefing.

CHAPTER THIRTY

The house seemed much quieter without Melissa and Mia but that would all change when he got his daughter back.

He turned the kitchen light on and stared at the cooker hood, imagining Melissa's dead body slumped in their carver chair. He placed his hands around his neck and began to squeeze, imagining how Melissa must have felt as the life was squeezed out of her. As his grip remained constant, he felt the need to gasp. Letting go, he sucked in the stale air of the kitchen. She'd have felt pain.

Through the darkness of the kitchen, he walked over to the table and kicked the chair. It fell to the floor, causing no damage whatsoever. He brought his heavy boot down on its solid frame and it shattered to pieces. His face flushed as he continued kicking until the pile of wood beneath him barely resembled a chair. He gasped for breath – he was so unfit it was embarrassing. He grabbed the padded seat and flung it across the kitchen, gasping and seething as it hit the pantry door. 'You got what you bloody well deserved Mrs.' He caught a glimpse of his clammy reflection in the stainless steel kettle. His hair seemed even greyer and his skin was almost ashen.

The hum of the fridge filled the room. He grabbed a beer and snatched the magnetic bottle opener from the fridge door, releasing a colourful painting. Mia's footprint dropped to the floor as he swigged the cold liquid. He grabbed it and walked through to the living room, sitting in the darkness with the curtains closed. He placed the picture of Mia's foot down and stared at the wall. It was

no good. He couldn't sit in all evening, alone. There was nothing
to do and the smell of death still hung in the air. He needed to
get out. He grabbed his phone from his back pocket and called
the only person he could talk to. 'Rob, coming out for a beer?'

'Not a good idea.'

'It is a damn good idea. My wife has just died. I'm also going
stir crazy and I've only been home a few minutes. I can't just
sit here with the telly on, watching crap. I don't even know
what's happening with Mia yet.' He thought of his daughter at
his brother's house. Every time he thought of that detective, he
wanted to wring her neck. He released his grip from the cushion.

'She'll be back with you soon. Start looking for a nanny or
something. That will keep your mind off things.'

'I've already contacted an agency. As soon as she's home, I'm
sorted.' Darrel paused and listened to the background noise
coming from Rob's house. 'Who's with you?'

There was a pause. 'The usual crew.'

Darrel grabbed his beer and walked to the window, his gaze
travelling along the drive, then onto the main road that ran out
of Cleevesford. His eyes focused on a car that was parked under
a streetlamp on the opposite side of the road. All his neighbours
had driveways with plenty of parking space. There was no need
for anyone to park on the road.

He ran to the back door and jogged along the hedge-lined
side of his garden. Whoever was in the car was too busy looking
down. In darkness he stared, willing the person in the driver's
seat to turn around and she did. DI Harte looked across at his
house. He flinched and kept close to the trees, out of her line of
sight. The very woman who'd taken his daughter now had the
nerve to sit outside watching his house.

'Are you still there?' Rob asked, holding the phone to his ear.

'She's here, watching my house,' he said as he entered through
the back door.

'Who?'

'That detective, Harte. The bitch who took my daughter. That woman is poison. She needs to pay for what she did.' He swigged the rest of his beer down in one and slammed the bottle onto the worktop.

'You need to get out of the house. But first, go freshen up, change your clothes, then take a walk to the Angel, enjoy a night out. Get hammered. Forget about that bitch.' Rob hung up.

After showering and putting on a fresh shirt, he reached for his jacket and left the house, not looking back at the car as he continued towards Cleevesford.

*

Selina smoothed her hair as Rob placed his phone on the coffee table. 'Selina, bring us something to drink,' he called. 'Make it snappy.' He laughed as he sat around the table in the dining room with four of his closest friends.

Selina hurried back through with a tailor's tape measure falling over her shoulders, smiling as she carried a tray of drinks. Rob lowered the lights in the room and Bruce began dealing the cards as he sucked on a cigar. 'We'll be here all night, love? All of us, here, playing cards?'

She nodded and smiled, wondering what was brewing amongst them.

'You can go upstairs now and work on your sewing, if you like. I'll shout if we need you. Have you finished your latest creation?'

'Almost, just adding the last few stitches.' She leaned over and kissed Rob on the cheek. She wanted to shake him and ask why he still didn't trust her enough to tell her what was going on.

Rob smirked as he finished dealing the cards. 'Dan got what I asked for too. Everyone's registered for council tax.' He passed a slip of paper to everyone. 'Use this information wisely. Actually remember the address on it and rip it up. Don't leave it lying around.'

Selina craned her neck, hoping to see the words on the slips of paper. It was no use. They all pocketed them before she had the chance.

Ben checked out his hand and winced. 'Must be a fix, I'm not playing this hand.'

'Get in there. I'm on a winning streak tonight,' Rob said as a grin spread across his face.

Rob pulled the card that DI Harte had given to Darrel after she'd seen him at the station the night Melissa was killed. He placed it on the table. Their newest member grinned and picked the card up.

As Rob dealt an extra card to every player, he took a moment to make eye contact with each person around the table. 'Highest wins. Selina, can you leave us to chat?'

Once again left on the outside. She lingered in the hallway. DI Harte again, she thought to herself, as she angrily walked up to her sewing room.

CHAPTER THIRTY-ONE

Gina slumped in the passenger seat of the car and watched as Darrel headed down the tree-lined verge before meeting the path. Soon he was completely out of sight. She stepped out of the car, placing the case notes on the back seat, ready to pore over when she got home.

The clear sky and half-covered moon lit up the rural setting. As she walked down the block-paved drive, she stared at the house. She needed to go around the back. In her mind, she kept thinking, *He has an alibi. It can't be him.* Who were his other friends? They had one full name on file, Robert Dixon. Dixon had to be the lead to follow and she would follow that lead as soon as she was back home. She walked around the large house and reached the kitchen door, the same door she'd entered only a few nights earlier before being confronted by Melissa's body.

The moon reflected in the window. She placed her nose close to the glass, to see inside. She hoped she'd see something, to see that he'd let his guard down. She almost wanted to slap herself for thinking it. It wasn't as if he'd come home with half a roll of blue washing line cord and dump it in the kitchen for her to see. She flashed her torch through the window. Everything was pretty much as she remembered. He'd barely moved a thing or added anything to the scene. She shined the torch nearer the back of the kitchen. A kitchen chair lay on its side, shattered.

A cracking noise came from the shrubbery at the side of the garden. She flashed her torch. 'Who's there? Darrel Sanderson?'

All was silent, except for her pounding heart. She watched as a fox darted towards the back of the garden. She laughed as she lowered the torch and pulled her phone from her pocket, noticing a missed a call from Jacob. She pressed the return call button. 'Jacob. What do you have?' she asked in a whisper.

'The analysis of Sanderson's computer has come back. He's definitely not the nice pleasant family man he'd like us all to believe he is. Good call on removing the daughter.'

'What have they found?'

'Our Mr Sanderson has been chatting in a lot of online forums. They are mostly disguised as men's rights groups but after taking a closer look, they are total woman haters. Believing in only traditional family roles work and sharing tips on how to use manipulation and even violence to control women. So much hate in these groups. I watched on as one member made suggestions on the lines of burning his house down with his wife in it, just because she said she wanted a divorce. They speak of women as if they are property. Honestly, it's disturbing stuff. He's a member of several of these types of group and regularly participates in discussions.'

'Bloody hell. We need to keep a close eye on him. Any news on finding his other friends?' She stared into the distance where the fox had scarpered.

'Not as yet.'

'Keep looking through the computer analysis and I'll give you a call in a minute, when I'm back in my car.' She began walking alongside the house and back towards the road.

'Where are you, guv?'

'Outside Sanderson's house.'

Jacob paused. 'What are you doing there?'

'I just wanted to take a look around.'

'He has the house back. Is he there?'

Gina gazed around in the darkness. 'No, he went out a few minutes ago. I don't know what I was hoping to find, some washing line cord, I think. I was hoping he'd get comfortable now he has his house back, slip up. I know it was a long shot but there we go. I was hoping to catch him out somehow.'

'You should get away from there. If he comes back, he'll be screaming harassment, especially if he catches you staring through his windows.'

She shook her head. 'If he comes back, I'll say I'm just following up on the investigation and give him a very superficial update. There are no issues here.'

'Whatever, guv. Just get back to the car and give me a call straight back. From what I can see, he's one dangerous man. He may not have killed his wife but I feel he sure wasn't sad about her death.'

Gina ended the call and began walking back. As she put the phone back in her pocket, she heard a rustling noise coming from the trees at the back of the garden. This time, it was too big to be a fox. Her heart began to thud against her chest as she spun around and stared into the darkness. Hand trembling, she held her torch up. 'Who's there?'

CHAPTER THIRTY-TWO

Becky paced back and forth. Ellie had been off the booze for so long now. Things had been going well. They were getting married. She enjoyed her job at the coffee shop. They loved their flat. What had happened? Ellie's last message had been so out of character and she never stayed out all night. She tried to call her again but her voicemail came on – again.

She tried to think back, working out where things might have gone wrong. Ellie had been late home the other day. When questioned, she'd just said she'd got caught up doing *things* but Becky suspected she'd gone back to the Angel Arms. Ellie's nightmares had become more frequent. She'd struggled to speak of her assault. Ellie had lied though, telling her that her lateness had something to do with a surprise for the wedding. Becky didn't believe her. She'd found a return bus ticket to Cleevesford, dated the thirteenth of April, in Ellie's pocket. She'd looked shaken and had gone for a lie down around seven in the evening and stayed in bed until the next morning.

She picked up the framed photo next to the phone and rubbed her half of the heart necklace. Whatever Ellie was going through, she'd see her through it like all the other times. Ellie looked so happy in the photo, outside the pub on the beach at Combe Martin. They'd just bought chips and a glass of coke each, then gone for a walk along the beach, checking out the rock pools. She smiled as she remembered the tide coming in and the sea flowing over the wall they were walking along. Ellie had been in fits of laughter as the sea soaked her jeans. They shivered all the way back to the caravan park as the wintery air chilled them to the bone. She shivered now as she thought of what Ellie might be up to. Something wasn't right. Ellie had always told her where she was, even when she'd gone totally off the rails. There was something her lover wasn't telling her.

She continued to pace back and forth, occasionally staring at her phone as she'd done all day. 'Please call me,' she said, as she felt tears welling up in her eyes.

CHAPTER THIRTY-THREE

Gina's heartbeat quickened. 'Mr Sanderson?' The sound of a heavy foot treading on undergrowth drew her attention back to the trees. She flashed her torch across the drive and the front garden. A figure in a forensic suit and a red mask emerged from between two trees. The eye area was covered with mesh that reminded her of insect eyes. Tallish, about six foot, straight waist, likely male. He waved a crowbar above her head. 'Stop, Police,' she yelled as he brought the metal bar down onto her shoulder.

The masked figure stepped towards her and brought the crowbar down on her head this time. The stars in the sky began to swirl as she fell to the ground. He sat over her, with his legs apart, pinning her down. 'Get off me,' she slurred as a piercing pain flashed through her head. She reached up, trying to gauge his eyes through the mesh, grabbing his face, pulling at the mask. She felt the back. The crisscross thread reminded her of a mask that a wrestler would wear. The material was thin but hard to tear. He returned her efforts with a punch to the side of the face. She had to get him off. She tried to bring her knee up between his legs but she was pinned to the ground. She wriggled as he grabbed her breasts and weaved his gloved hands underneath her shirt, then he reached for her groin, trying to get into her underwear.

As she lay there dazed, her mind went to Terry and the times he'd attacked her. Remaining still was always her solution back then. She'd never dare to refuse what he wanted. Not this time. Her victim days were well and truly over.

She grabbed his growing erection and squeezed. The masked man let out a yell. She reached around and grabbed the hair at the base of his head, pulling until she'd ripped out several strands. He continued yelping and holding his groin as he pulled away, stumbling as he stood.

She rolled over onto her front then managed to stand. The world spun. Her heart threatened to burst from her chest. She put her fingers to her head and could feel the hot sticky blood that was matting into her hair. She held the torch above her head and ran in his direction, preparing for impact. As she reached him, he brought the crowbar down once more. As he caught her wrist, she dropped the torch. Her attacker limped down the path as he rubbed his throbbing groin. She fell to the floor as she went to grab her torch and landed at an angle, bending her wrist. Through the pain, she smiled as she closed her eyes and gripped the hair in her hand.

Her mind drifted back to Terry. She'd never have fought him off. 'That was for you, Terry,' she said as she lay on the damp overgrown grass, welcoming the darkness as she slipped into unconsciousness with only the scent of his musky aftershave lingering in the air. It wasn't a scent she recognised. She had come face to face with the devil and she'd fought with all she had.

The world above swirled as a sharp pain travelled through her head. As the stars and moon disappeared, she clung on to the bit of evidence tightly. *Don't let go of the hair*, she kept telling herself. *Don't let go of the hair*, as she lost the battle to remain conscious.

CHAPTER THIRTY-FOUR

Monday, 16 April 2018

Terry tied his red eye mask at the back of his head, then slowly turned. With his eyes covered, his other features blended into nothing more than a skin coloured blotch. Shaking her head, she tried to shift the wooziness. She felt the mattress dip as he kneeled on it and kissed her with his beery breath. As little Mia cried, her heartbeat increased. She had to save Mia before he could get to her and hurt her. She always had to be there, ready to step between Terry and Mia. She would die for that little girl. He ripped open her nightshirt and lay on her naked body, pinning her to the bed. She screwed her eyes to get a better look at him. His jaw was too defined and he was tall. It wasn't Terry.

'Mia,' she called. She'd always been there to protect Mia from the devil that came for her. Never would he get to the child – never. Through chattering teeth, she tried to call again, but the demon clasped his large scaly hand across her nose and mouth. As she panicked for air, stars filled her eyes, she knew her end was near. 'Mia!' She sobbed as she wondered who could protect Mia now. She should have left him, ran away, gone to a refuge, anywhere. It would too late as soon she'd be gone and she'd never know what had happened to little Mia.

*

'Mum.' Gina opened her damp eyes and gasped for breath. The brightness of the stark white room sent pain shooting through her head. 'Mum, you're in Cleevesford Hospital. It's me, Hannah.'

Gina reached with her jittery hand and placed it over Hannah's. Her daughter allowed her hand to remain but didn't respond. Although their relationship had improved a little since she'd opened up to her daughter about her abusive past, it still wasn't right. She'd left things too late, as always.

She looked up at her daughter's blonde straggly hair and pale face, and she knew it had been a long night for her. 'Where's Gracie?'

'Greg's looking after her. I couldn't bring her here to see you like this.' Hannah sat beside her on the hospital bed. 'You were just calling for someone called Mia.' She flinched as she grabbed a glass of water from the bedside table. 'Who's Mia?'

'It was just a dream, that's all.'

Hannah removed her hand. 'Can you remember what happened?'

Gina took a sip of water. It was the best drink she'd ever had in her life, relieving her bone-dry throat. She could see her daughter waiting for her to give her more details of the attack, but she wasn't going to tell her that some man pinned her down and groped her, shoving his gloved hands in her pants. She swallowed and looked away. The shame of being a victim of sexual violence still burned, smouldering her spirit. Discussing bruises would have been fine, but sexual violence, never. 'There really is no need to worry. It's just a few bruises. I'll be okay and I'll catch whoever did this. My shoulder hurts like hell though.' She flinched as she reached up with her bandaged wrist and felt the material tightly wrapped around her head.

'Your wrist is sprained.'

'I can tell. What time is it? I need to get to work,' she said as she stared through the window, feeling the warmth of the sunshine flooding into the room.

'Mum, you've got a slight concussion. I don't think you'll be going anywhere at the moment. The doctor said you won't be driving for a few days either. One of the officers took your car home so you don't have to worry about that.' Her daughter paused. 'I brought you some clothes to change into later.'

Gina held her wrist up and saw the bandage covering it. 'I'm not staying here.' She sat up and tossed the blankets aside, revealing a hideous hospital gown. She felt a draft up her back and knew instantly that she had no underwear on. 'Pass me the clothes you brought me.'

'Mum, you have concussion. Just stay in bed.'

'I feel fine. Look,' she said as she forced a smile. As she went to stand, the room swayed, almost making her stumble. She stood her ground. Hannah wouldn't see that she wasn't feeling anything but ready to leave the hospital.

'Look, Mum, just get back in bed and drink some more water. You've just woken up after being beaten up and you have concussion. You need to take this slower. I know you want to get out of here, but you've got to be sensible about things. What if it was me? Would you let me just get up when I could barely stand and then let me walk out of here, discharging myself? If you do—'

'What?'

Hannah's cheeks reddened. Gina knew her daughter had a point but there was no way she'd stay in hospital a minute longer than she had too. If she could walk, she was walking right out of the door.

'Just stay here! What is your problem? I've had enough. I'm going home to see Gracie now. The police bagged your clothes up so you've got some of mine. There's a pair of joggers, a T-shirt and one of my gym hoodies.'

Gina shook her head. 'Look, don't worry – really. I'll be fine. I'm sure they'll let me out in a bit. I'll call you later. I need to speak to Jacob, DS Driscoll. Have you seen him?'

'He's hanging around outside, waiting his turn. I'll tell him to come in, shall I so you can get on with your work?'

Gina placed her hand on Hannah's. 'Thank you for the clothes. I do appreciate you being here.'

'Anyway, get some rest. Speak later.' Hannah stepped backwards, allowing her hand to drop.

Gina waved as her daughter left, then Jacob entered. 'Alas, I disappoint my daughter yet again! How did they find me last night?'

Jacob sat in the upright chair next to her bed. 'You didn't call me back and I got worried. I called you but you didn't answer. I knew something was wrong. You never ignore your phone. I came straight over to find you lying on the pavement outside Sanderson's house.'

'I must have crawled there. I was attacked on the front lawn. Was there anything found?'

'Only the hair that you kept murmuring about. I bagged it up. Bernard has it for analysis. The results are being fast tracked and will be with us tomorrow. Can you remember what happened?'

Relieved that her attacker's hair had been bagged, Gina yelped as she propped herself up. The gash on her head rubbed against the dressing and her shoulder felt as though it had been severed. The internal bruising made it hard to move. Jacob leaned in and helped her with the pillow. 'Thanks. I'll be all right in a bit, just need some painkillers. Right, I remember speaking to you on the phone. I came from the side of the house and heard rustling coming from the trees. A man walked towards me.' She scrunched her brow as she thought back.

'Can you describe him?'

'He was wearing a forensic suit, boot covers and this red mask that covered his face, oh and gloves.' Her mind went back to the previous night. 'The mask he was wearing, it was like a wrestler's mask. I could feel that it was threaded and tied up at the back. His eyes were covered with a fine mesh that he could see through. He reminded me of an insect. He came at me with a crowbar and hit me on the shoulder, hit my head and I can't remember the other hits, I know he hit me again. I remember going at him with my torch. I just wanted one hit. I'd have brought him down.' She paused. If she wasn't in so much pain, she'd have punched the bedframe. 'He had me pinned to the ground…'

'What happened then?'

Gina realised she was being interviewed and shuddered. She'd become the victim. 'He straddled me and was feeling my breast and groin area but I hurt him. I managed to grab him between the legs and I squeezed like hell. I hope he's walking with a limp today.'

'Bloody hell, guv. I hope that hair identifies him. We all want him caught. I wished you'd have told me what you were doing last night. I could've gone with you.'

She knew Jacob was disappointed. 'I was just going to take a look.' She paused. 'Was it him? Did you question Sanderson?'

Jacob nodded. 'He was in the Angel Arms until close. It was the first lead we followed up on.'

'That was convenient. Whenever anything bad happens up his neck of the woods he's in the Angel Arms.'

'We verified the fact. The bar staff and the CCTV both confirmed he was there.'

Gina leaned her head back on the pillow and swiftly sat back up as the room began to sway. 'He's got to be behind this, I know he is. Was last night a warning?'

'Look, guv. Take a rest and I'll get back to the station for the briefing and tell everyone what you've told me. Can you tell me anything else?'

'Yes. He's about six foot. His weapon of choice was a crowbar. Like I said before, there was mesh over the eyes of the mask so I didn't see them, and it was dark. He was wearing aftershave but I couldn't tell you which one it was. I'm not really up on aftershave. I hope he's in as much pain as me today.'

'Me too, guv. Is there anything I can get you? Some chocolate, bunch of grapes, anything, you just name it.'

'A time machine. I'd like to go back a day.' She smiled.

'If only. Oh, I just remembered.' Jacob pulled a lunchbox from his satchel and passed it over. 'O'Connor sent you some coffee cake. His wife made it ages ago. He pulled it from the freezer when he heard you were in hospital. It should be defrosted now.'

'He knows me well. Thank him for me.'

'Will do. Will you be okay?'

There was a knock at the door and Briggs entered. 'I'll be fine just as soon as I get out of here. Just find out who attacked me. I'm sure that whoever attacked me killed Melissa. We found forensic suit material at the scene of Melissa's murder and my attacker was wearing a forensic suit. We have his hair. Keep calling Bernard. Get Keith on the case with him too. Blow the budget. Let's get the results and catch this killer.'

'I'm on it, guv,' Jacob said as he left.

Briggs watched as the DS walked down the corridor, then he closed the door. 'Sir,' Gina said.

'Are you okay?' He walked towards the bedside. She could tell he wanted to hug her but she turned away.

'I'll be fine, sir,' she said. A tear slid down her cheeks, dampening the white hospital pillows. He placed his hand over hers. She couldn't hold the emotion in any longer. What would her attacker have done if she hadn't fought back and hurt him? Would he have raped her? Would he have killed her like he killed Melissa Sanderson?

'You're not fine.'

She leaned back on her pillow, creating a safe distance between them. 'Thank you for coming.'

'I'm so sorry I tried to push you to open up to me. I know you have a past, something that makes you unhappy, but you didn't want to share it with me. I should've respected that and shut the hell up. I know you said it was because you didn't like hiding our relationship but I know better. I'm not stupid. Can I please help you through this? As a friend and colleague? I promise, no more questions. We can go back to friendly beers, working together out of hours. We make a good team when it comes to crime fighting.'

'No more questions. Friends,' Gina agreed.

She told him about the case and he listened. They even lightened the atmosphere with a few jokes but as soon as he closed the door, she swung her legs over the bed and grimaced as she stretched to grab the joggers and hoodie that Hannah had left for her. She wasn't about to waste any more time lying in a bed.

CHAPTER THIRTY-FIVE

Selina sprayed the windows at the back of the drawing room, rubbing the same pane over and over again as she listened. 'What's all this about? I'm meant to be at work,' Dan asked.

'It's okay, Dan, we have all we need for now. Our mate is on his way. We just needed a catch up on last night,' Rob replied.

'What exactly happened last night?'

What happened? Selina wanted to know everything. Rob nodded in her direction. She knew his nod meant he wanted her to fetch refreshments. She left the window and hurried, grabbing a tea tray from the kitchen. Dan stopped talking and looked flustered as she re-entered, placing a couple of glasses of iced tea on the coffee table. Rob smiled. She was a woman who knew exactly how to keep her man and how to behave. She was everything the others desired. She grabbed the window cloth and continued wiping the same patch of window. If they wouldn't tell her what was going on, she would find out.

Dan began to scratch his head.

Selina watched their reflections in the glass as Rob's voice became no more than a whisper. She clenched the cloth as she glanced over her shoulder. A few flakes of dandruff fell from Dan's head as he scratched like a flea-ridden mutt. She cringed at the thought of cleaning his chair when he left. 'Look. There's no need to panic, and for heaven's sake stop covering my Chesterfield with pieces of your head.'

Dan placed one hand in his lap and snatched the glass of iced tea with his other hand. 'I shouldn't have given you all that address.'

'Look. It's just an address, chill out.'

Dan sighed and ran his fingers through his hair, once again releasing a flurry of dandruff. 'I know but I can't afford to lose my job. It's all right for you lot, you work for yourselves. I work for the council.'

'Don't be daft. No one's going to check. Do you think the powers above haven't got better things to do? I have two members of staff out for appointments this morning. I don't care. They're good hard-working men and I know they'll catch up.' He looked at his watch.

There was a knock at the main door. Selina went to answer it and Rob's new friend barged in and stood in the middle of the room, pacing back and forth with a bit of a limp.

'That cow is going to get it,' he spat as he sat next to Dan.

'He's messed up, hasn't he?' Dan said to Rob and, once again, began to scratch his flaky head.

'I didn't mess up. How dare you!'

'What went wrong?' Rob asked as he placed his glass on the table. 'Nothing can go wrong, can it? It's not just your liberty at stake.'

'It's not about what's going to go wrong or has gone wrong, don't worry – nothing is wrong. This is totally personal. Get me a drink, a stiff one and I'll fill you in.'

Selina swallowed hard. Her husband was getting too involved in something. What did he mean by things going wrong? She knew he'd always been a man of principle but something inside her wanted to scream at him. Tell him to quit whatever he was into. Was it something to do with DI Harte?

'Selina? Can you leave us to it and close the door?'

She wanted to throw the window rag right in his face. She deserved to know what was going on. Her husband had trusted her with everything before his old friend came back on the scene. Why was Dan fishing around for addresses at work? She needed to find out what was on the pieces of paper that were being passed around the previous night. Maybe it was the address they kept talking about. What had Ben and Lee got to do with it all? She'd never betray Rob, she just wanted to be included. She gripped the rag. She'd never really thrown anything. Throwing things just wasn't ladylike. She forced one of her sweetest smiles and left the room, closing the door and leaning against the grain. All went silent until Rob opened the door. As it moved, she'd almost reached the stairs. He watched as she continued up before heading to the kitchen. Was he onto her spying ways?

CHAPTER THIRTY-SIX

Gina handed the taxi driver cash before stepping into the cool sunshine. The run-down station almost looked pretty with the morning sun brightening up the one wall, its light concealing the damp patches. She caught her reflection in the main door. The purple hooded top, pink T-shirt and navy joggers did nothing for her image. She knew Hannah had meant well by bringing a bag of her comfortable clothing but it didn't feel right on Gina. Her hair resembled an overused, dried out mop. She had tried to dampen it down but as soon as it dried out, it had gone awry again. She really could have done with washing it in a nice hot shower but she wasn't spending a moment longer in the hospital.

With every step, her body ached but she wasn't about to sit back and do nothing. This case had now become personal and the only thing on her mind was catching her attacker – and the man who had killed Melissa Sanderson. As she went to open the door with her bandaged wrist, she flinched. Nick, the desk sergeant, left the youth he was booking in to open the door for her. 'Here, let me help you, guv.'

'Thanks, Nick.'

'Should you be here?'

'Damn right, I should.'

As she entered the incident room, O'Connor and Wyre turned from their computers and Jacob entered with a coffee. 'What on earth are you doing here, guv?'

'Why is everyone looking at me as if I've just fallen from the sky? I work here, don't I? We have a murder to solve? Why on earth would I not be here?' She knew full well what they were seeing. They saw her frailty. They saw the bandage on her wrist. Thankfully she'd binned the bandage from around her head when she'd left the hospital. All they could see was the red bump and gash that had been hidden underneath. She hobbled towards them. She knew she felt fine and she was well enough to be back at the station. No one was going to stop her being there. 'Right what have we got?' The room swayed slightly. She wasn't fine at all, but she would be.

Jacob placed his cup down. 'Okay. The tests on your hair and clothes and the hair in your hand haven't come back yet. As I mentioned earlier, Sanderson has an alibi for the time of your attack. Briggs is preparing an appeal for witnesses with the press. That's where we are, guv.'

'Shortbread, guv? Mrs O made them at the weekend. You look like you need building up?' O'Connor held a lunchbox full of biscuits towards her.

'Thanks, but I'm fine. I ate the coffee cake while waiting for the taxi to turn up. Thank Mrs O for me.' She sat at the main table and rubbed her head, feeling along the bump.

O'Connor and Wyre swivelled in their chairs back to their computers.

'You should be at home, guv. Really, you look like tripe. You shouldn't be here.' Jacob bit into wedge of shortbread while awaiting her answer.

'I know you're right but you know me and that's not going to happen.' She turned to go to her office.

'Harte. Why on earth are you here?' Briggs bellowed. 'Your office, now.' She marched along the corridor feeling like a naughty schoolgirl who was about to be taken to task by the headmaster. 'What are you doing here, in this state?' Briggs closed the door behind them. 'You really have come straight from the hospital, haven't you?'

She flinched as she slumped in her chair. 'I need to be here. It's my case. I'm SIO. It's important that I don't miss anything. I feel fine. The doctor said I could go and to just take painkillers, which I've done.' It was only a small lie. They were talking about discharging her later that day.

'I want you to go home, get some rest; have a shower and a bite to eat. You were attacked last night. I don't expect you to leave the hospital and come straight back here. In fact, you should be having a few days off to recover—'

'I don't need a few days off. I need to be here. I'm going to catch him.' As she reached the end of her sentence, she realised she was trembling. In her mind, she could smell his aftershave, she could feel his weight on top of her. She closed her eyes and turned away, hoping that she could contain the tear that was threatening to escape.

Briggs placed a hand on her shoulder. 'Let me drop you home. Just for a shower. I'll make sure you don't miss out on a thing, I promise. Besides, you can't wear those clothes all day. Do you trust me?'

She opened her eyes and nodded, biting her bottom lip. 'A shower would be great. I'll take you up on the lift. The doc says I'm not allowed to drive until next week as I may have mild concussion. I'm fine to work though, no dizziness or nausea; it's just a precaution. I agree with you. These clothes need to go. I don't think anyone will take me seriously dressed like Honey G's sister. My daughter just forgot to pack the baseball cap.'

'Come on.' He smiled as he held a hand out, helping her to stand. Feeling her hand in his was as familiar as morning. As soon as she was upright, she let go. She wasn't going there, not again. That part of her life was over. She only hoped he could see that. Something told her he thought there was a chance.

CHAPTER THIRTY-SEVEN

Her cat, Ebony, meowed as she opened the kitchen door and entered the sun-filled room. Spring mornings were one of life's simple pleasures in her opinion. She gazed out of the kitchen window and noticed that new leaves were sprouting from the trees. The daffodils had already reached maturity and the foliage on the trees and shrubs at the end of the garden now covered the old road behind, making the greenery stretch as far as she could see. She reached for the cat biscuits and struggled to refill the almost empty cat feeder, spilling the biscuits on the floor.

'Looks like someone's missed you.' Briggs took the box from her bandaged hand and completed the task. 'You should really use the other hand for a while. You don't want to hinder your recovery. Go upstairs, take a shower and get changed. I insist. I'll make you a bite to eat while you're up there.'

'But, Chris—'

'I'm not taking no for an answer. You could use a hand and I'm here. I'm hoping you have some cheese in the fridge. I make the best cheese sandwich in the world, as you know. I'll leave it on the side for you and pop back in a bit.' She wanted to argue with him, tell him it was no use clinging onto what they had but she needed his help. Besides, a shower and a sandwich sounded like her idea of heaven.

Grabbing a plastic bag, she taped it around her wrist. 'Best not dampen my bandage.' She smiled at him, then felt his gaze on hers for a few seconds longer than normal. She remained at arm's length, fully aware that her emotions were all over the place following the attack. She didn't need complications. She needed to catch Melissa's killer. 'Right, I'll see you in a bit.'

A shower had been most welcome. The black trousers and purple roll neck jumper were more 'her'. The home phone rang. She grabbed it as she swallowed the last bit of cheese sandwich. Briggs would be back in half an hour to take her to the station.

'I can't believe you left the hospital, Mum. I just called them to ask how you were and the nurse said that you'd walked out.'

'I'm fine. They were talking about discharging me later anyway. I'm not sitting there while they fill out paperwork and make me wait there for hours.' Ebony jumped on her lap, making her flinch as she rubbed against her wrist.

'Unbelievable. You just couldn't stay away from work, could you? I bet you've already been in. I'll pop over later with Gracie, Mum, and I want you to be in. This is ridiculous.'

Gina nudged the cat off her lap. 'I know what you're thinking and, yes, I am going back to work. I don't expect you to understand but that's the way it is. I have a killer to catch and someone attacked me. You think I'm going to sit here all day, watching crap on the telly because you think I should?'

Her daughter sighed. 'I don't believe it. Three hours ago you were in hospital, looking like you didn't know what day it was, and now your back home and going to work. Why can't you just have a couple of days off?'

She couldn't explain to her daughter what a couple of days meant when it came to an investigation. 'Because a woman was brutally murdered. I'm not going to sit at home, drinking tea while a dangerous killer is out there. If she was a friend of yours, would you want to know that people like me were doing all we could? Course you would! Look, I know you're only thinking of me and I love you for that but I know what I need to do, so can you please spare me the telling off?'

She pictured Hannah's face reddening and braced herself for her reply. 'Whatever.' Hannah went silent. 'Can you just try to stay safe?'

Gina could feel the tension between them as she waited for more. A trail of tears slipped down her cheeks. 'I will do, love. Thank you. Give Gracie a cuddle from her nana. Speak later.' She placed the phone down, more sure than ever she was doing the right thing.

There was a knock at the door and her mobile rang at the same time. She took the call as she opened the door. Briggs was there to drive her back to the station as promised. 'Jacob.'

'We've just had a woman call, reporting a missing person. Given what happened to Melissa Sanderson, I think we need to follow up on this without hesitation.'

'Great, Jacob. You're driving. I'm on my way to the station. Meet you in the car park.'

CHAPTER THIRTY-EIGHT

Jacob opened the passenger door and smiled. 'How's your head, guv?'

'It's been better. But I'm okay. Look.' She responded with her goofiest smile. 'I'm fine and I don't need help getting out of the car. I can still walk, well to a certain degree.' She stretched, feeling every muscle twinge in her body. 'What's the woman's name?'

'Rebecca Greene.'

Jacob waited as she caught up. The block of modern flats looked pleasant enough and was within walking distance to the town centre. A couple of young children threw a ball back and forth on the patch of grass out the front. The main door opened, as if Rebecca had been waiting for them to arrive.

'Thank you for getting here so soon.' The woman led them to the living room of her first-floor apartment. The room was small but cosy with a Juliet balcony at the far end. Gina picked a photo up. Rebecca and Ellie were both smiling in the image. 'Can I get you both a drink?'

Gina shook her head and thanked her. She'd already lost valuable time after her attack, she wasn't wasting any more. 'Can I just confirm your name? Rebecca Greene?' Jacob made a note.

'Call me Becky, no one calls me Rebecca.'

'Is this Ellie?' Gina placed the photo back on the shelf.

Becky ran her hand through her short brown hair, took her square glasses off and rubbed her eyes. 'Yes. That's Ellie. I don't know where she's gone.'

'When did she go missing?' Gina flinched as she tried to find a comfortable position to sit in. Her injuries were making *comfortable* near impossible.

'I haven't seen her since Saturday night. She said she was popping out, had to do something. She wouldn't tell me what, but I could sense she wasn't right.' The voile blew as a light breeze passed through the slightly open door.

'Could she just be with friends?'

Becky wiped a tear away. 'Ellie didn't have friends. She was introverted, preferred her own company. If she had time, she'd normally be painting. We have two bedrooms, she uses one as her studio.'

'What's Ellie's surname?'

'Redfern.'

'Tell me a little about her.'

Becky began playing with the heart-shaped pendant dangling on a chain around her neck. 'We both have one of these. We're getting married in the summer, finally. Ellie manages a coffee shop. Just a small independent in town. Her big passion is art. She was meant to study fine art at Edinburgh University after school but she didn't have it easy. She couldn't cope with life.' The woman rubbed her eyes.

'Go on.'

'She paints portraits, professionally. The word's been spreading and she gets a lot of work. She did that one of me.'

The small painting that hung on the wall looked very professional with a modern twist. The face and features were painted almost traditionally, but the paint had been left to drip in places and the colourful background had not quite reached the edges of the canvas.

'It's a lovely portrait.'

'I'm so proud of what she's achieved.' She wiped away an escaping tear. 'Ellie was going through a bit of a thing. She wanted to face her past so she could move on as we were getting married. I'd managed to get her to open up to me a little.' Rebecca paused and looked down. 'I've never tried to push her too much through fear of driving her away.'

Gina could relate to that comment. She too had a past that people were hell bent on trying to delve into. Her daughter, Briggs – they wanted to know things, things she didn't want to share.

'She's had a few days off work. I called her when I got home on Friday, wondering where she was. I'd been shopping and when I arrived home, she'd gone out. No note, nothing. When she got home, later that day, she looked ruffled. I was worried she'd started drinking again as she used to have a drink problem. That's another thing. She's fallen off the wagon more than once but she's always allowed me to help her, never shut me out. On the Friday, when she arrived home, I couldn't smell drink on her but when I asked her where she'd been, she said she'd been doing secret wedding stuff. But she'd been having nightmares and there was something that didn't seem right. You know when you can't put your finger on it, but you just know?'

Gina nodded. 'Did you find out where she'd been?'

'Yes. As soon as she walked through the door she got in the shower, which was odd. I searched through her coat pocket and found a bus ticket to Cleevesford. Ellie won't open up to me, but what I do know is that twenty-five years ago, when she was eighteen, she was attacked in the Angel Arms car park. She won't tell me about the attack or any of the details. It hurts that she can't confide in me, but I accept her wholeheartedly – I love her. I just want her to come home.'

'You're doing really well, Becky. We need to know what happened after.'

'That night, last Friday, she only wanted toast for tea, said she wasn't feeling too well. She went to bed and slept all night. I had to go to work on Saturday so I was up early. I work as a retail manager and do lots of weekends and evenings. When I left about ten she was asleep. I kissed her on the head and told her I'd see her later, and I haven't seen her since. I tried to call her when I returned home on Saturday evening but she wasn't answering. She never goes out at night. I called her but she kept cutting me off. On Sunday morning, I received a text from her phone.' She read the text aloud. '"Met an old friend at the pub and had a few. Slept on their sofa. Love you." I know this isn't her. She was out all night and she sends me this? She's an ex-alcoholic and she's a very serious person. She wouldn't say something like that. She goes out chasing her past, being all secretive, and then this text comes through. This isn't Ellie. Something has happened to her, I know it has.' The woman broke down.

'Do you have a recent photo of Ellie that we could take with us?'

The woman opened a drawer under the coffee table and pulled out a postcard. 'She got these made when she had her last exhibition. She gives them out. They have her contact details on the back.'

A round-faced woman, with a black fringe and sharply cut bob, looked back at her from the postcard. She could tell that Ellie had been uncomfortable when she'd had the photo taken as she'd barely managed a half smile. 'Thank you. Is this up to date?'

'That is how she still looks.'

Gina passed Jacob the photo to go with the notes he was taking. 'Can you tell us what she was wearing? Maybe you know which items of clothing are missing.'

'Yes. She always wears a cropped faux leather black jacket. Jeans, she always wears jeans and her flat black boots are missing. Her wardrobe is pretty predictable. She wears black nail varnish and quite bold make-up. Don't mistake her bold image for confidence though. I'm always reassuring her that she's beautiful. She never believes me.'

Gina walked towards the Juliet balcony. In the distance she could hear clunking noises coming from one of the factories located in the nearby industrial estate. The children laughed and yelled as they ran past, bouncing their ball. As she watched people pass, and cars come and go, she wondered if Melissa Sanderson's murder could be linked to Ellie Redfern's disappearance. Maybe Ellie was just with a friend. Maybe there was more to her relationship with Becky than Becky was telling. But maybe something far more sinister could be behind her disappearance. Her mind kept going back to the Angel Arms – the link. Given the fact that a woman, in a town close by had been murdered last week, she would be taking this seriously. If they weren't related, good. If they were, she wasn't going to be accused of ignoring the link early on, especially as the press were becoming so involved.

She thought about Melissa Sanderson. The two women were worlds apart. Melissa had a home that resembled something out of a lifestyle magazine, she had a young daughter and she was married. Ellie lived in an apartment in Redditch, lived with Becky, no children, but she had a past she didn't want to speak about that had possibly contributed to her drinking habit. She was even more certain that the common factor was Cleevesford and the Angel Arms. Darrel Sanderson had been in the Angel Arms while his wife was being killed. Ellie had also mentioned the Angel Arms and she had a bus ticket to Cleevesford in her pocket.

As they left the apartment, Gina pulled out her phone and called Wyre. 'I'm going to message you a photo of Ellie Redfern in a minute. Look into her past, anything. We're taking a diversion.'

'Are we?' Jacob pulled his car keys from his pockets and Gina smiled.

'Too right.'

CHAPTER THIRTY-NINE

'Oh, you know how much you love this place, guv.'

She laughed as Jacob pulled up in the Angel Arms car park. 'You know me well. Smarmy Samuel Avery, it's been too long. He hears things, he see's things, he causes an awful lot of trouble around here. The idiot was cautioned for being in a fight last week, another disgruntled husband. I just don't know what women see in him. There must be something strange in the beer.'

As they approached, Gina glanced through the leaded window. Her mind was briefly taken back to the last major case she worked on. This pub had been the centre of the most notorious kidnapping to ever come from Cleevesford. This place was well and truly on the map. Real life crime fans treated it like some sort of Mecca equivalent, boosting Samuel's footfall and profits.

She led the way. 'Samuel Avery, I see you're still profiting from this poor woman's misfortune,' Gina said as she pulled the poster from the wall, advertising a crime walk that began at the pub and ended at the woman's old house. 'I don't know how people like you sleep at night.' He'd driven the kidnap victim and her family out of their home and town with his sick tours, all for a few quid.

'Some of us have got to eat, Detective. Unless you are here for a drink, I suggest you go. You've seen better days, haven't you? I thought you were a bit of a looker last time we met but now you've let yourself go. Someone get fed up with your probing and give you a smack?' His liver-spotted hands trembled as they gripped a brandy glass.

Refusing to rise to his petty insults she took a seat at the bar. She would never give him the satisfaction of seeing how much she hated him. 'We're investigating the case of a missing woman who was seen in here last Friday. We can either chat here or at the station. Being the last person to have seen her, we just wanted to have a chat, that's all.'

'Not again. Mind you, the last one has been profitable. As I say, always willing to help the pigs. We can't have helpless women going missing, can we?'

He really was despicable. She clenched her fist in her pocket. She'd love nothing more than to grab the glass from his bony fingers, pour his drink over his revoltingly loud shirt and fling the glass at his head, but she wouldn't.

'Do you recognise this woman?' Gina held the postcard close to Samuel's eyes.

He squinted and grinned. 'Ahh, the cheeky bint. That one gave me a bit of lip. She was hanging around outside, last Friday. She came in and I must admit, she caught me staring at an arse and gave me a mouthful.' Gina liked her already. 'I basically told her to mind her own business. She took her drink and sat over there by the window. That's all I know. Haven't seen her before, haven't seen her since. Sorry I can't be of more help but I'm sure she'll turn up. I'd wonder if she'd pulled some bloke or something, maybe gone off with him but there aren't many who'd put up with her. She seemed like a handful.'

'Did she leave alone?'

'I don't remember. Jill might know more, she was serving. She's on her break, in the garden. Is that me done?'

Gina wondered for a moment if Ellie had seemed like a challenge to him, after all, he was used to getting his way with women. A woman verbally attacking him might have turned him on. She watched as he rolled a cigarette.

'Do you know a Lee, Ben and Dan? They maybe come in with Robert Dixon and Darrel Sanderson?'

'I see lots of people, Detective. If I think of anything, I'll give you a call.'

'You do that. One woman has been killed and another is missing.' She stared at him, waiting for him to crack or look away, but he didn't. 'We'll need access to your CCTV, starting with Friday morning, up until now.'

'Always happy to help.' He winked as he left the bar to get what she needed. She was thankful he was cooperating. She shivered as he left and she led the way to the garden.

'What do you think, guv?' Jacob asked as he tuned to a fresh page in his notebook.

'I think he's a disgusting human being. He makes my skin crawl. I want to know what he said or did that made Ellie so angry. Maybe Jill can fill us in. Something's not right here, but then again, it never has been.'

Jill was throwing bits of sandwich to the blackbirds at the end of the unkempt beer garden. A wonky wooden bench took pride of place. The Angel Arms certainly wasn't ready for spring. Cigarette butts littered the grass and the patio area.

'Jill, I'm DI Gina Harte, this is DS Jacob Driscoll. Do you mind if we have a word?'

The woman flicked her long red auburn hair aside and smiled. 'Of course not. How can I help you both?'

'We're investigating a missing person. Do you remember seeing this woman last Friday?'

Jill scrutinised the photo and smiled. 'Yeah, I do. She didn't half give that slimeball I work for a telling off.'

'What happened?'

'I was getting her a drink. Samuel must have said something about me or given the others at the bar a look. The woman asked him what he was staring at, or something like that. I can't really remember now. I just remember thinking, nice one.'

Gina felt her vision swimming a little, and hoped that Jacob and Jill wouldn't notice. She leaned against the wall. 'Did you see her before that, or after?'

'She looked really upset outside, before we opened. I asked if she was all right and she didn't say much. She just walked around the car park, which was a bit odd. She came in, bought an orange juice and that was it. I remember she went to sit by the window, next to the entrance. I don't remember her leaving. That really is all I know.' The woman ate the last piece of her sandwich and the blackbirds flew away.

'Do you remember who else was in the bar?'

'Not really. I haven't been working here long so I'm not that familiar with the regulars.'

'Going back to last Thursday, do you remember Robert Dixon and Darrel Sanderson being in here?'

'Yes. I told the other detectives everything I know. They were just sitting at the bar, drinking. I don't remember much more. It's terrible what happened to that man's wife, while he was here. I tell you something. I not only lock all my doors and windows, I've been pushing a bookcase against my bedroom door. That really freaked me out. I hope you catch the person who did it so we call all sleep better at night.'

'We do too. Thank you for your time. Here's my card, should you remember anything else or should she turn up, give me a call straight away.'

'I will do.' The woman sat on the broken bench, enjoying the last few minutes of her break.

Gina shuddered as they re-entered the pub. 'Let's grab the CCTV and get back to the station. There has to be something we're missing. What is it with this place? It seems to entice trouble. A woman is murdered while her husband is here and, in such a short space of time, a missing woman is last seen here. I hate this pub.'

CHAPTER FORTY

Darrel darted across the kitchen and grabbed his mobile off the side. 'Rob, you all right mate?'

'I've had a copper at my door asking if I was acquainted with a Lee, a Ben and a Dan. Why would she ask that?'

He kicked the kitchen door and stared into his garden. His daughter's trike was upside down on the grass. 'It wasn't me, Rob. I've said nothing. We've all been to the pub together, maybe it was someone at the pub or the landlord, or that Charlene, the gossipy witch behind the bar.'

'Maybe. Just be cautious.' Rob ended the call.

Darrel threw his mobile down and slammed his open palm onto the worktop. He grabbed the chopping board and hurled it across the room, marking the door. Not only had they taken Mia, they were prying into his life, finding out who he was acquainted with. He grabbed a bottle of brandy from the island and poured himself a large one, necking it back. Had his cheating wife told her lover more that he thought? He hadn't banked on her being a gossip and sharing private things about him with other people. She'd have known what she'd have got if she did. It didn't matter. He didn't kill her. He was at the pub, with Rob.

He shivered. The house was cold and empty. This isn't how he imagined it would be. Where were the neighbours with home-cooked casseroles? Where were his sympathisers? He couldn't even go and see his brother, Alan, while Mia was living there and being assessed. He kicked the kitchen door and poured another brandy.

Maybe he'd just get wasted while he toiled over that bitch of a detective. If she dared to watch his house again, interfere in his affairs or generally make a nuisance of herself, he'd get her. She wasn't going to ruin everything.

Insurance was about calculating risk. He calculated risk for a living. How much 'at risk' did he think applied to his current situation? He hadn't told Rob about the bruising on Mia. There was a risk that Rob might find out and what then? He knew what they were capable of, he was part of it. They wouldn't want him to talk. His friends were on his side at the moment. It was Melissa's fault he took his anger out on Mia. While she lay in a stupor, he'd had to deal with a screaming two-year-old. She'd become incapable. He went to pour another drink, then stopped. Even if the police knew the name of all who were part of their little exclusive club, what could they do? They all had alibis: low risk. Other risks: lover boy. What had she told him? That was a question he couldn't answer. He was unable to calculate that risk. He hated being unable. It wasn't in his vocabulary. What did Phipps know and what did he tell the police while trying to save his own skin? There was the unknown variable.

Someone hammered at his door. His heart pounded. The police. They were back. He ran to the door and looked through the spyhole. Rage travelled through his whole body.

'Open the door! I know you're in,' the man slurred.

He'd open the door. He'd let the bastard spill in. Intrusion, that's what it would be and he'd show him what he'd get for sleeping with his wife.

'She wanted to be with me. She wanted me!' the man yelled as he opened the door. So this was Jimmy. Poor drunken Jimmy slipped on the step. Darrel kneeled and aimed a punch at Jimmy's face but the man shifted to the left as his fist hit the floor.

'She was never going to be with you. Look at you. You think she'd leave all this for a loser like you?'

Jimmy punched him, catching the side of his chin. There was no power coming from his punches. Darrel tussled with the man on the floor, eventually grabbing both of his arms with one firm hand and landing a punch on the man's chin. 'That's for shagging my wife. Now get out of here. The next time you come back, I won't just land one on your chin. You'll wish you were never born.' He grabbed the man by the coat and flung him out of the door. Her feeble lover was no match for his strength even though he had let himself go. Underneath his beer belly was a six-pack waiting to be freed.

For now, he hoped the loser would just crawl back under his rock. His analysis. High risk: lover boy.

CHAPTER FORTY-ONE

'Right, Wyre. I spoke to Samuel Avery earlier and he didn't give me much. How are we getting on with tracking the men that James Phipps mentioned? Did you speak to Robert Dixon again?' Gina sucked air in as she rubbed her aching wrist. The painkillers were wearing off quickly. She popped a couple into her hand and swallowed them down with coffee. Her stomach was beginning to rumble. The thought of food made her mouth water.

Wyre flicked through her notes. 'I caught up with Dixon earlier today at his house and asked him if his circle of friends included a Lee, Dan and Ben. He just kept asking why I'd want to know that and seemed a bit cagey. He said he had lots of friends.'

'Did you get surnames?'

She turned the page on her notebook. 'Yes. It didn't take long. We have a Lee Munro, Ben Woodward and Dan Timmons. Munro is a carpentry sub-contractor, works for himself; Woodward actually works for Dixon's electrical wholesale company as head of sales; Timmons is in a supervisory admin role at the local council.'

'We need to speak to them in turn. Can I leave that with you? See what they know. Where they've been. How well they know Darrel.' Gina held her hand to her head and fell into a chair. She needed food and her injured head was stinging.

Wyre nodded. 'There was something at the Dixon house that made me almost laugh out loud. Mrs Dixon.'

'What about Mrs Dixon?' Gina massaged her temples.

'Are you all right, guv?'

'No. I need to get home, but not before you tell me about Mrs Dixon. I need cheering up.'

Wyre smiled. 'She looked like a "Stepford Wife" with this silly looking frilly apron and neatly pinned hair. She rubbed Mr Dixon's arm and gazed at him, like she worshipped him. She offered me the most perfectly made home-made cookie I've ever seen and she served tea from a pot. I know I'm sounding critical and I know Mrs O likes a bit of baking—'

O'Connor swung from side to side on his chair wheels. 'She doesn't worship me though and frilly aprons, no way. That sounds so antiquated.'

'Something didn't sit right but who am I to judge the relationship of others. They are totally weird though. I stand by that comment.'

Gina let out a small laugh. 'And we come across the weirdest of them. Make sure you put that in your notes. It may tell us more about Robert Dixon. Did you manage to garner how often the group of friends met up?'

'I did. They play cards together at Rob's house most weeks. There are no set days. On the night of Melissa Sanderson's murder we already know Rob was with Darrel at the Angel. I need to check the whereabouts of the others.'

'Lastly, any further results from forensics?'

'Not as yet. We are chasing, but they're overloaded and understaffed, as usual.'

Briggs walked in with Annie. 'We've just been talking about the missing woman. We thought, given that you suspect there may be a link, it would be best to issue a press release, appealing for her to make contact. At the moment we only have circumstantial evidence that connects Melissa Sanderson's murder with missing Ellie Redfern. Even the MO is different making it less likely.' The method of murder for Melissa Sanderson involved coming to her home, tying her to a chair and strangling her. With Ellie, she'd just gone missing. The common denominator was still the Angel.

'I agree.' Gina watched as Briggs sat next to Annie. Her tight wrap-dress enhanced her voluptuous bosoms. The newly-divorced woman had grown in confidence over the past few months and she oozed appeal. Her wavy hair almost reached her lap, looking like something from a shampoo advert. Briggs smiled as Annie delivered her recommendations on how they should deliver the missing woman's information to the press. Gina hoped Briggs would see that Annie liked him. It was time for him to move on.

'Did we have any luck confirming if Ellie had been in the Angel last Friday, any CCTV?' Briggs asked.

Gina swallowed. 'I've just finished watching it. She went into the pub at 11.50 a.m. The CCTV shows everything. From 11.15 a.m. she was standing in the corner of the pub car park before it opened, not by the door as if waiting, but in the corner by the shrubbery. What's disturbing is it shows her kicking a bush several times as if she was really angry. When they opened, she entered the pub, bought an orange juice, had a bit of interaction with Samuel Avery, then sat near the window, cowering. The image is really grainy so we can't see exactly what she was looking at. She seemed to be transfixed with the bar. A man arrived, had a drink, then left. She left soon after, taking a right onto the main road. We lose her there.'

Wyre looked up. 'I checked, there is no further operational CCTV to track her movements further.'

'As we know, she went home that night, but what was upsetting her?' Briggs questioned.

'I questioned Jill Keller, the bar server. She said that Ellie had said something to Samuel about a gesture or comment he'd made and that was all she had to add,' Gina said. 'I asked Samuel, he said he'd only looked at Jill and Ellie flew off the handle. Again, he gave us full access to the CCTV without arguing. Said he's always happy to help the pigs.'

She leaned back and stared at the board. Nothing had changed with Avery. He was the same Avery that treated women like meat but they still flung themselves at him after he plied them with free drinks. The same Avery that had been involved in spats with husbands after affairs with their wives. The police were on record as visiting on several occasions over the past few years after husbands had tried to assault him. He'd never been caught breaking the law though. 'He's full of charm – not. I flicked through the CCTV after that and the next day. It appears she just went there the once but it needs a closer look. So what happened on Saturday? People don't just disappear. Her partner, Rebecca Greene, showed us a text message she sent on the Sunday morning saying she was staying at a friend's place. She's convinced Ellie wouldn't have sent that message.'

'Maybe Ellie had felt guilty after turning back to drink,' Briggs added.

'Maybe. I hope so, for her sake, but Rebecca Greene was so sure Ellie would never have sent that message.' Gina yelped as she stood and began hobbling towards her coat. Her muscles seemed to be seizing up. Adrenalin had kept her going during the day but she needed to give her body a rest. 'Right, I think I'll carry on working from home. Any volunteers available to give me a lift?'

Wyre held her car keys up. 'I'll drop you off, guv. Just coming up to the end of my shift. Don't worry though, I'm taking the rest of my notes home and I'll get them on the system.'

'Take care. I'll call you later when we've finalised the press statement,' Briggs called from across the room before quickly getting back to his conversation with Annie.

CHAPTER FORTY-TWO

Shaking, Natalie opened the new diary. Write down your feelings the self-help book had said. She remembered when she used to write song lyrics for what Bruce had termed, her 'stupid little band'. She used to love writing songs. As she reread her entry, she couldn't forget the woman who her husband had left in their spare room. She trembled as she heard the woman stirring. She could pop in there when she started to yell, release her, and face Bruce when he got home. That would be the right thing to do. Tears fell as she finished reading her passage. Her inner feelings stared back at her from the crisp white sheet.

> *I am the crack that runs through the mirror, and I'm scared of reaching the edge. One wrong step, one wrong word, one wrong look, and I'll shatter. All that will remain are fragments, fragments of me that can no longer be fixed. A carpet of chaos spread across the floor. Unrecognisable reflections of a shattered face will stare back. I am the crack that runs through the mirror and that crack is ever stretching, further and further, towards that edge. When will I shatter? Or will that crack remain forever within its confines, never quite reaching the edge, petrified of what lies beyond. Will I remain a crack, ever running through a mirror?*

'Shit!' It was all a load of shit. As tears mingled with the ink on the page, she tore it up and flung it in the waste bin. Her stupid little band days were over, Bruce had been right. She grabbed the stupid self-help book and threw that to the back of the wardrobe. She'd just work on mindfulness. The woman screamed at the same time the front door slammed. He was back and she was awake.

She ran downstairs and watched as Bruce placed a piece of paper on the kitchen worktop. It contained the personal address and mobile phone number of a DI Harte. Where had he got that information? He'd been out with friends, that's all he'd told her. They'd only been in Cleevesford a couple of days. She heard him on the phone talking to someone but she'd never heard any names mentioned. He rubbed the back of his head and walked with a slight limp. She daren't ask. Natalie poured him a coffee and passed it to him.

'It's too milky,' he said as he passed it back to her. She held back the tears as she made him another. Nothing was ever right. How could she forget how her husband liked his coffee?

As she passed him another, tears began to well up in her eyes. There was the matter of the woman her husband was keeping in their house. This was much bigger than coffee. 'I don't know what to do. We can't keep her here. We have to let her go.'

'Don't you even think about it!' He cupped her chin with his other hand and stared into her eyes. 'You'll ruin me, us, our life, the business, our lovely house and for that I'd never forgive you – never.' He dropped his hand and took a swig of the drink. She wiped her face. 'That's much better. See you can do it. Imagine having to leave here and start afresh all on your own, without me to do all the things you can't do because you won't leave the house?'

She began to shake and her skin prickled. He was right. A weal began to form on her neck and she gasped as she held back her sobs.

'She hasn't eaten and she's started screaming again. I'm worried. What if she needs a doctor?' She almost hyperventilated as she wiped her eyes on the sleeves of her jumper, her wild hair falling over her face.

'I'll check on her and don't worry, the tablets I gave her, they're just some of your sleeping tablets. They won't harm her. She's up there in the spare room having a lovely sleep. That's all. I just don't need her screaming all day while I decide what to do with her.'

As she slumped in the chair, she turned on the television in an attempt to mask the sound of her rapid breathing. A photo of a missing woman, Ellie Redfern, filled their screen. Bursting into tears, Natalie turned away from the television and stared at him.

He checked his watch. 'What are you staring at? Go and get little Ellie another one of your lovely pills. Grab the whisky too.'

Tears soaked her face as she followed his orders. She couldn't bear to anger him any more.

Bruce ripped all the sockets out of the back of the television and the room went silent. Natalie had seen enough television. He'd tell her it was broken. She had no idea where all the leads went. He took a swig of the coffee and almost spat. She couldn't do anything right. He'd show her again how to make coffee exactly as he liked it – milky. After that, he'd start preparing for what he had to do next.

He rubbed his groin. Pain still radiated from where the detective had grabbed him. He grinned as he opened his briefcase looking at the contents. 'I'm coming for you,' he said aloud.

CHAPTER FORTY-THREE

The figure watched from the back of the garden as the DI placed a takeaway bag on the kitchen table and poured a glass of water. As she unlocked the back door, the watcher shifted into the corner, hidden by a clump of shrubbery. 'Ebony,' she called as she rattled a box of cat food. The cat was going nowhere while it was being gripped this tightly. Just as she gave up and slammed and locked the door the cat began to wail. The figure let the panicked animal go and it scurried off, over the fence, into the wilderness beyond.

A gentle breeze whipped past the watcher's ears as they zipped up the forensic suit, covering their whole body. The waiting game had come to an end. It was just past eleven, she'd have to go to bed eventually. The watcher grinned. She'd left the key in the door. She had to have left the key in the door. She wasn't holding it and she hadn't placed anything down. Getting into DI Harte's house was being made even easier. As the kitchen light went off, the figure darted across the unruly lawn, ready in wait. After all, there was no rush to be home.

CHAPTER FORTY-FOUR

Gina turned the volume down on the television after watching the press release. She was impressed at how efficiently it had reached the local news station and she was sure it would be in the online local's before their paper publication day, which was Wednesday. She really hoped that someone would come forward, telling them where Ellie was. She saw the distress in Becky's eyes when she'd spoken of Ellie going missing. She shook her head and began ploughing through the day's notes on her laptop as she tucked into her takeaway chips. The phone rang – Briggs. 'Hello.' She took a swig of water and a couple of codeine-based painkillers. She needed to sleep tonight.

'I'm sorry we didn't get to talk before you left. How are feeling?'

'Sore.' She placed the plate of food onto the coffee table. 'I feel like I've been beaten up.'

He paused for a moment. 'Do you need anything?'

'I'm fine. I'm going to take a couple of painkillers and try to get rid of the aches and pains, ready for tomorrow.' She knew he was hoping she'd invite him over but she wasn't going to.

'Well don't feel like you have to rush in. I know you're not feeling good and no one expects you to be rushing around. You've had a bad twenty-four hours and you should be taking it easy.' She exhaled, glad he'd shifted the conversation.

'I would, take it easy I mean, if we didn't have a murderer on the loose and a missing woman. I only have aches and pains to contend with. I'll be okay. See you tomorrow, sir.'

Her joints began to relax, giving her a welcome sinking feeling, inviting her to close her eyes and sleep. The tablets were taking effect. She left the greasy chips on the table, turned everything off and yawned as she fell into bed. She heard the cat flap banging in the kitchen. Just Ebony returning from her night-time adventures.

CHAPTER FORTY-FIVE

Tuesday, 17 April 2018

The figure sat in the darkness of the moonlit room watching DI Gina Harte's chest rise and fall. Her digital clock read five past one in the morning. It had been a long night but so worth it. The DI was a woman who needed to be taught a lesson.

The cottage had been easy to enter. She lived in the end plot of a small row of terraced houses, in a semi-rural area. All the cottages had long gardens that were tree-lined at the end and were separated by mature hedges, as well as a fence, in between each plot. The rusty back gate hadn't even been locked and the kitchen had been easy to enter. People were always warned about leaving keys in doors, especially when they had cat flaps. Getting the hanger in the right position had been tricky but not impossible. As the keys clashed on the tiled flooring, there was the worry that she'd stir, but she'd slept right through. Silently, the back door had been locked again and the key had been positioned back in the keyhole. The front door would be the best exit route. That way there would be no sign of a break in. The police might even think she let someone in, leading them to suspect someone she knew well. Maybe they'd even suspect a copycat killing. That would throw an element of confusion into their investigation.

Wrapping the cord around the gloved hand, the watcher walked over to where she lay. The suit chaffed a little, making a slight brushing sound with every step, but nothing too loud. She opened her mouth and began to breathe heavily, flinching in her sleep, murmuring words that couldn't be deciphered. Her head thrashed and she turned to face the intruder. The quilt that covered her slipped down a little as she stretched out, revealing an open nightshirt. Sweat mingled with the smell of fruit penetrated the material of the thin mask. Her hair smelled of coconut. Such sweet smells for a person who had caused so much upset. The watcher caught sight of a photo on the bedside table as the clouds dispersed, allowing a bit of moonlight to shine through the window. So DI Harte did have a family. The young women in the photo shared her eyes.

The watcher flinched as the DI half called out. Little beads of sweat slipped down her cleavage, glistening in the moonlight as she whimpered while dreaming. Her nightmares would soon be over though.

The thought of wrapping the cord around the DI's neck was very appealing. She seemed so defenceless and vulnerable while sleeping. She would probably be a little easier to take on than Melissa had been.

She began wittering away in her sleep as she turned away. Before she woke, the intruder knew they needed to loop the cord around her whole neck and pull as hard as possible, just like the other night. They might end up wrestling on the floor, but there would be no letting go until she had passed away. This would be the ultimate lesson. Shame she wouldn't be around to learn from it.

Her phone began to buzz on her bedside table. The DI stirred.

It would be impossible to take her on alone if she was awake. Being in the police, she'd know how to defend herself. She'd fight to the end. Heart hammering, the figure crawled across the bedroom floor onto the landing as the DI came round, and crept downstairs and out of the front door. She'd keep – for now.

CHAPTER FORTY-SIX

She felt for the phone, trying to press the answer button as she prised her eyes open. Sweat ran down her forehead as her heart hammered in her ribcage. It was a withheld number. 'Hello. DI Harte.'

The caller was silent until she heard a whimpering sound coming from the other end. 'I don't know what to do.' A woman with a shaky voice began to sob and hyperventilate. 'I'm scared he'll kill the missing woman.'

'What's your name?'

'He could be back any moment.'

'Where are you? I can come straight there. Give me your address?' Gina sat up in bed, almost crying out as she leaned on her bad wrist. Her sweaty nightshirt clung to her skin.

'I have to help her. I must go. He'll be angry if he knows I've called. I can't do this.' The woman cried as she hung up.

Gina forced her aching body out of bed and stood as she called the station, knowing O'Connor was on a late. 'It's DI Harte. Get me a trace on a call to my phone, made at one sixteen. Then call me back.'

She called Jacob. Several rings later, he answered. 'Hello.'

'Jacob. I just got a call from a woman. I've called it in and I'm hoping for a trace. It was a woman saying that she was scared that he'd kill the missing woman. I'm thinking Ellie Redfern. Someone has her.'

Jacob cleared his throat. 'Are you sure it wasn't a prank?'

She headed down the stairs and flicked the kettle on. Her head was pounding from her injury and the abrupt awakening. 'She sounded petrified. It didn't sound like a prank, I know what a prank sounds like. This all has to be connected. Ellie, Melissa, my attack right outside Darrel's house.' She stared at her back door key in the lock and noticed it was leaning out of the keyhole at an angle. Shaking her head, she pushed the key in properly. She jumped as Ebony dived through the cat flap and rubbed her body against Gina's legs.

'Guv?'

'I'm still here. My cat just gave me a scare. I'm a bit on edge as you can probably tell. The woman said that he, whoever he is, would be back at any moment and that she needed to help the woman. What the hell is going on?' Her phone buzzed. Another call was coming through. 'Wait on the line; I have another call coming through. It's O'Connor.'

'We have a number but the phone isn't registered, guv. What's this about? I tried to call the number but the phone was turned off.'

'Thanks. I'll call you back in a minute to report what happened. I'm just on the line to Driscoll.' She ended the call and transferred back to Jacob. 'The phone wasn't registered. It'll be a while before we get an approximate location but O'Connor's on to it.' The kettle clicked and the corner of the kitchen filled with steam.

'Great. Do you want me to pick you up? Do we need to go to the station or are you staying at home until morning?' She could sense that Jacob hoped that she'd tell him to go back to bed.

'I'm going to stick around here for a while. I may try to grab a nap before we head back in. Would you pick me up for seven? I'll update my notes on the call and give O'Connor a call back.'

'Will do. Try and get some rest, guv. You've had a rough time of it and you need to heal those wounds if you're to be on top form.'

'Goodnight, Jacob.'

'Night, guv.'

Gina poured a coffee and sat at the kitchen table, taking a moment to enjoy the warmth of her favourite beverage. She leaned over to the back door and unlocked it. She closed the door again and locked it, noticing that the key stayed firmly in the lock. She rattled the doorframe. The key still didn't budge. How had the key ended up hanging slightly out of the keyhole?

She stepped through the house and shook the front door by the catch. It was firmly closed. She was becoming paranoid. The codeine-based painkillers she'd taken had sent her a bit funny, giving her nightmares, and unnerving her. Between that and the strange call, there was no way she was going back to sleep. She grabbed her phone and called O'Connor as she stared through the back door, into the darkness of the trees at the back of her garden. From what she could make out in the moonlight, the gate was closed. What she couldn't see was the figure watching her from the back of the garden, hidden in the dark shadows.

CHAPTER FORTY-SEVEN

Ellie's head felt like lead against the pillow. She tried to force her eyes open but they were barely responding. She remembered back to the warmth of the alcohol sliding down her throat, then she'd fallen into a deeply satisfying slumber. She dreamed of being in Combe Martin with Becky. They'd been sitting on a bench, staring up at the stars. The stars had descended from the sky like fireworks, a display for their eyes only. Becky had been smiling and holding her tightly on that cold night as they shared a flask of hot chocolate.

'Hey. Wake up.' A woman was calling her. That wasn't Becky's voice. 'We haven't got much time.' The room filled with sobbing and wailing, and kept repeating itself. 'Wake up.' Her head began to swim. She needed to sit up, drink a glass of water – shake off the heaviness that was weighing her down. She'd had a drink. She wasn't meant to drink again, ever. Why had she accepted a drink? She closed her eyes, they were too heavy to open and sleep was welcoming. She hadn't finished her dream. She tried hard to be back in Combe Martin.

Her mind flashed back to the night of her attack. 'Go away,' she tried to say. 'Leave me alone.' She wanted Becky and Combe Martin back but she wasn't in control of this dream. It was like she was reliving what had happened to her all over again.

'Wake up,' the woman called as she shook her. She felt her hand drop beside her, followed by her other hand. Her legs, she couldn't move them. She prised an eye open and saw the wild-haired blonde woman messing around with her feet. She tried to move them again, they were free.

She pulled herself up in the large metal-posted bed. It was all coming back. How could she have slept through all that was happening to her? The thought of waking up in a pub car park, before a judgemental stranger, now seemed like the better option.

'You need to go before he comes back.' The woman tried to drag her by her hands to a standing position. She was free from the bed that she'd been tied to. His wife, Natalie, was helping her to escape.

Pain flashed through her head as her gaze momentarily met the moving light bulb that dangled from the ceiling, causing shadows to dart around the room. The visual noise was too overwhelming. She needed a dark room in which to nurse her hangover. Holding her arm over her eyes, she tried to stand but her legs buckled. 'Help me,' she said as she grabbed the woman's arm to steady her balance.

'We don't have long. Hurry.' The woman helped her to the bedroom door, one step at a time.

Her throat was like sandpaper. She tried to swallow. Her jeans felt cold and damp. Had she urinated? She was sure she had. She had no recognition of the landing and had no idea how she'd ended up in the bedroom, tied to the posts. An image of her rapist forcing her to eat toast and drink whisky filled her mind. She remembered almost gagging as he kept telling her to swallow it. The woman dragged her down the stairs and she slipped down the last few, landing with a thud onto her bottom.

'Get up.' The woman ran to the window, shaking as she checked for signs of life outside. 'You don't have much time. He could be back at any moment,' she called, wiping her runny nose with her sleeve.

'Thank you.' Ellie grabbed the stair rail and pulled herself up. With each step along the hallway, her legs wobbled then she finally stumbled out of the open door. Linking her arms in the woman's, she took a step outside, almost buckling again. The world was spinning and her head pounded. She was so familiar with that feeling. Why were her stupid legs like jelly?

'I can't help you any further.' The woman fell to her knees and began to hyperventilate as she gripped the doorframe. 'Go.' The woman's sobs filled the night air. The security light came on as Ellie staggered through its trigger zone. The path was long. She had to keep going. She tripped over the uneven block paving and hurtled forward, into a pile of slimy moss. 'Get up. You have to hurry,' the woman yelled as she clung onto the door.

Her life depended on her getting her act together. Her legs were beginning to wake up as more blood flowed through them. Standing, she went from a slow walk to a slight jog, weaving her way down the long driveway.

A car squealed down the country road and turned into the drive. Dazzled by the full beam headlamps, Ellie was blinded. She went to dive onto the grass but just before her body landed, she wheezed as the car caught her hips and legs. Pain seared through her body as she half rolled over the corner of the car and landed in a heap, unable to catch her breath. All she heard was the sound of the engine humming and Natalie's piercing cries coming from behind her. 'Let her go.'

Pain ran through Ellie's whole body. She tried to shake her legs but they were so stiff. Reaching down, she felt a wetness spreading from her knee. Blood covered her hand and she yelped as he dragged her towards the boot of the car. 'You shouldn't have come back.' He stood above her, his shadow elongated over the full length of the overgrown lawn. After fumbling in a briefcase in his car, he grinned as he dangled a length of blue washing line in front of her.

'Get away from me.' She tried to shuffle away, further towards the back of the garden but she was too weak and he was too fast.

He leaned over her and began to wrap the cord around her neck. Batting his arms out of the way, she struck his throat, causing him to gasp and cough. She had to get away. She dragged her body closer to the hedge, hoping to find a gap and hide but he'd regained his composure.

His face had reddened and it almost looked like the veins on his neck were close to bursting. Wasting no time, he soon caught up with her. Within moments, her breath was being stolen by the cord cutting off her airflow. She grabbed for everything and anything but there was no point. He was strong. As little blotches of light teased her vision, she cried, knowing she was never going to see Becky again. She wondered if Becky would forever think that Ellie had chosen a life of drink over her. That hurt more than the thought of death. Hurting Becky was more than she could bear. Her vision deteriorated further and her body lost its rigidity. As she slumped, she shed her last tear for Becky, their wedding and the future she'd been so looking forward to.

CHAPTER FORTY-EIGHT

Natalie's stomach turned as she watched her husband. The pleasure on his face as he gripped the cord around Ellie's neck told her everything she needed to know. As she trembled in the garden, he ran over. 'Get in the house. Now!' She went to speak but she couldn't utter a word. She couldn't scream, she couldn't reason with him, all she could do was remain mute. 'Did you hear me?'

She nodded as she looked away. He grabbed her by the arm and dragged her across the drive and flung her into the hallway, slamming the door as he left. Natalie crawled on her knees across the floor. She stared through the letterbox as the man she thought she loved dragged the body into the back of their son's car. She shook her head. It wasn't real. Just something else she'd imagined. She checked again. It was real. He jogged towards the door with a look of rage on his face and placed his key in the lock. She ran to the living room as he let himself in. She had to get her phone and call the police. If he could kill once, he could do it again. As she grabbed her phone, he was upon her, twisting her hand until she dropped it. 'Bruce, please, you're hurting me.'

'How do you think I feel? My own wife, about to betray me.' He gripped her arm, pinching the skin. 'Get up,' he yelled, dragging her across the carpet, through the hall and along the drive.

'Please. Stop it. You're hurting me. I don't feel well.'

'You brought this upon yourself.' He shoved her into the passenger seat of the car. 'One movement or sound from you and it's game over.'

As the car rumbled off the drive, her heartbeat went into overdrive. The dark outside seemed to be shifting in position every time she moved her head. Disorientating her. Teasing her senses. One minute, the fields ahead looked like dark mounds, the next, they looked like they were growing in height and were about to suffocate her like some biblically proportioned land tsunami.

As the car rumbled over the country lanes, Natalie sobbed and gasped for air. He put his foot down, almost speeding along the lanes. Where was he taking her?

All she could hear was her hammering heart. She wanted to kick him, tell him to stop the car and shout, but she was incapable. Was she imagining everything? After all, her memory had been playing up something rotten. She'd lost keys, boxed bathroom items with kitchen items, failed to remember how her husband liked his coffee. She'd lost things and had no recollection of where they had gone, not even after a while. Bruce had been nothing short of understanding as he'd cared for her, encouraged her to rest and brought her food and drinks to bed when she was feeling ill.

Maybe there wasn't a dead woman in the boot. Maybe the woman he called Ellie didn't exist. It wouldn't be the first time she'd mentioned someone and Bruce would tell her he'd never heard of that person. She had been beyond sure that they'd had visitors in the past but he'd deny it, saying that she'd been asleep and must have dreamed it. Her sleeping pills were strong but she had been so sure.

A thought flashed through her mind, one of her recent episodes. She dreamed of another person in the house. She didn't recognise the voice. It was a couple of nights before they'd moved and she'd taken one of her tablets after a stressful day of packing. Had she opened her eyes and discovered Bruce talking to someone in their old house at Stratford, or was it her alternative reality? In her reality, she'd staggered down the stairs in a stupor and spotted her husband unpacking the washing line. Was it real? She kept trying to remember the voice but she couldn't recall it. It was no use. It wasn't real.

She inhaled and counted, then exhaled and counted. She'd read that this helped with anxiety. It was no use. She gasped and began to hyperventilate as a tremor travelled through her whole body, forcing her to shake against her will. She couldn't do this. She needed to go home and be safe behind the closed door of her house. 'Take me back,' she stammered between gasps of breath. She stared at the streetlamps ahead and saw a sign pointing to Cleevesford Community Park. It was a park she'd never been to before but Bruce had told her about it. He'd played there as a child and it contained a small pond where he used to collect tadpoles. Cleevesford was nothing like Stratford-upon-Avon, which was enriched by its Shakespearean history. She'd loved their house in Stratford but Bruce had insisted on moving close to where he'd lived as a child – wanting to show off his success to all who had known him. The boy who'd grown up on a council estate and made it big.

'I knew I'd need to deal with Ellie, for us, but not now. You did this. You killed her.' There *was* a woman in the boot. She hadn't imagined it. She pinched her hand as her breath began to quicken and the shakes came back. She needed to ground herself. That was something else she'd read. Be in the moment. Feel, hear, touch and smell. It wasn't working. Her mind kept coming back to the fact that there was a dead woman in the boot. She hadn't imagined it. Her husband had murdered the woman.

He reached out to her, tried to calm her down, but she struck him on the back of his head. 'Don't you dare touch me. You killed her! You're going to kill me too.' Her wet face glistened in the moonlight as he turned into the deserted car park. No one visited the park in the early hours of the morning. She was alone with a madman, and that madman was her husband.

CHAPTER FORTY-NINE

He slammed the brakes on as he pulled up. 'Just shut up. I did what I had to do, to protect us, to protect you. How about our son? What would Craig think?'

Nothing but a field surrounded by trees stared back. She knew she had betrayed him by helping Ellie. But what was she meant to do? It was all real. She'd watched the woman lying in their spare bed, tied to the posts, sleeping in her own urine and she couldn't bear to have that happening in her home any longer. She'd tried to call the detective but her nerves had got the better of her. Maybe the detective had traced the call and was coming to help. She wondered if she'd kept the call open long enough or if the phone had even been registered. After all, it was an old pay-as-you-go phone that Bruce had kept topped up so that he could call her if she was working in the garden.

'I can't have you playing me up tonight, not now. Open your mouth?'

She shook her head as tears streamed down her face. He wiped her tears and kissed her cheek.

'Look outside. Does it make you anxious? How would you like it all to go away? Look, my love. I can help you. We're in this together; just you and me. I'm going to deal with it all. You've had her in the house, tied up to the bed too, not just me. You helped me – remember? If we get caught, we both go down for murder. Craig is twenty now, at university, in his last year. What would this do to him, knowing his mother and father were murderers?

Open your mouth, now!' He held the pill between his fingers and tried to shove it through her pursed lips.

She shook her head. She wasn't a murderer. She'd tried to help the woman get out of the house but he'd come back, and he'd forced her into the house and killed the woman. She turned away from him. She wasn't taking the pill.

He grabbed her chin and squeezed her nose. 'Okay. We'll do it the hard way. You know I always win. I'm doing this because I care. Remember that.' As she opened her mouth and gasped for breath, he dropped the pill down her throat. Grabbing a bottle of water, he poured it into her mouth and clamped a hand over her lips. She had no option but to swallow.

As he removed his hand, she burst into sobs. 'You're going to kill me.' He poked his finger around her mouth and under her tongue as he felt for the tablet. She could bite him – hard. She began to clench her jaw, but stopped. There's no way she had the energy to fight.

'Close your eyes. I'll have you back home and in bed soon. You've just had a bad panic attack. Go to sleep.' He left the driver's door open as he dashed to the boot. A chilly blast of air filled the car as the breeze picked up a little. She wished he'd shut the door.

Natalie closed her eyes, hoping he would leave her alone. He opened the boot and she listened as the woman's body thudded onto the ground, followed by a dragging noise. He stopped and paused before closing the boot. She inhaled – petrol. She opened her eyes and pinched her skin once again. The tablet would totally take effect soon and she'd be good for nothing and at the mercy of her killer husband. She turned the rear-view mirror so that she could see. The white overall her husband was wearing stood out against the darkness of the hill. As he disappeared, dragging the body along the path that led to the play park, she flung open the passenger door, prodded a finger down her throat and shuddered as she vomited. There was no way he was sending her to sleep.

By morning she'd be convinced that nothing had happened. She knew what was happening right here and now. She couldn't risk forgetting. She was reaching her edge and was about to topple over into the unknown. Regardless of whether she could be fixed, she was no longer going to resist. 'I am the crack that runs through the mirror,' she whispered as she stepped out of the car, avoiding the small blob of vomit. The fear of shattering and losing herself forever was weaker than usual.

With every step she took, she knew there was no way back. Bruce wasn't going to forgive her for assisting the woman's escape and he wasn't going to forgive her if he found out she'd called the detective.

She'd spent too many years gazing into a mirror and tracing the outline of the stranger that always stared back. No longer would she be a stranger to herself even if she lost herself in the process. Maybe she could be fixed, maybe not. As her breath quickened, she inhaled and tried to ground herself. She could smell earth and cut grass. She listened. The sound of water trickling in the distance, then the couple of cars travelling along the dual carriageway that led to the town centre, further verified the here and now. She felt a bramble bush as she passed and was careful not to prick her fingers. She'd reached way beyond the edge of her safe zone and suddenly she could breathe. It was like she had just been reborn. Maybe she could be fixed. She sniffed the April air once again and shuddered as she inhaled smoke. As she staggered along the path, she almost fainted at the sight. What she saw could never be fixed.

She had to get away and quick. If he could do that to Ellie, he could do it to her. She didn't want to be murdered, tied to a roundabout and set alight. The sight of flames licking the skies above and the smell of cooking flesh overloaded her senses. The heart rate she'd done so well to control began to ramp up. The light of the fire swirled into shapes as she glanced back. She'd brought the tablet back up. She shouldn't be feeling woozy. Little imp-like creatures that her brain teased her with began to emerge from the flames, leaving the smouldering woman behind. They flew at her, grinning as she staggered, threatening to set her alight.

As she slipped and ran down the bank, she headed towards the trees at the back of the field. A hand grabbed her shoulder. The imps had caught up with her. They'd come to take her away. The earth began to bend and swirl. The sky above was now the sky at her side. The moon was laughing as she lay on her back. Her eyelids felt heavy. She'd left it too long to get the tablet out of her system. Some of it was still in her. It was too late.

Her husband leaned over and scooped her up as her heavy eyelids closed, against her will. A tear slid down the side of her face. The image of the dead woman, burning on the roundabout where children would soon be playing, was all she could think about. In her mind, the little fire imps were eating away at her, finishing her off, until there was nothing but charcoal left.

CHAPTER FIFTY

The fluorescent clock on the taxi driver's radio told Gina it was almost 5 a.m. 'Just here will be fine.' She stopped him at the entrance of the parking area and handed him some money. The forensic vans were in the car park and in the distance she could see the battery-powered lights, marking the spot. She thought back to the phone call from the mystery woman and the words *he'll kill the woman* ran through her mind.

She nodded at PC Smith as he began taping off the outer cordon. 'Another murder in less than a week, guv. How are you?'

Several other PC's assisted with the scene, going about their business under torchlight. Crime scene investigators walked back and forth to the van. One headed back towards the scene with a clipboard, another carried a camera.

'Still tender but there's no time to stay at home and lick my wounds.' Smith simply nodded as Gina passed him. He too looked exhausted. She yawned as she made her way across the bottom of the car park, towards the park, flinching with every step. The pain from her attack had set in even worse after she'd been woken up by Jacob's call; face buried in a cushion, on the settee.

A crime scene investigator intercepted her. Gina held up her identification. 'You need these on,' the woman called as she handed Gina a forensic suit, some gloves and a pair of boot covers. 'We're trying to preserve the car park too. Bernard's just over by the tent and he's waiting for you. Keith's on his way to assist. Follow the stepping plates around the edge of the park.'

Gina turned back to see Smith telling an early morning dog walker to take an alternative route.

'The investigators have made a start and erected a tent. Hope you don't mind us starting without you,' Jacob said, walking towards her. Gina shook her head. Jacob knew the drill and was all suited up. She trusted Bernard and Jacob to work the crime scene thoroughly. 'There's no way any member of the public should catch a glance of this. I don't know who we're looking for but this is awful, guv.'

'What do you know?'

'I've been here about fifteen minutes. The fire service was first on the scene. They put the fire out, but touched nothing. Smith turned up soon after, followed by an ambulance.' Jacob wiped his brow with his sleeve. A few strands of his sweaty hair had been left behind, sticking to his forehead.

'Who found the body?'

'The woman sitting in the ambulance. She's being treated for shock. She was just jogging and saw the fire.' Gina cried out in pain as she turned. 'Should you even be here, guv? You look rough.'

'I need to be here. Who could do this to someone? Set them on fire?' She shivered as she watched Bernard stepping out of the tent. 'Bernard!'

He removed his mask. 'Detective Inspector Harte. I was hoping not to meet you again so soon. What the hell happened to you?'

She touched her sore head. 'Oh this, I'm still trying to work that one out. Any first thoughts or initial observations?'

Bernard ran his fingers through his beard as he spoke. 'We'll be able to tell more after the post-mortem. On first glance, it appears that the victim was either dead or unconscious when the burning took place. The position of the cadaver. There is no tension. When a person is being burned alive, they normally clench their fists or show some signs of tensing up. There is no tension at all in our victim. The body appears to have been positioned on the roundabout in a sitting position, legs straight in front and together, and the body has been tied to the centre pole. The position is too neat for a living or conscious person. They would've thrashed about. We won't know for definite if the victim was dead or alive at the time until we've analysed the lungs, and we won't know if they were drugged until we analyse the blood results. We can check the skeletal remains for trauma during the PM. We'll then know if our victim was assaulted.'

'Thanks.' Gina grabbed her pad and managed a bit of scribbly writing with her left hand. As a right-handed person, with a sprained right wrist, she was struggling. The gloves weren't helping either, especially the one covering her bandage and the tips of her fingers, which looked fit to burst. 'Time of death? How was the fire started?'

'We could smell petrol on the grass. The charring certainly follows the pattern of accelerant being poured on the victim's head and trickling down. The feet and legs are barely burned but the head, chest and arms are fully charred. As for the time, not one hundred per cent, but given the damage and the state of the body when we arrived, I would say the cadaver was set alight within the past hour. Again, I can't confirm this fact just yet.' Gina continued scrawling notes onto her pad. 'So many people walk this route which, as you can appreciate, has made things more difficult. What we did find in the car park was a small pool of vomit and several steps leading from that pool of vomit. We've measured them and it looks like that person is a UK size five. There are also tyre tracks which we will crossmatch against the database. Also, we have drag marks from the car, along the car park and grass, which lead straight to the roundabout. We're just collecting and collating at the moment. Once all the samples are properly catalogued, we'll let you know straight away of any results.'

'Anything else?'

Jacob ran back towards Gina, a CSI trailing behind him. 'They've just found a broken necklace at the foot of the round-about, where the drag marks end.'

'Was there a pendant?'

'Yes, it was a little further away from the necklace, but it was half a heart.'

Gina rubbed her temples. 'Ellie Redfern. Our missing woman. We need an immediate briefing. Bernard, you and your team, work the hell out of this scene. I want to know everything as you find it. I want a sample of the vomit sent straight to the lab, see if we can get a DNA match. Size five shoe. That's a small foot. A woman, maybe? Our victim? Jacob, I need a statement from the woman in the ambulance. You do that while I make my notes legible and finish talking to Bernard, then you can drive me back to the station.'

One of the CSI's walked around the tent with a camera, taking photos of everything. Every time the flash was triggered, the park lit up. Gina gazed over the pond and saw a couple of moorhens swimming. They were soon joined by a few ducks. The sun was just starting to emerge. Soon it would be daylight and the officers would have their work cut out, keeping pedestrians, joggers and dog walkers away from the scene. Within no time, the news would be all over social media. She reached inside the forensic suit, swapped her notepad for her phone, and struggled to call Briggs. He'd need to prepare a press statement. Another plea for witnesses.

When she came off the phone, she approached the tent and went inside. She pulled the facemask over her mouth. Outside the tent, she could hear Jacob relaying all they knew so far to Wyre and O'Connor, who had just turned up. As she stepped forward, the smell penetrated the mask's fibres, becoming more intense, acrid, nauseating and sulphur-like. Within moments the dense smell almost blocked her nostrils and hit the back of the throat.

She stepped out of the tent, removed the mask and took a deep breath. 'Not good in there.'

A CSI looked at her sympathetically. She needed to go back in. The victim's head was completely charred, all her hair singed. Her shoulders, chest and back, along with the centre pole of the roundabout were also charred. A deep mix of red lesions stood out from the sooty skin, as did the victim's teeth. The victim was wearing jeans and boots. Becky had told them that Ellie always wore jeans and black boots.

O'Connor opened the tent flap and leaned in, grimacing as he covered his mouth. 'Guv. They've just found a small sample of blue washing line cord out here.'

'Blue washing line? Could it be the same blue cord that had been used to strangle Melissa?

'Get it bagged and sent straight to the lab. Looks like our killer has struck for a second time.'

CHAPTER FIFTY-ONE

The early morning sun shone through the incident room window. Gina stood beside the board and re-read all the information they had so far. 'How did you get on with interviewing the witness who discovered the body?'

Jacob leaned back in his chair. 'Forty-two-year-old Elouise Flanders. She was out jogging. She normally starts work as a carer at six. On her work days she always runs for twenty minutes, starting out between four and four thirty. She basically described the scene as we saw it and she touched nothing. She said the park was deserted, not another person in sight. Basically, apart from being heavily traumatised by what she saw, she has nothing to add.'

'Okay, moving on. We have discovered a small sample of blue cord at the scene. On first glance it looks like the same blue cord that was used to kill Melissa Sanderson. The cord is currently at the lab for testing, and Bernard and his team are still working the scene which is why they're not with us now. Our victim was either unconscious or dead before being set alight and was also wearing black boots and jeans. The victim's boots are a size seven which means they do not match the size five prints we found leading from the pool of vomit in the car park to the roundabout. I checked the details we have on Ellie and she is a size seven. I will also add that the victim's boots match the description Rebecca Greene gave us of Ellie's boots.'

O'Connor and Wyre watched as Gina relayed all that they'd found. 'Here, guv.' Jacob passed Gina a cup of coffee.

'Thanks. What I can't understand is the two different MO's. The modus operandi for Melissa Sanderson was totally different to that of Ellie Redfern. Melissa – assaulted on the stairs, was then tied to a chair in her own kitchen, no sign of forced entry. She was then strangled with what we have confirmed to be blue washing line. Ellie appears to have been brought to a park, tied to a roundabout and set alight after being either killed or rendered unconscious. Both are totally different. We have found blue cord at the scene and on face value it looks to be the same as the blue cord found at the scene of Melissa's murder. Who is shoe size five? We know from the markings on the grass and car park that the body had been dragged over one hundred meters. That's not an easy task. Whoever did this had to be physically strong unless there were two of them.'

Gina took a marker pen and drew a shaky line on the large map of the park with her left hand, showing the route in which the body had been dragged. She then began adding the information that they'd received onto the board. She stepped back, just about able to read her spidery writing.

'Shall I take over, guv?'

Gina nodded and passed the whiteboard marker to Wyre. She rolled her achy shoulder, feeling a grinding pain with every movement. Her painkillers were wearing off.

'Thank you, yes. What do the two women have in common? Melissa was thirty-five, Ellie, forty-three. Melissa was a married, stay-at-home mum, with a two-year-old. We know she was having an affair with James Phipps. We need to investigate any links between Phipps, Melissa and Ellie. Ellie was an ex-alcoholic who was facing some element of her past which we don't know about. It relates to a past assault. This past brought her back to Cleevesford and the Angel Arms. She worked in a coffee shop and was in a relationship with Becky. We haven't had a formal identification as yet but let's work on the information that we do have. A necklace matching the description of one that Ellie owns was found at the scene. The victim was wearing the same clothes that Ellie was known to be wearing when she disappeared. The only connection I can find, again, is the Angel Arms. Darrel Sanderson was drinking with Robert Dixon at the Angel on the night of Melissa's murder. Ellie went back to the same pub to confront her past. What could Ellie's past have to do with Melissa Sanderson? Maybe there's a link somewhere, I just can't see it.'

The other detectives looked as blank as Gina felt. She took a swig of coffee, trying hard to remove the acrid taste of burning flesh that lined the back of her throat. She imagined being at home and scrubbing away at her mouth and gums with her toothbrush until they were bleeding. Anything to get rid of the taste. As she blinked, the charred body flashed through her thoughts. Choking on her coffee, she grabbed a tissue and coughed hard, spluttering. 'What is it we're missing?'

O'Connor stopped chewing the end of his pen. 'I've got Daniel Timmons coming in for his interview at ten this morning? He's one of Darrel Sanderson's and Robert Dixon's friends. Phipps mentioned him and we managed to track him and the others down through Robert Dixon. Also Samuel Avery of the Angel Arms called today, said he had spoken to a couple of detectives and remembered some names. He confirmed that the group of friends we were asking about are fairly regular, sometimes visiting the pub in different pairs of the same friendship group and very occasionally attending as a group.'

'I wished he'd just cooperated when we were there!' Gina said.

'I know. We have a Lee Munro and a Ben Woodward also coming in later. Avery mentioned another friend of Rob's who had started coming to the pub, a Bruce Garrison. Maybe we should check him out too.'

'Has the press appeal gone out yet? Someone must have seen something at the park, either a car or a person.' Gina placed her empty coffee mug on the desk.

'Yes. Just sent it out,' Briggs replied as he entered.

'Great. Someone had to see something. Let's hope we get some good leads from the public.'

'They want to put something on air this evening and have requested a formal press release.'

'As SIO, I'll deliver it. What time?'

'Annie has arranged it for 5 p.m.'

'I best pop home and change. Can you all keep me updated on the interviews? We need to speak to Darrel Sanderson, Robert Dixon and James Phipps too. I want to know where they were between two and four this morning. I'm going to give Bernard a call on site and find out how he and the team are getting on. I'll do that while I'm getting ready. We also need to formally identify our victim. Jacob, will you contact Rebecca Greene and break the news? We need her to identify the necklace, the boots and the jeans. We will look at confirming the identification through Ellie's dental records. I will attend to that as well as continue working on the evidence we have and the evidence that keeps coming in. We have a lot to be getting on with. As you find anything out, update me. I'll do the same.'

Gina's shoulder began to throb. Her phone rang. As she struggled to answer with her left hand, Briggs stepped in and pressed the answer button. 'Here you go.'

She smiled and held it to her ear, pausing as the lab relayed their information. 'Thanks for letting me know. Are you emailing the report over now?'

Everyone in the incident room waited for the update. 'It's the DNA results from the hair I pulled out of my attacker's head. There's a match.'

CHAPTER FIFTY-TWO

The incident room was instantly silenced by her words. 'On Friday, the twentieth of February 1998, a woman was raped behind a shop in Camden. DNA was retrieved and it matches my attacker's DNA. The file is on its way over. This person is not on our database and has never been caught.' Gina gulped. The warmth of the sun shining through the window did nothing to disguise the tremble that was working its way through her body. 'It was a violent attack, leaving the victim in critical care for almost two weeks. That's all I have for now.' She left the room, gasping for breath as she reached her office and slammed the door closed.

Her mind flashed back to her ex-husband Terry. The nights she'd cried, begging him to stop hurting her. The sounds of Hannah's cries coming from her cot. Mia flashed through her mind. In her mind she was right there with Melissa as she died listening to her crying child, never knowing what happened after her demise. She wanted to hug the woman and tell her that her child was safe, but she'd never get that chance.

Trembling, she slid to the floor, leaning against the door. No one was coming in. Briggs knocked. 'Gina.' He pushed the door, sliding her along the floor as he entered. Sitting in front of her, he placed his arm around her and she nestled into his chest as she burst into tears. 'I'm taking you home, now. I mean it. You've been through a traumatic time and I insist that you speak to a counsellor.'

'I'm okay, sir. It was just a bit of a shock knowing how close—'
She stood and walked over to her computer. She needed to see
the information they had on her attacker. She opened the email.
'I'm going to find this bastard. I mean it.' She slammed her left
fist onto the desk, causing her keys to bounce. 'Someone is going
around killing women in our town. Someone attacked me and
it's all linked. I've been close to him, I've smelled him, touched
his hair, felt his strength. I'll know if we find him and I'm going
to be the one to arrest him.'

'But for now, I want you to go home, take some painkillers and
book in for a counselling session. As your superior, it's an order;
once you've done those things, you can come back. No counselling
booking, no press release. I will take over if you don't comply.'

She knew his conditions were non-negotiable. 'I'll do everything you said and I am coming back. I'm going to deliver that
press release and we're going to find him.'

'I'll be back in ten minutes to drive you home.'

As he left her office, she stared at her computer as details of the
historic rape case filled her screen. A pretty young woman with
dark eyes and hair stared back. She scrolled down, revealing the
way that same woman looked following the attack. She barely
recognised her under her bloody nose and swollen eyes. His
victim, a nineteen-year-old Spanish exchange student called Lucia
Ramos, had been at a friend's apartment and had left to go home
at around 1 a.m. She'd taken a short cut between two shops. It
was at this point that she reported hearing footsteps catching up
with her. She'd sped up but he'd soon caught up with her. He'd
grabbed her from behind and slammed her face first into a wall,
instantly breaking her nose, after which he raped her. Gina wiped
a tear from the corner of her eye.

She skipped the details and moved onto the evidence. They
had his DNA. He hadn't used a condom. They'd taken samples
from all the surrounding streets and many people had been

around that night. No one saw this man following Lucia. She gazed over the still photos taken from the CCTV and they were all unusable. She did note that the blurry figure walked with an upright stance. She watched the clip. He was wearing a hat and keeping his head down, never once looking up. Even if he had given them a glimpse of his face, the quality of the recording was so poor it wouldn't have been useful.

'Right. Home time.' Briggs entered her office and jangled his car keys.

'I'll do as you say, book a date with the counsellor. I'll have a rest, have some food, freshen up, then I'm coming back and I'm going up before the reporters. We need to let people know that there is a dangerous individual out there and to be on guard. This will be national by the end of the day.' She turned her computer off and grabbed her coat.

Briggs intercepted her as she walked towards the door. 'I'm with you all the way. Look, if you need to talk, anytime, I'm here as a friend and a colleague.' He moved aside and followed her out.

For now, she needed an afternoon alone to prepare for the press release. She couldn't talk to him – she wouldn't ever.

CHAPTER FIFTY-THREE

Gina read all the gruesome details of Lucia Ramos's attack several times before slamming down the laptop lid and turning the kettle on. The painkillers were beginning to take effect and that had allowed her to comb her hair and iron her jacket as best she could with one hand. She caught her reflection in the door. The gash didn't look too alarming now she'd covered it with foundation and hidden the bruise on her forehead with a few strands of hair. Both would have journalists sensationalising the story if they looked too closely and spotted them. As the kettle boiled and began to steam up the window, her phone rang. 'Wyre. What have you got for me?'

'We've just interviewed Daniel Timmons. Thought I'd call and update you. I'll update the system as soon as I get off the phone.'

'Hit me with it.'

'On Thursday the twelfth of April, and on the night of your attack, and in the early hours of this morning, he was at home with his wife, Alison. When questioned about his friendship with Robert Dixon and Darrel Sanderson, he claims to have known them most of his life. They grew up in Cleevesford. He has no prior record and has worked for the council in the revenues department since leaving school. He occasionally visits the Angel pub, often meeting up with Robert or Darrel, but hasn't been for a couple of weeks. I checked all his information out. His wife's story matches his version of events.'

'What did she say?'

'She claimed he was in all last night and never went out. They went to bed around ten, as they normally did. She said the same for the night of the twelfth.'

Gina poured the water into the coffee as she leaned sideways, wedging the phone between her ear and shoulder. 'Did you manage to speak to Avery at the Angel again about Timmons?'

'When I spoke to him, Samuel Avery confirmed that it had been a couple of weeks since Daniel had been into the pub. We verified this through Daniel's Facebook records. He'd tagged himself at the pub on that night, and had also tagged Darrel in his post. Avery claimed they were laughing and drinking, and then they walked home. This was nothing unusual to him.'

'And his workplace?'

'We had no trouble obtaining information from them after we said we were investigating two murders. We confirmed his job with the council. He has indeed worked there since leaving school and is currently working at middle management level. They did have a couple of things to share on his record that may be of interest. He received a couple of official warnings for bringing his volatile home life to work. Staff had heard him arguing with his wife and it involved a bit of unsavoury name calling, mostly of a sexist nature. After the warnings, the behaviour stopped. There is one other thing I noticed, guv.'

'What's that?'

'He is only about five foot five inches tall.'

'Which means he couldn't be my attacker. He'd be too short even with shoes on. We can't discard the fact that there may be more than one person involved. Whoever dragged Ellie's body had to be strong.'

'He's also quite portly and sounds out of shape. He was a little puffed out after walking to the interview rooms. He couldn't wait to light up a cigarette after he left either. He'd have trouble carrying a bag of potatoes, let alone dragging a body over one hundred meters.'

'Okay. Keep on with the interviews. I'll be back in a bit for the press release. Having to attend to my clothes and hair with only one good hand is proving to be a little tricky.'

There was a pause on the line. 'I really admire you, guv. With all that's happened this week and you're still going out there in front of the press. We're right behind you. Oh, one last thing, the call that was made to your mobile. It was made in the Cleevesford area. That's all we managed to get from the signal. There's a mast on the edge of Cleevesford, just by the main island as you enter the town. The signal came from the west side of that mast. There are a lot of flats, houses and businesses within that area. You already know the number is unregistered.'

A lump formed in Gina's throat as she ended the call. Her mind went back to the scared woman who made the call. She looked at her watch, only three hours to go until she had to perform.

Wyre's words almost caused her to gag on her coffee. Would they all really be behind her if they knew her past? The look on Terry's face as his hands windmilled down the stairs and the sound of his body thudding on the ground made her flinch. After all she'd been through at his evil hands, the feelings of guilt still never left. She'd often questioned herself. If she hadn't left it so long before calling an ambulance, would he have lived?

'Pull yourself together, Harte,' she said as she grabbed her phone and called the counsellor to book her appointment.

CHAPTER FIFTY-FOUR

Coughing, Natalie tried to sit up but was swiftly wrenched back by something tugging at her bare wrists and ankles. The pitch-black room was spinning. 'Stop,' she croaked as she closed her eyes and took a deep breath, swallowing to try and lubricate her throat. She wrenched her wrist to try and shake off the binds, but they weren't loosening. Where was she? She remembered the fire imps, chasing her. Was it real? It was real. She knew he'd convince her she'd imagined it because he always did. If it wasn't real, why was she bound in darkness, unable to move? She opened her eyes again and managed to focus on the moon's outline through the curtains. Then she saw the grainy outline of the chest of drawers and the door to the built-in wardrobe. She stared at the chair in the corner. There was more to the outline than just the chair.

Lamplight filled the room, almost binding her until her vision adjusted. 'My darling wife. She who must obey.'

'Untie me Bruce.' Tears slid down the side of her face, wetting the pillow beneath.

'You betrayed me. Everything I did, I did for you, for us. Now look what you've done. I'm not going to let you ruin Craig's life. I've gone beyond caring about me, or you, but he will never know.'

'You hurt her, didn't you, you killed Melissa Sanderson?' Natalie cried as she spoke. There had been no mention of the details surrounding Melissa's death but she'd seen him using blue cord to strangle Ellie and she knew. She'd watched the news report before he disconnected the TV, and she'd overheard him speaking on the phone to Darrel Sanderson. He had been Bruce's friend from the past. 'You killed your friend's wife. How could you?'

'She deserved everything she got. Like you, she was a disloyal bitch who couldn't be trusted. Like you, she was self-centred, lazy and unloving. Toxic is the word for a woman like her. All this time, I thought you were better.' He pulled his office keys from his pocket, the original set with his bottle opener key ring attached, and he grinned as he dangled them in front of her. 'You were so easy to fool. Poor little Natalie with her anxiety. Poor little Natalie forgets everything and can't leave the house. You made it so easy which is why you're lying in that bed and I'm sitting here, deciding your fate.'

'Did you ever love me?'

'You had to get pregnant, didn't you? I know you lost the first one, but I was committed by then. Thought I'd persevere with what we had, settle for this! Don't get me wrong, I love Craig but a sprog was never really on the cards. Enjoyed trapping me, didn't you? I put up with you all these years for our son. I suppose the only pleasure you gave me was the game. I enjoyed that.'

She tensed up and yanked the binds, but they weren't budging. 'Let me go,' she cried. She now realised what a monster her husband really was.

'Let me tell you about Melissa. Did you know Melissa was shagging some theatre luvvie? I bet you didn't.' He roared with laughter. 'What am I thinking? You never leave the house. You don't know any of my friends. How could you? You haven't attended a social event in years. No wonder I am the way I am. Here goes. Melissa was going to leave Darrel for that idiot and take his child. Did he deserve that?'

She shook her head as tears flooded her face. 'But she didn't deserve what happened to her.'

'You make me laugh. Are you sure I did it? You think you know everything just because you saw what happened to Ellie.

Let me tell you something,' he spat, 'I admit to being a very bad boy in the past but I hadn't killed up until little Ellie. Oh yes, I tied her up and I confess, a part of me was a little turned on. Kill Melissa – no. That's one cord I didn't pull.' He walked over to her and kissed her forehead. 'You know why I'm being so straight with you?'

'No.' A lump formed in her throat and her nose ran. She turned, unable to look into the eyes of the man she no longer recognised. She knew what he wanted her to say but she wasn't going to say it. The only way she would leave that room was to die. 'Who killed Melissa?' She had to know.

He smiled and stroked her head. 'Wouldn't you like to know? That's not for me to tell. Open wide.' He grabbed a bottle of water from the bedside table and poured. Her hungry mouth opened, gulping all that he'd give her. Without warning, he popped a tablet in her mouth and continued pouring. She knew she'd swallowed it. 'Have a lovely sleep and I'll see you soon. I've very important work to do.'

'No. Don't leave me here. Please, let me go. I won't do anything wrong. I'm sorry.' It was no good. The light went off and the door closed. She yanked at her binds but they were going nowhere. She heard him on the phone, something about him getting some help was mentioned. 'Help,' she yelled. Maybe the person on the phone would hear. Her husband didn't sound worried by her yelling. They were all in on it, she knew it, and she was next.

The neighbours wouldn't hear her yells for help. They lived in the country, a good distance from the next house. They had a long drive and a long garden and double glazing. She thought of Craig, named after the brother she lost to sepsis at only twelve years old. Craig, her boy, who she was so proud of for following in his father's footsteps and studying accountancy. If only he knew who his father really was. Bruce had been her saviour during her episodes, but now it was all beginning to make sense. He'd carefully engineered her path to anxiety, he'd made her ill and she'd trusted him fully. Soon the outline of the moon through the curtains became fuzzy around the edges as she drifted off to sleep thinking about Craig, wondering if she'd ever wake up. 'Please, I don't want to die.'

CHAPTER FIFTY-FIVE

Gina stood tall on the temporary stage that had been erected in the conference room, lights blinding her, fading the journalists' faces that filled the room. As she finished relaying the information relating to Melissa Sanderson and a second murder victim, she suddenly felt a lump forming in her throat. The journalists were hungry for their next story and were awaiting their moment. Her aches and pains controlled her every move. She knew they could see her discomfort.

As soon as she opened the floor up to questions, it wouldn't end. Not one of them sat on the tired-looking chairs that had been laid out, all preferring to stand next to their camera and boom operators. Flashes filled the room. More photos, all of which would be appearing online soon after the interview, and then in the morning papers. Her bruised head and bandaged wrist would take prime position in their articles. She knew the intense lighting was probably melting her foundation.

'As you can appreciate, the person who did this is dangerous. If you have any information, please do not hesitate to call the number on the bottom of the screen.' Gina stared at all the faces before her. 'Any questions?'

Briggs stood tall, beside her, as she waited for the flood of comments to come forth. 'DI Harte, can you confirm that the Cleevesford Killer attacked you on the night of Sunday the fifteenth of April?'

The 'Cleevesford Killer', that's what they had decided to call the killer. 'As yet we can't confirm that the same person was responsible for the deaths of Melissa Sanderson and the victim who's yet to be identified. We are waiting for the forensic reports to come back.' She held her trembling fingers out of view. They weren't going to make her a victim all over again. If she verified that it was her who had been attacked, they'd press for details. Not only were they holding the finer details of the case back to protect the integrity of the investigation, some of those details were personal to her and she didn't want the press sensationalising her story. Her neck began to prickle and burn up.

'I asked about your attack.' The journalist dragged her cameraman through the mob to the front of the room and several other journalists fought her to get into prime position. Gina felt her face redden. It didn't take long for word to get out. They had been informed that there had been an attack within the police as there had been a witness appeal. They had seen her injuries and put two and two together, taking a gamble on the 'Cleevesford Killer' link.

'We're here to discuss the murders in the hope of receiving witness information. Please keep your questioning on track or I will end this interview now.'

The journalist sighed. Another called out. 'You made an arrest this week. The public deserve to know who you arrested. Is it James Phipps? Is he a suspect?' It was Lyndsey Saunders of the *Warwickshire Herald*.

'This is an ongoing investigation and no one is detained in relation to that investigation, at the moment. We can only keep suspects if we have enough evidence against them.'

Several journalists called out at once.

'People are scared. Could you have let the killer go?'

'What leads are you following?'

'Is the husband, Darrel Sanderson, a suspect?'

'Is there a link to the Angel Arms?'

'There's a murderer out there, people need to know what you're doing about it. How close are you to catching the killer?'

'Is it true that your attack occurred outside the address of the first murder?'

'Did you see the Cleevesford Killer?'

Questions came from everywhere. Flashes blinded her. She'd given them the information she had set out to relay. She wasn't about to share the details of her experience with them. They knew there had been an attack. They knew of the location, the time and the date. That was all they needed to publish a witness appeal.

The door at the back of the room crashed open. Rebecca Greene staggered through, closely followed by PC Smith. She shook him off. Mascara ran down her tear-filled eyes as she slurred her words. 'What are you really doing? I know my Ellie is gone. I know that bastard killed her.' Rebecca almost toppled over. Every member of the press turned; all cameras were now on her. 'I don't need to wait for your dental records to prove anything. They found her necklace, they found her—' The woman burst into tears and let out a piercing scream as she collapsed into a heap in the aisle. Instead of helping her, the press crowded around, shouting question upon question as the woman broke down.

Gina barged through the crowd, flinching as she pushed through with her bruised shoulder. 'Move away from her. She needs help. Stand back, I said.'

'Ellie who?' one of the journalists shouted. 'Is she the second of the Cleevesford Killer's victims? The public deserve to know. Or is she the third, DI Harte?'

Gina stared into the camera.

'Get away from her,' Briggs called as he pushed his way through, breaking Gina's stare. He helped drag the wailing woman to the front of the building and through the back door, closing it on the rabble. They had all they were going to get for the day.

Rebecca fell into a chair. 'It's Ellie. I know it,' she cried as she buried her head in her arm and PC Smith came to take over.

Briggs pulled Gina aside. 'It's all going to go berserk in the morning. Who knows what the press will make of this.'

'Stuff the press! I'm going to chase up those dental records. We need a positive identification. I know the post-mortem is in progress and they were prioritising the victim's dental records. Jacob is there at the moment. I'll give him a call. Rebecca can't go through this uncertainty any longer. Look at her.' Gina rubbed her throbbing temples, knowing it was going to be a long evening. She felt Rebecca's heartache as the grieving woman cried out. Her phone rang. 'O'Connor. We're heading back now.' She paused as she listened to what he had to say. 'Yes! Make sure everyone is in the incident room for when I arrive.' She ended the call.

'What is it?' Briggs asked.

'We have a lead.'

CHAPTER FIFTY-SIX

Gina wiped the sweat off her brow and flung her jacket over a chair. 'Bad news. The cat is out of the bag on Ellie Redfern. Rebecca Greene turned up at the press release and gave the vultures a feast. The press have Ellie's name and they are pursuing James Phipps. The post-mortem is still in progress but we know the cadaver's dental records are being prioritised. I'm hoping to have that confirmation any time now.'

'Sounds like I have my work cut out.' Annie frowned and looked across at Briggs.

'We had no way of knowing Rebecca would turn up like that and, yes, the press are going to be on to us non-stop now. They were also speculating that it was me who was attacked. They are indeed right. I don't think I successfully convinced them otherwise. What else do we have? O'Connor? Tell me about the call, in more detail this time.'

Briggs sat at the head of the table. Wyre turned in her seat and O'Connor stood in front of the incident board. Two officers removed their headsets and turned to face O'Connor.

'We had a call from a Mr Sid Boucher. He delivers milk for Avon Dairy King, based in Studley. He was just driving his lorry through Cleevesford when he saw the only car on the road, pulling into the park. He said, as a night-shift lorry driver, he often sees the odd car in the night so nothing really stood out. The information he did manage to give was the driver had a passenger and was driving a black saloon car. He didn't take notice of the make. He did however notice a slight dent to the driver's side panel. I asked if he saw the driver or passenger, he said no.'

'What time was this?'

'He said he'd just listened to 'Bridge Over Troubled Water' on the local radio. He didn't clock the time. I called the station and they said that the song started at three fifteen. Our killer and a passenger entered the car park between three fifteen and three twenty.'

'Two people in the car.'

'Yes. It sounds like he had our Ellie Redfern in the passenger seat.' O'Connor grabbed a cookie. 'Help yourself by the way. Ginger and raisin.'

Gina's stomach ached for a bite to eat. Despite the acrid film that still lingered in her nostrils, she needed something otherwise she'd almost certainly feel nauseous. 'Or, he had his accomplice in the passenger seat. Going back to the scene at Melissa Sanderson's house. Could there have been two people? The assault on the body, tying her up, strangulation with a cord. One person could've done that. That murder seemed so well planned. No traces of anything except forensic suit material and a small piece of denim, both from the same person, caught at the same time. Maybe there were two really well-prepared perps. Now, look at this morning. The perp wasn't as prepared this time. We have tyre tracks, vomit at the scene, drag marks, a different MO, but the same cord was used on the victim. Was it the same two perps? Then there's my attack. He was alone, and once again very well prepared. Face covered with a mask, full forensic suit. Something happened that he wasn't expecting. He wasn't expecting Ellie. She came back to confront her past. Was he her past? Did my attacker rape her?' The room fell silent as everyone's minds whirled.

'Any more on the historic rape?' Wyre tied her hair up as she asked.

'Not as yet. What did the interviews drag up?'

'Ben Woodward and Lee Munro, they both have alibis for the night Melissa Sanderson was murdered. They both separately stated that they were at Lee's house on the night of the attack. Lee's wife, Jennifer, confirmed that he was having friends over for a game of cards and she went to her friend's that evening. When she arrived home at 1 a.m. Lee was in bed and his friends had gone home.'

'Did she see his friends?'

'No. They arrived after she left. She did make a point of saying that there were beer cans all over the coffee table and the place was a mess. She did mention Bruce. His details were provided by Lee and are on file. We need to follow up on him. I left a message for him to call me back.'

Gina began rubbing her head. Sounded like the same Bruce that Avery had mentioned. Her wrist was throbbing and her shoulder had taken a bit of a bump while rescuing Rebecca from the press. She fell into one of the plastic seats around the table and began eating a biscuit. 'And James Phipps?'

O'Connor rubbed his hands together, dispersing biscuit crumbs all over the floor. 'I paid a visit to the Eagle pub in Redditch. Two members of staff confirmed that, on the night of Friday the thirteenth, he was telling the truth about being there all evening and he got absolutely wasted. They refused to serve him after eleven. He wasn't being abusive; they were more worried for his health. He'd been downing rum by the double. He staggered out of the pub at closing time and the landlord worriedly watched as Phipps unlocked his car, which was parked on the opposite side of the road, in front of a row of terraced houses. He said that Phipps opened the back door and curled up on the back seats. He locked up after that. CCTV confirmed that Phipps stayed there all night. The time he left ties in with us picking him up on Saturday the fourteenth at 6 a.m.'

'Will someone check on him? It appears the press have his name. They're probably camped outside his block of flats now.

Right – thanks, O'Connor and thank Mrs O once again for the biscuits. I'm going to head home, I'm really not feeling so good. I am on duty though. If you hear anything, call me first.'

Wyre picked up the ringing phone on her desk and relayed the message. 'It's Jacob. The post-mortem results will be in first thing. They can confirm without any doubt, that the body we recovered from Cleevesford Park this morning was that of Ellie Redfern. The dental records are a match.'

'Would you please pop over to Rebecca Greene's and give her the bad news? I called Smith just before I got back here. He was taking her home. She wasn't in a good way at all and I don't feel well enough to be there.'

Wyre placed her pen on the desk. 'I'll get over there now, guv. Hope you're feeling better in the morning.'

'Thanks. Any volunteers to give an injured detective a lift home?'

'Nothing but the best for my team. I'll drop you home in five.' Briggs stood and pulled his car keys from his pocket.

CHAPTER FIFTY-SEVEN

Briggs helped her out of the car and into the house. 'Right, I'm putting the kettle on before I go. Do you have any food?'

She shrugged her shoulders and let out a yelp as a pain shot from her wrist to her shoulder. The bruising was really coming out and the term *mild concussion* sounded better than it felt. Her head ached, she was overtired and her muscles felt as though they were seizing up. 'Can you grab me a couple of painkillers from the side?'

Briggs passed her the bottle and a glass of water. 'Where do you keep the food? I checked the fridge and the cupboard. There's some old food in a plastic tub.'

'It's not old. It's a perfectly good piece of quiche; it's only two days past its use by date. I was just going to warm it up. I have some thoughts on the case, we can share the quiche and talk them through.'

'Can I make a suggestion first?' She nodded as she swallowed a couple of tablets and washed them down. 'Can we order some food in? I'm starving too and I don't think that leftover whatever-it-is will feed the two of us, and your mouldy bread might kill us.'

'Sounds like a plan.'

After he ordered a pizza, he poured two glasses of cola. 'Here, get this down you.'

'Thanks.'

'What do you want to talk about?'

Gina stared at the flickering lights behind the grate of the electric fire. 'I was thinking of upgrading to a log burner. That old thing looks like it belongs in the last century. What do you think?'

'You want to talk about log burners?'

Her deflection had sounded ridiculous. She shook her head. 'No, sorry. I wanted to talk about the case and us. I mean me. I know our relationship was getting complicated. I mean we'd hidden it well for months. I'm not good for a relationship and the holiday gave me some clarity of thought. I just didn't want that to affect our working relationship and friendship—'

'Stop. You don't need to spell it out. There's no denying I feel something for you but, mostly, you are one of my best detectives. You know what I'm trying to say. Of course we're friends. That's not the reason why you pushed me away, is it? Call it instinct but I am a detective and this didn't really challenge my detective skills.'

She shook her head and sipped the coffee. 'You're too good at this.'

'It's the nature of our job. You knew you weren't convincing either, didn't you?'

She nodded. 'Nature of the job. Bloody hell. It could be a long evening.'

'As long as our phones are on, I have all evening. And we still need get some work done at some point.'

'I don't know where to start.'

'The beginning? I'm also a damn good listener.'

'I wasn't straight with you about my past relationship, my main one – my marriage. If I were to be, I'd have to speak about things I'm not comfortable about.' Her heat rate began to pick up. What was she doing? Terry – always there, always in wait to ruin another evening or relationship. No more. Every time she kept her secret, it gave Terry strength.

'Should I be worried?'

'No, of course not. I know I said I'd been made a fool of in the past. We both laughed it off a little, agreed that was a normal thing. You know my first husband died. What you don't know…' She wanted to say, what you don't know is I shoved him down the stairs to his death. I didn't call an ambulance. I watched him die and only then did I call for help. I held my crying toddler in my arms on that thundery night as I watched him take his last breath.

He waited for her to continue. 'You can tell me anything. What you say to me won't go any further.'

'For years, he used to beat me, abuse me and do worse things. That's what I was holding back. Gina Harte – Detective Gina Harte, once allowed herself to be treated like a victim.' She stared ahead, into the fireplace willing herself not to cry as her trembling hands betrayed her.

'Gina. You're the strongest, warmest person I know. To come through all that and become the success that you are, is nothing short of amazing.'

'I feel like such a fool. I allowed him to do all those things to me. I could have taken Hannah and left. I should have left. I allowed him to beat and rape me and the other night, when I got attacked—'

He held her. 'Shh. No one allows someone to beat and rape them. Do you hear me? You're not a fool. Don't say that.'

Had she done the right thing, telling him? 'I don't like to think about it, ever, but I can't get it out of my head, especially since the other night. Get this, I was convinced someone had been in my house the other night. They hadn't been, but all these thoughts about Terry have been messing with my mind.'

'Did you book that appointment with the counsellor? You really need to talk this through, especially after the attack. You should take a few days off.'

'I don't need a few days off. What happened to me, in the past, is what has driven me in this job. I love this job. Gina Harte, child protection and domestic abuse – that's where I started and it's still close to my heart. Ellie Redfern, she was battling something from her past and we were too slow to help her. I'm certain her past involved the man who attacked me? Was she raped? Melissa

Sanderson – why was Melissa always alone at home, drinking? Darrel Sanderson, the bruises on his daughter, the damage to his wife's body. We have taken that little girl out of harm's way pending further investigation. Of course, he blames Melissa. Easy target now she'd dead. James Phipps, what is he in all this? Clever murderer, or just some sad man who loved a woman who was out of his league? The press will be all over him now. At least if he is the murderer, he's not going anywhere tonight. This case and others like it, they are the reason I get up every morning. I get up so that we can catch people like the animal I was married to and bring them to justice. I will continue getting up every morning to do my job so long as there are still people out there who need me.' A stream of tears ran down her cheeks. Briggs wiped them away.

'But what do *you* need, Gina? Look at you. You're in pain, emotionally and physically. You need to look after yourself too.' The doorbell rang. Briggs paid for the pizza and placed it down on the coffee table. 'What I'm saying is. It all starts with you looking after yourself. Eat.' He grabbed a slice and placed it in her hand.

She blew her nose and bit into the pizza. 'You know what? I'm ready to face all this shit, including my past, well as ready as I can be, but first, I'm solving this case before someone else gets hurt.' She paused and took another bite of pizza. 'The perpetrator or perps didn't plan Ellie's murder as well. Too much was left behind. There was an element of the unknown with this one, something unexpected that caught our murderer off guard. Melissa Sanderson's house was so clean of everything.'

'I think you're right. Murder one was well planned. Even your attack was well planned. He'd come prepared.'

'Darrel Sanderson and his friends. Someone isn't telling the truth. Or are they all telling the truth? They are all giving each other alibis, which seems convenient. Between each of them and the Angel Arms, it seems they are all in the clear but something isn't sitting right. Did Lee Munro's wife come home to a well-staged men's night in? Will you pass me my laptop?'

'Only if you eat another slice of pizza while we talk it through. Shall I grab my computer from the kitchen?'

'I feel I need to be alone with my thoughts tonight. Is that okay?' He nodded. She could see he was a little disappointed but she didn't want to give him the wrong impression just because she'd confided in him. As he packed up to leave, she followed him to the kitchen. She played with the key in the door, eventually locking up. She knew better than to leave keys in doors. The other day had acted as a reminder of how she'd compromised her security. She grabbed one more slice of pizza and handed Briggs the box. 'For when you get home. I'm sorry. You understand?'

'Goodnight, Gina.'

'Night, sir. See you tomorrow.'

CHAPTER FIFTY-EIGHT

Wednesday, 18 April 2018

Gina had been exhausted after putting her work away at just before 1 a.m. and now she was back at the station for a 7 a.m. briefing. Briggs had dutifully turned up at six thirty to pick her up. Trying to flex her wrist under the bandage caused her nothing but pain and the stiffness in her neck and shoulder prevented her from turning right. The grey skies cast a dull hue into the tired room. Wyre, who sat next to Jacob, squirted a small mist of air freshener to mask the damp odour before she took a seat at the end of the table. Bernard began unloading paperwork from his bag

'As we know, the forensic report will take some time to be delivered but after attending the autopsy, there are some things that Bernard and I can share with you. You will also see that the photos have been added to the board, and we will add further information as we talk it through.' Gina rubbed her shoulder as she gazed at the photos of Ellie, charred and tied to the roundabout.

'Bernard. What can you tell us?'

He grabbed his beard and stroked it from top to tip as he spoke. 'Our tests prove that Ellie Redfern was dead before she was set alight. There was no smoke in her lungs.

'I think the burning was a poor attempt at concealing her identity. The killer didn't think that we'd find out who she was from her dental records. He probably never for one moment thought that so much of her would remain intact,' Gina said.

Jacob leaned back in his chair and chewed the end of his pen.

Bernard began to coil the wispy end of his beard around his index finger. 'We tested the cord that was found at the scene and made a comparison to the cord that was used to asphyxiate Mrs Sanderson. There was a direct match. Again, the cord was a standard polypropylene washing line cord. The blue colour was an exact match too.'

Gina rolled her shoulder and leaned forward. 'Thanks, Bernard. As we know, the first murder appeared to be well planned. Darrel, the husband, goes to the pub, leaving his two-year-old and wife Melissa at home. On his return, he finds her tied to a chair and asphyxiated. The subsequent report shows that she was killed by the hands of the person who used this piece of cord, the same cord that was found at the scene of Ellie Redfern's murder. Do we have the results back on James' Phipps collection of denim?'

Bernard scratched his grey hair. 'Yes and there are no matches to the denim that we found at the scene of Melissa Sanderson's murder.'

'Unless he disposed of the jeans after spotting that they were torn.'

'There is that,' Jacob replied.

'I read the interview transcripts of Lee Munro and Ben Woodward.' Gina looked up at the board. She could see that Wyre had added Lee and Ben to the board, with relevant notes. 'We have Benedict Woodward. Head of Sales for Robert Dixon's company. Forty-seven – married to Janet. One teenage son. Then we have, Lee, a carpenter, fifty-one and the host of the so-called party on the night of Melissa's murder. Each one of the friends have claimed that they were together that night, at Lee's house. His wife Jennifer was out, at a friend's house. From what I read, they were having a game of cards.' She gazed at the board. Her mind kept coming back to the night of Melissa's murder and the party they were all attending. Robert and Darrel were at the pub together. 'Have we confirmed Jennifer Munro's whereabouts?'

'Is she a suspect?' Wyre asked.

'Everyone's a suspect until we can rule them out. It's not confirmed but we may be looking for a second perp, probably wearing size five shoes. Will you chase up Jennifer Munro, Selina Dixon and Bruce Garrison? I want their whereabouts checked out on the nights of Melissa Sanderson's murder, my attack and Ellie Redfern's murder. Anything not adding up, I want to know immediately.' Gina's head began to pound and the room swayed a little.

'You really don't look well, guv.' Wyre gave her a sympathetic look.

'I'm fine. If we didn't have a double murderer on the loose, believe me, I'd be at home resting, but we don't have time to rest. There is too much to do, not enough people to do it all and very little time. Two people were seen in the car by our lorry driver when he passed the park. Was Ellie with him, sitting in the passenger seat or was it an accomplice? If Ellie was with him, did he asphyxiate her with the cord when they were in the car, then drag her to the roundabout, tie her up and set fire to her? Why tie her up if she was dead? Was it for effect? To keep the body in place? Have we had any matches on the tyre tracks as yet?'

Jacob shook his head. 'Not as yet.'

'Anything come back on the vomit found at the scene?'

'No, guv.'

'I'll be in my office. Wyre, will you visit Jennifer Munro and Selina Dixon? O'Connor, Smith will be back in this afternoon. Will you call Bruce Garrison and ask him to come in voluntarily and then interview him? If you can't get hold of him, take a drive up to Stratford and visit his place of work. Jacob, we need to bring James Phipps back and verify his whereabouts for last night but I suspect that will be straightforward if the press have been camped outside. I'm going to try and make sense of all this information. Keep updating me as you find out new things. Jacob, also contact the DVLA, see if any of our new names have a black saloon car registered to them?'

'Will do, guv.'

As she stood, the room felt as though it were moving. She wanted to be out there, interviewing, but her body was telling her otherwise. 'Do you need a hand?' Briggs asked as he helped her up.

'I'm all good, thank you. I'm going to put out another press appeal and email it to Annie. Someone else must have seen a black saloon car between three and three thirty on the morning of Ellie's murder, and they might just be able to give us a description.' She pushed the chair under the table and managed to reach the corridor before leaning against the wall. She had to get through this pain. She had to find the killer.

There had to be a connection, something she was missing. The answer was close, she could feel it. Her mind flashed back to Wyre's description of Mrs Dixon as a Stepford Wife. Then her thoughts came back to the Angel pub. Her past dealings with Samuel Avery, the landlord, had shown him to be a pest when it came to women. He knew the men that associated with Darrel Sanderson. He hadn't told her their names when she spoke to him at the pub. Were Robert Dixon and Darrel Sanderson the same as Samuel Avery? Were they pests towards women? Were they all friends? Was Avery part of the trusted group? Was Phipps more calculating than he seemed? Darrel Sanderson's little daughter, Mia; Mrs Dixon in her apron working in her kitchen – these mixed images flashed through her mind. Ellie – what did Ellie know? Had she confronted her past a little too closely? Had Gina almost confronted Ellie's past? Would he have stopped at rape this time? Did he stop at rape or did he murder Ellie? As she stepped along the corridor, it seemed to shift slightly to the left, then the right. Eventually, she reached her office and slammed the door closed before exhaling and falling into her chair. Whether her light-headedness was all down to concussion, she'd never know, but she was feeling sickly and anxious. In her office was where she'd remain for the rest of the day.

She logged onto her computer and began checking on the news. She cringed when she saw herself featured on the front page of the *Herald*, staring directly into the camera, bumps and bruises on show for all to see. There was another photo of Rebecca slumped on the floor amidst the reporters. Ellie's identification was out of the bag and the 'Cleevesford Killer' was now hot news. James Phipps name was mentioned everywhere. She threw her pen at the wall.

CHAPTER FIFTY-NINE

'Wakey, wakey, rise and shine,' Bruce said as he opened the curtains. Natalie prised one eye open and was faced with grey miserable skies. A slight pattering of rain tapped on the window-pane. She lifted her arm, realising she was no longer tied up. He grabbed her under the arms and dragged her forcibly down the stairs before she'd had the chance to feel her feet on the ground. As they reached the kitchen, he threw her into a chair and began tying her up with the same blue cord that she now knew had killed Melissa and Ellie.

'Are you going to hurt me?' she stammered as he pulled the blue cord around her ankles and wrists, securing her. A quiver ran through her. She was cold, so cold. It was April but when the sun wasn't out and clouds filled the skies, it was still chilly. In the thinnest of nightdresses, she shivered as she waited for his answer. Her groggy head filled with conclusions that all involved a painful death.

'You had to interfere. Instead of just sitting back or sleeping like you normally do, you had to stick your nose in. I had it all under control—'

'You killed a woman.'

'I didn't want to kill her. She came to our home, threatening the life we'd built. Threatening Craig and all that I've worked so hard for all these years, and you, you took her side. My own wife betrayed me just like Darrel's betrayed him. I suppose the next thing you'd have done is sold me out, told the police. You'd have laughed while I was rotting in a cell. Sitting here in our lovely house, already paid for, operating a successful business that already runs itself with barely any of my input. You had it all with me, but I'm not letting you have any of it without me. I'm an all or nothing kind of guy and you know that. You're going to vanish. They'll never find you. Maybe—' Bruce sneered as he walked over to the cooker, turned the gas hobs on and snatched a lighter from his pocket. 'Maybe you die tragically after leaving the gas on. After all, you have history of being forgetful. Calling the docs all the time for more of your sleeping and anxiety pills. Getting rid of you will be the easiest so far. I collect the insurance, maybe even move back to Stratford if I have to and start again. Something I've considered before. I could have it all. You know Sheryl, the junior accountant, she's always making moves on me. She's young, full of energy, fun to be around, not a neurotic mess, like you.'

'It wouldn't take you long to turn her into a neurotic mess. You made me this way.' Natalie began to sob as the smell of gas filled her nose, making her nauseous.

He teased her with the lighter and grinned. 'Just one flick and I could end you. One. Little. Click.'

She screamed as she tugged at her binds, unable to budge them, even a little. 'Let me go. Stop this. You don't need to do this, please.'

He kissed her on the forehead. 'You're right. I should think this through. I quite like this house.' He placed the lighter back in his pocket. 'I'll have to be a bit more creative. Maybe set you up as another Ellie, somewhere out there, flames coming from your head until you burn to a crisp.'

The times she'd genuinely thought he cared for her. She'd lived a life, bound by fear and he'd been the understanding constant in her life. The one who'd never pressured her to leave the house. He'd helped her, so she'd thought. He'd really been her oppressor, gaslighting her at every opportunity. If anyone had been disloyal in their marriage, it had been him. He'd lied to her, abused his power and her trust in him. Now he was deciding the best way to make her disappear. 'All these years, there was nothing wrong with me. Before you I had everything, a promising career in floristry and I was in a band, until you told me I didn't quite have the voice. You told me I was bad at everything, everything! I made the last garden nice and it wasn't good enough. Everything I did was never good enough. The only thing that wasn't good enough was you.'

'Believe what you like in your airy-fairy brain, under that hideous hair. You wouldn't have made it with your half-soaked songs, and those idiots you called band members were just that, idiot simpletons. Yes, the garden was okay. You did a good job of the garden. Feel better now that I've complimented you? Back then, you got pregnant and I did the right thing.'

'I lost our baby and you didn't care, even back then.'

'And did I leave you? No! Then we had Craig. I married you, took care of you both, and paid for everything. I've worked like a dog for all this,' he yelled as he turned off the gas. 'So you can sit here all day in a pretty little house playing with flowers.' He kicked the kitchen cupboard, making a dent in it.

She could see the cracks beginning to show. She wasn't the one who was cracking any more, it was him. It was always him, she just couldn't see it. He was the one who was close to shattering. 'You can't keep me here. It doesn't need to be like this. You can just let me go and we can carry on.' Tears streamed down her face.

He laughed manically and kneeled to her level. 'You can't fool me at all. Remember, I'm the master of manipulation. Let you go?' He burst into fits of laughter as he massaged his temples and stared out at the garden. He grabbed his mobile as she sobbed, realising her fate. 'Shut up with the crying. Shut up or I'll shut you up. Do you hear me?' He stepped into the hallway.

She tried to twist the cord and loosen it. With every movement her heart rate increased. The room began to move and every word her deranged husband spoke seemed to blast her eardrums. The grogginess she'd felt when he'd woken her had been replaced by a need to escape, to break free.

Her husband hurried along the hallway with the phone pressed against his ear, until he was out of sight. 'I know about what was on the news. Okay, it was me. That bitch followed me and was threatening to destroy my life so, yes, I killed her.' Bruce paused. 'Yes. I'll be here, waiting. Thank you. We will all get through this.'

'Who's coming over?' she shouted.

'Someone needs to help me clean this mess up.'

As she tugged, she realised there was no escape. Her yells echoed through the kitchen but her husband didn't answer. Someone was coming to clean her away. The key moments in her life flashed through her mind. She'd never see Craig again. Her boy, her son, the grown-up man he now was. She would never see him marry, have his own children or graduate. Her husband would get away with her murder, just like he'd got away with everything he'd done so far.

She trembled as she thought about death. Many times in the past she had considered ending it. She'd imagine herself staring at her reflection, a sight she detested with a passion. She'd smash the mirror into a thousand pieces, take a shard of glass and slice her wrist with it, watching the deep crimson liquid slipping out with ease, draining her of life. She'd mostly wanted to end it all on the days she had been too scared to leave the house, when she'd dwelled on the past and all the opportunities she'd missed out on. The days after Craig had left for university, leaving her feeling lonely and hollow. The days when her anxiety had hit with a crippling force, totally imprisoning her. She now knew it was all carefully engineered by the man she trusted, the murderer who now paced in the hallway, awaiting back up, to end her life. She wanted to fight. She would fight them to the end. It wasn't her time to die, it was her time to fight. She closed her eyes and imagined that mirror, scattered on the floor. Slowly, she visualised the pieces of mirror floating back up, slotting into place until it was once again whole and perfect. In her mind the mirror could be fixed and she was going to fight to fix it once and for all.

He ended his call and paced back over to her. 'Swallow it.' She shook her head and pursed her lips. He'd kept her in a drug-induced trance for years. She didn't want another pill, not now. She wanted to live. He clasped her nose between his thumb and finger. She couldn't hold her breath in any longer. As she gasped for air, he threw a sleeping pill down her throat, almost choking her as he held his hand over her mouth. She swallowed the dry pill as tears fell down her eyes. 'You're a devious bitch.' He snatched a roll of tape from the top drawer and wrapped a strip over her mouth and all around her head. 'There will be no spitting that one out.' Soon the world started fading away and she was being dragged along the hallway with no idea where she'd wake up, if indeed he'd ever allow her to wake up again.

CHAPTER SIXTY

Natalie's eyes flickered. She wanted so much to wake up but her eyelids still felt heavy. One minute she was aware of someone creeping around her, the next she'd fall into a slumber.

She was falling and falling until she awoke to find herself lying in their new garden. She knew it was unkempt and she'd been convinced that she'd be well enough to eventually get out there and make it beautiful. She brushed a clump of dried mud from her hair and stood.

There were some amazing trees, mostly small fruit trees. In the summer, apples, plums and apricots would adorn them. The brambles would provide an abundance of blackberries. In her dream it was a beautiful, late summer's day. The sun was high and she was wearing a hat. She watched as a bee buzzed amongst the honeysuckles that bordered the garden.

The gate rattled. Startled, she turned. It rattled again. She wouldn't venture as far as the gate. It was too risky. That gate was the only thing that protected her from the dark woods. The entanglement of trees with all the chaos that they brought would trap her in their branches, suffocating her as they tightened, squeezing the life straight out of her. She would never open the gate – never. She wasn't about to let in whatever evil resided behind the gate.

The gate banged and banged, almost coming off its hinges. Something was trying to ram its way into her garden. As the banging boomed through her head, rain fell, then hailstones, then snow, until the whole garden was coated in a dusting of white. The life that filled the garden was now all dead – all killed without warning. She gasped but couldn't catch her breath. The gate creaked opened, revealing a framed tableau of darkness. Branches weaved in and out of each other until they spilled into the garden, displacing the snow. They surged closer to the house like an uncontrollable tsunami, chasing her to the door. Just as she felt that her heart was about to fail, the branches grabbed her by the feet, lifting her high into the snow-filled skies, taking her further and further away until she could see nothing but white. The pain in her chest stabbed away. Heart attack – that's what it had to be.

'Shh. It's okay. You're perfectly safe,' came the gentle voice of the woman in white. She tried to open her eyes further. She wasn't wearing all white, she was wearing a white jumper. It wasn't just white, it was pristine, exactly how a brand new white jumper would look.

A phone rang. Natalie's heart was humming away. Was she still dreaming? The woman scrutinised the screen, swore under her breath and dismissed the call.

Natalie attempted to speak through the tape over her mouth. The woman reached over and ripped it away, tearing a piece of skin on her top lip. 'You have to get me out of here. My husband, he's gone mad. Untie me,' she called as she began to struggle.

The woman nervously looked away. 'I'm just looking after you until he gets back. He said you're sick.' She sat back in the chair in the corner of the bedroom. Natalie was back where she started, tied to the bed in their guest room.

'You don't understand. He's keeping me here against my will. I need to get out of here. He's killed a woman. We're in danger.' As her eyes focused, she couldn't see any binds on the other woman. She didn't even recognise the other woman. 'Who are you?'

'You're not well. I'm trying to help you. I'm just here to care for you.'

Was she seeing an angel? The woman's hair was beautifully pinned up in a classic French pleat. Her fitted jeans complimented her perfectly slim frame with precision. She was quite short, with the most petite of features. The woman pulled the bed sheet back up to Natalie's chin, revealing her French manicured nails. She'd never seen anyone so perfect, not outside of a magazine anyway. Maybe this woman was a figment of her imagination, the woman she'd like to be. 'You're not real. You're not real. You're not real,' she kept repeating.

The woman began humming a tune she didn't recognise as she picked up a sheet of blood red material and began to sew. It was all too bizarre. She needed to wake up. No way was there a pristinely dressed woman in her spare room, sewing. She clenched her eyelids shut and tried to go back to sleep, to block out the surreal situation that was slowly appearing to be real.

'When you marry someone, you promise to honour and obey. Wedding vows are very important, you know. A good wife should know her role.'

Natalie wanted the voice to go away. She never used the word obey in her wedding vows. They'd had a modern ceremony in a hotel. 'No. Get me out of here. You need to untie me before he comes back. We'll both be in danger if he sees you here.'

'A good wife is never in danger. Don't worry about me. I'm perfectly safe. It's not too late, you know, to become a good wife. He just needs your understanding at the moment. He has a lot to attend to with your illness. He's told me how poorly you are.'

'Shut up.' Natalie writhed in the sweaty bed sheets. She was covered up to her neck and the heat was unbearable. She needed to free her wrists from the posts and pull the bed covers down before she melted. Her heart began to pound – louder and louder. She panicked as the hotness radiated from her core to her numbing extremities and she began to hyperventilate.

'There, there. You go back to sleep. A rest will make it all better. You'll see everything more clearly when you wake up properly.' The woman began to stroke her brow.

'Untie me now,' she yelled as tears flooded down the sides of her face, soaking her ears and hair.

'I'm disturbing you. I'll sit outside the room. Just get some rest and you'll feel much better.' The woman wiped her damp hair from her face, turned the lamp off and left the room, taking her sewing with her. Natalie stared at the window and watched as little droplets of rain tapped against the pane. Shadows from the woodland trees danced around the room, leading her gaze everywhere. She felt like she was being watched; by whom, she had no idea. As the room began to turn, she clenched her eyes closed and tried to think of better things but it was proving difficult. She had to get out of her binds. She tugged and tugged at the blue cord. She'd keep tugging, even if she lost a layer of skin along the way. As long as she could break free, she didn't care. If she didn't get free, she was dead.

CHAPTER SIXTY-ONE

Gina held the phone to her ear. 'Bloody hell,' she said as she dropped the phone on her desk. Knowing she had a sprained wrist was one thing, remembering not to use it was another. The pain throbbed as far as her fingers.

'What happened, guv?' Wyre asked.

'Just my wrist. I've swapped hands now. Go on.'

'I managed to speak to Jennifer Munro earlier. Jennifer swears she left husband, Lee Munro, getting ready for his friends coming over on the night of Melissa's murder. She can't however provide an alibi for him. She was at her friend's all evening. He did text her that evening saying that all was going well, that they hadn't wrecked the house. She'd also replied, promising that she wouldn't be later than they'd agreed, that she'd be back by one in the morning. She showed me the messages.'

A heaviness crept over Gina, forcing her to close her eyes while they continued their conversation. She wanted nothing more than to be at home wearing more comfortable clothing in her warm house. Her shoulder had stiffened almost to a freeze. 'How about the Stepford Wife?'

'Mrs Dixon.'

'That's the one.'

'I called her house and her husband answered. He said his wife was on a shopping day in Worcester and she was apparently stopping off at a friend's house before coming home much later. I have her mobile number. I tried to call but it went straight to voicemail. I'll keep trying. It's all really strange, guv.'

'What do you mean?'

'Jennifer Munro is just like Selina Dixon. Weird. It's like walking into another era. The way they talk, the way they dress and their demeanour. It may be that I'm as working class as they come but Mrs Munro was arranging flowers while wearing the most pristine apron I have ever seen. I know I'm neat but this woman was perfect, like she was trying really hard to impress, but she carried it off with ease. Lee Munro's slippers were placed on the floor, perfectly aligned and ready for him to step into. The newspaper was placed on the kitchen table and the seat was out at an angle, like she was ready for his homecoming and the set up was all part of a ritual. The coffee pot had a filter in it and there was a cup next to it, containing milk. She was prepared for him coming home at any time. When I asked her what time he'd be home, she said he finishes anytime between two in the afternoon and six, depending on how busy he was with work. Get this. I checked with her friend, Penelope Lewis, an old friend of her mother's. She said that Jennifer Munro was with her all that evening. The friend did however say their night-time get together was a rarity, that Lee Munro didn't like her going out of an evening and forbade it most of the time.'

'Forbade it? What century is this?'

'Exactly. It doesn't sit well with me but, as yet, we have nothing on Lee Munro. He is also too tall to be your attacker but that's not to say he couldn't be party to what has happened. There's still no getting over that he has alibis.'

'Alibis I don't trust. The more I think about it, the more it all seems too convenient. It's no good me thinking all this though, we need to find a crack in the story, a breakthrough in evidence. Any matches on the tyre tracks as yet?'

'No. We do know the tyres are badly worn down though. There's hardly any tread on them – totally illegal.'

Rain pelted against the window. The April showers were out in full force. 'When you eventually track down Mrs Dixon, give me a call and tell me what you find out. I want to know where she was on the night of Melissa's and Ellie's murder.'

There was a tap on her office door. 'Come in.' She yawned.

'Tired, guv?' Jacob asked.

'Groggy and lightheaded. Any information on the black saloon car?'

Jacob sat in the chair opposite and dropped his notebook on her desk. 'None of Darrel's associates currently own a black saloon car. No black saloon cars are registered at any of their addresses. Rebecca Greene doesn't drive. No one working at the Angel Arms owns one either. I'm clutching at anything here.'

'We only have the lorry driver's word for it. Any black saloon cars showing up on CCTV in the area?'

'As you know, there's hardly any CCTV outside the centre of Cleevesford. The park is nowhere near the centre. Nothing useful as yet but we'll keep looking. I went over to James Phipps's flat. He was absolutely hammered earlier today and was unable to say much when I questioned him about where he was at the time Ellie was murdered. He had a bit of a shiner though and a sore on his chin, don't know how he got them. The press that are camped outside his block of flats are having a field day with that. As it stands, we have nothing more to bring him in on at the moment. He claims to have never heard of Ellie and when I showed him her photo, he said he'd never seen her before in his life. He wasn't looking good though and I could barely follow what he was saying. He was in an unbelievable state.'

Gina squeezed her shoulder and closed her eyes, willing the aching to go away. The more she willed it away, the worse it got. 'He's too much of a convenient scapegoat. Again, everything's coming back to Darrel for me. Darrel was very conveniently in the Angel Arms when his wife was killed. Get this, Wyre refers to Selina Dixon and Jennifer Munro as the Stepford Wives. Maybe Melissa Sanderson didn't fit their expectations. She wasn't pretending to be happy within her marriage to Darrel. She was drinking alone, depressed and having an affair. We know she was confused if we're to believe Phipps. He wanted her to leave Darrel and be with him, but instead she finished it with him. She'd confided in him about Darrel's friends – then I was attacked. I was the one who made the decision to remove Mia from Darrel's care. Doesn't it all seem like a coincidence? I want Darrel brought in again and questioned. If he did have anything to do with his wife's murder, we're going to nail him.'

'Shall I get on to that now?'

'No point delaying.' Gina almost cried out as she turned. 'I'm not feeling so good.'

Jacob walked around the desk and kneeled beside her. 'You okay, guv? Look at me.'

'It's okay. I can see you fine. The doctor said I'd feel like this for a while. I'm feeling a bit nauseous. Can you drop me back home? I'll base myself at my kitchen table for the day.'

'Of course. I'll drop by Darrel Sanderson's house on the way back and I'll let you know what happens.'

'I'll give Briggs a call when I get home, tell him I'm basing myself there. Has anyone contacted Bruce Garrison yet?'

Jacob opened the office door. 'Tried to. I tried his house, no answer. I went to his accountancy firm also. His receptionist, a woman called Sylvie, told me he was out at a client's that day. I asked who, but she was unable to tell me. The only thing he'd put in his diary was on-site auditing for the next two days. She had no idea where. She said they have hundreds of clients and she couldn't just guess where he might be. She also said, as he's the boss, he didn't have to account for his whereabouts like the rest of them. He's proving to be a hard man to track down.'

'Keep trying. Do we know anything about him?'

'Forty-five, wife called Natalie and a son aged twenty called Craig who's away at university. He has a Facebook profile but never posts and has very few friends. He owns an accountancy firm in Stratford and has recently moved back to Cleevesford, the town he grew up in.'

'How recently?'

'The house sale went through two weeks ago, so any time since then.'

'We need him in. I need you to keep calling, will you do that?' Jacob nodded. 'Call me when you've made contact with either him or his wife.'

As Jacob left, her phone rang. 'Harte.'

'How's the investigation going?' asked Briggs.

'Jacob's dropping me home. I'm going to take some pills and change into something more comfortable, then go over all the case notes. There has to be a clue in all this somewhere. It's all just a mess at the minute. Every time I think it could be someone, someone else comes into light. Or maybe it's just my concussed head playing tricks on me. Either way, I need to be at home. I'll be back in first thing.'

'When's your appointment with the counsellor?'

'Next Monday. The only problem with my head is the pain but as you made it a condition—'

'For good reason. I want my team to be at their best and that's the end of it. I'll pop over to yours on my way home, check how you're doing. I could bring a bite to eat? Nothing funny, we can just talk about the case.'

She smiled. 'Thanks. And thanks for listening the other night. I really don't need counselling but I know you have to do what you think is right. And, yes, there's a few things about the case I'd like to bounce off someone else and, yes, to the food. These people are strange, odd, and another pair of ears and eyes might help. We can run through Wyre and O'Connor's interviews.'

'Can't wait. Take care of yourself, Georgina.'

'Don't call me that.'

'Point taken, Harte. I'll be with you as soon as I'm able. Won't be long. Get the coffee pot on. It will be a long night.'

'The coffee pot is never off.' She ended the call and smiled. Things didn't feel awkward with Briggs any longer. They wouldn't be the first or last detectives to have a fling and just get on with things after.

She pressed play on the fuzzy CCTV showing the lead up to Lucia Ramos's rape and watched as her attacker followed the woman between the two shops. She kept rewinding it over and over again, trying to fix his gait and presence in her memory.

CHAPTER SIXTY-TWO

Darrel stared out at the pastures that backed onto the detective's cottage. He'd been staring at the same view for a couple of hours and he had no idea how much longer he'd be staring at that same view. He belched, trying to relieve his indigestion, wishing he hadn't had a greasy bacon sandwich for lunch.

Darkness fell as the rainy afternoon turned into early evening. Bruce grabbed the blue cord with his gloved hands and began playing with it. Every time he twisted it, Darrel wanted to grab the cord off him and fling it out of the window. Everything had seemed so clear a few days ago. He hated the detective, he really did. His hands shook. Killing a detective was in another league. *Cop killer.* That label was etched into his brain. Bruce flexed the washing line once again, a grin forming across his face as he anticipated his next move.

DI Harte lived in the end plot of a nice little row of terraced cottages. They'd backed the car in, along the rough lane behind them. The long gardens ensured that they'd kept their distance from her house and the others in the row. DI Harte's garden was a little unkempt and mostly paved, and the grey stone exterior was far from warm. When they had been in the back garden earlier, scoping it out, Darrel had noticed how bleak the interior was through the kitchen window. He'd also seen her little black cat. The creature had welcomed him into the garden and enjoyed the leftover bit of bacon sandwich he'd fed it. Part of him had wanted to wring its scrawny little neck, after all, the detective had taken his daughter away from him. He could take something she loved from her. His head was everywhere. He wanted her to pay but the 'cop killer' label kept milling through his mind.

The days had passed in a blur for Darrel. His brother wasn't speaking to him after he'd seen the bruising on Mia. He'd sworn it was Melissa in her drunken state but Alan had remembered the way he'd been treated by his brother when growing up. Darrel thought of the times he'd get Alan in a headlock and force him to eat a spoonful of mustard or the times he'd pulled his shorts down and kick him into the brook. Alan knew him more intimately than anyone and, deep down, Alan knew that he was the bully he pretended not to be. He'd tried to call and ask how Mia was but his calls had been blocked. All this because of Melissa. If only Melissa had been the good wife she'd promised to be when they had married. But no, she had to shag a stupid drama teacher and neglect their daughter and home, the home he had worked so hard to provide.

Bruce wrapped the blue cord around his wrist, coiling it until he ran out of length. 'Can you stop doing that?' Darrel snapped as he watched the house. The detective's house remained deserted.

Bruce unravelled the cord and placed it in his lap. 'Feeling a bit nervy, are we?'

'What do you think? I shouldn't be here. If I'm seen here, we've all had it. Did you think about that when you stuffed up?'

'I didn't stuff up! Everything I did was to protect the group – to protect you.'

Darrel shook with anger as he stared at Bruce. 'Protect me. More like protect yourself. I don't know you—'

'You were happy with me helping to take care of your wife problem. She'd been drinking and disrespecting you, not looking after your kid. Well, the deed has been done and it's payback time. Did you think it was all about you? This society we live in, it's diseased. Rob puts it so well. Melissa was a part of that decay, we dealt with her and we're all in the clear. We'll deal with the detective and we'll all be in the clear. After all, you were at the pub with Rob and I'm not even on the scene yet. Lee will also swear I was with them. It's all going to be fine. Anyway, you could be enjoying this rather than looking so tetchy. Remember the other night, when the detective was outside your house, how angry you were? You wanted me there, teaching the bitch a lesson. You wanted it. Don't pretend you didn't. After all, you made the call to Rob.'

He couldn't answer Bruce. He had called Rob and Rob had said he'd sort everything, and he had. Had they let their personal feelings go a bit too far? He should've played the game, stayed in, let the detective sit and watch. Instead, he'd been angry, wanted to teach her a lesson. He slammed his fist into the car door, rattling its frame. He was just as much to blame for things getting this far and he had to own that failure. 'Everything is going wrong. This wasn't meant to happen.' His hands visibly trembled.

'Look. Just calm it down. I'm going in there, alone this time. I'm going to wrap this cord around her neck until she turns blue. I'm doing this for you too. She's coming for us. She took Mia from you. She can't get away with that. After this, the police will have no clue as to who did what. The Cleevesford Killer did it, that's who.' Bruce laughed as he grabbed a forensic suit from the back seat. 'When she gets back, I'm going to watch her until I know I can get in and be in a good position to take her on. All you need to do is have the car ready to pull away. There are three possible routes just down the road. We take the first one and keep going until we reach Rob's.'

Through a crack in the trees, they spotted a car rumbling past. The detective's lights were switched on a moment later.

Darrel began to shake. All he had to do was drive away as soon as Bruce emerged from the back of the house. They were killing a detective. He shuddered as the fantasy became a reality. 'I don't know if we should do this.'

'Too late,' Bruce said as he pulled the thin red mask over his face and grabbed the cord and forensic suit. 'There's no going back now.'

CHAPTER SIXTY-THREE

Gina opened the front door and Jacob followed her in. The air smelled damp and the room was a little chilly. He turned the gas fire and lamp on. She passed him and headed towards the kitchen, knowing she needed Jacob to leave soon. She didn't want Briggs to turn up with dinner while Jacob was still here. 'I'll be okay now. Thanks for the lift.' She closed her eyes and held on to the doorframe.

'You don't look so good. I can stay for a while, make you a cuppa. It's been a long time since we've had a catch up. You can tell me about your holiday and all that's been going on.' Gina carefully stepped towards the kitchen table and sat. 'I'm seeing someone, did I tell you?'

She looked at her watch. Ten minutes and he had to be gone. 'I hope it all works out for you this time.' She booted her laptop up.

'It's early days. I met her on Tinder. She's called Amber and lives local.' She could tell he was trying to stick around.

She ran her fingers through her hair. 'Good for you. I really could do with being alone. I have a lot to crack on with and I know you have to drop by Darrel Sanderson's. It's getting late in the day.'

'We care about you, guv. That's all. Are you sure you're okay?'

She smiled. 'Stop fussing, Driscoll. I'm a big girl. All these symptoms are normal. I just need to be left alone, in quiet, with my trusty cat, then I'll feel better. Go and get on with your tasks. We have a killer to catch.' He paused and smiled back. 'Go,' she repeated.

'Anyone would think you're trying to get rid of me. Call me if you need anything.'

She gave him a smile. 'Will do,' she called as she heard him leave.

It was almost seven in the evening. Very soon Briggs would arrive with some food. Even though there was nothing between them any more, she still didn't want Jacob to hang around. She swallowed. She really wasn't too hungry. 'Ebony,' she called. The cat normally came home to greet her but not today. She walked over to the back door and stared into the dreary brambles and trees that almost covered the back gate. The back door key was fixed firmly in the keyhole. She pulled it out and slotted it back in a couple of times. Fixating on the other night wasn't getting her anywhere. She'd obviously left it hanging out when she'd locked the door. She turned the key and opened the back door. A gust of wind caught her face, blowing her hair everywhere. 'Ebony,' she called. There was no sign of the cat. She closed the door and sat at the kitchen table, booting her laptop up.

She clicked into the information that had been uploaded on Bruce Garrison. The only person they hadn't managed to interview yet. He graduated in accountancy at London Metropolitan University. She flicked to another window and opened the case notes on the rape in London and re-watched the fuzzy CCTV as the attacker followed Lucia Ramos between the shops. Her attacker was broad shouldered back then, and still was. Quite tall and imposing, he walked with a purpose. She paused the footage and zoomed in. There was no use trying to identify any of his features. She zoomed out and continued playing the clip, watching him walking, trying to commit his movement patterns to memory.

As she flicked to another page, Ebony crashed through the cat door. The back door flew open and she felt a sickening blow to her head as she toppled off the chair onto the kitchen floor.

A distorted version of her own reflection stared back at her in the cooker door. The man standing over her was wearing a red mask – that same red mask she recognised from her attack. Her attacker was back to finish the job. Her reflection began to sway. *Don't lose it,* Gina thought, as she tried to drag herself under the kitchen table. Her laptop crashed onto the floor, cracking down the middle. Ebony screeched as her attacker went to grab the cat. She kicked out, catching his shin. No one was hurting her cat! The man yelled. The cat clawed his arm, shredding the forensic suit. Roaring like an angry lion, the man pulled at her feet with one arm and batted Ebony away with the other. As he dragged her along the floor, she tried to grab a chair leg, or anything. He couldn't get her into the open. She clasped both hands around the leg of a chair and it jammed against the table leg. The room ahead swayed even more as she began to see double. A hint of the same sickly aftershave she'd smelled on the night of her attack assaulted her nostrils, nauseating her. Blood trickled down the side of her head and smeared the tiles. Ebony – she forced her stiff neck up and couldn't see the cat.

He struck her hand and she felt her fingers losing their grip on the chair leg. She was in the open. Out of the corner of her eye, she spotted Ebony fleeing. Her cat was okay. Bringing her loose foot back as far as she could, she kicked out, trying to catch him in the groin area, but missed. He forced his leg between hers and pinned her to the floor, fixing her arms above her head.

Her mind flashed back to a night when Terry had her in a similar position. She'd begged him leave her be but he'd ignored her pleas as she cried her way through the ordeal.

She wasn't begging this time. She escaped his clasp, reached out and poked a finger through the mask, piercing the cheek. He retaliated with a punch to her face, her blood smeared all over his gloved hands. 'Get off me,' she yelled as she tried to bring her knee up. He had her pinned with his hefty weight. He was at least fourteen stone's worth of solid muscle. He punched her one more time. She felt her resolve weakening as everything around her went blurry. For a second, she thought he was Terry until she opened her eyes once again. His mask was tickling her face. Every muscle in her body felt like it was made of lead. 'Let me go. I'm a police detective. You know what that means.'

She exhaled when he straddled her and sat up, catching his breath. He reached inside his forensic suit and pulled out a piece of blue cord. Her body trembled beneath him. She brought her hands up and began punching him in the neck. He leaned back, evading all her punches. Laughing under the mask, he used both hands to turn her onto her front, then he threaded the cord underneath her chin. She thought of Hannah and Briggs. In her last moments, that was all she could do. She stared into the cooker door and saw him grabbing both sides of the cord. Shaking all over, she closed her eyes. She wasn't going to plead for anything from this monster.

Just as she was about to black out, he stopped throttling her with the cord. Her head hit the floor, catching her nose. She inhaled sharply and coughed. Her attacker barged out of the back door and ran. She listened as a car engine started up, followed by her back gate slamming. That same car screeched as it pulled away.

Light shone through the front bay window. The hum of another engine was halted. She recognised that sound. It was Briggs's car. Her attacker had seen him pulling up and had fled. Her cat wandered over and began nuzzling her neck. Dragging herself up, she grabbed onto the worktop and stumbled through the lounge towards the front door. Briggs rang the bell. She had to let him in but he couldn't know how bad things had been. He wasn't going to take her off the case. Seeing double or not, she was cleaning herself up and getting on with her work but this needed calling in. 'I'm coming,' she croaked as she held her neck.

Stumbling to the door, with trembling fingers she fumbled with the lock. 'I've just been attacked. You have to find them. Someone else was waiting in a getaway car at the back of my house. They've been gone about two minutes. Go quick or you'll lose them.' They'd already lost her attacker and she knew it. Given the three roads that they could have taken at the end of the through road, she knew getting the cavalry onto them wouldn't happen quickly enough. They could be two to three miles away in any direction now. She slid down the wall, dragging the coats off the hooks as Briggs ran back to his car, pulling his phone out of his pocket. He dialled the station and placed it in the holder on his dashboard.

'I'll be back in a minute. I'm calling it in as I go. Help is on its way,' he shouted as he wheel spun the car off the drive.

As she sat there, in her hallway, fine rain blew into her face and tears meandered down her cheeks. Her attacker had been so close to killing her and she'd had no strength in her, none at all. Despite all the self-defence classes she'd taken over the years, she'd come to realise that when you're spent, you really are spent. She sobbed, knowing that the only way she had survived that ordeal was because Briggs had arrived. Had he not planned to come over, she'd be a rotting corpse, lying on the kitchen floor, waiting for Bernard and his team to come and assess the evidence. Ebony ran over and nuzzled her once again. She picked her up and held her close, stroking her soft fur. Her mind mulled over the attack. Her attacker had struck twice. Same mask, same subtle aftershave. This was personal.

Ebony had clawed him. She grabbed the door handle and pulled her aching body up with one hand, almost stumbling back to the floor. She staggered back to the kitchen and fumbled in the cupboard behind the door until she managed to grab hold of the cat basket. Falling to her knees, she pushed the struggling cat in and tied the strap, trapping the cat. 'Sorry, Ebony.' Ebony's claws could contain his DNA. She had to contain the cat until Bernard arrived.

They couldn't see her like this. She wasn't going to hospital. She ran the cold tap and swilled her face, washing the blood away. It now just looked like a bit of a scratch. The mark on her neck was a light pink colour. Her vision began to fade back into normal mode and she winced as she stretched. An ambulance pulled up and blue lights shone through her window. Briggs pulled in behind them.

'I lost them,' he called as he ran back into her house through the open door. She gazed around her house and it no longer felt like a safe place.

'I can't be here tonight and I don't want to scare my daughter. Can I stay at yours?' A tear slid down her face.

He nodded. 'Of course you can. We need to get a statement first. Can you do that now?' He placed his hand on her shoulder and sat beside her in the living room.

She nodded. 'I'm going to catch that bastard.' She grabbed a congealed coffee cup from the hearth and flung it at the wall. She was not powerless, she was not vulnerable. She was DI Gina Harte and she was going to find out who did this to her. She was going to find out who had killed Melissa and Ellie and she was going to make them pay.

'You're not doing anything tonight.'

'Watch me. Get me a new laptop sorted. We're going to yours and we're going to stay up all night until we come up with something. I need access to all the interviews, the photos and the evidence. You can help me or you can have a good night's sleep and I'll do it all myself.'

'I'm with you on this one.' She could see her own steely determination reflected in his gaze. As a paramedic entered, he nodded, then left the house to meet Jacob, who had just pulled up.

'That looks like a nasty blow.' The young female paramedic shone a pencil torch into her eyes.

'I can see perfectly well,' she said through gritted teeth as she held back her yelps. 'Please, just patch it up.'

'As a precaution, it would be best if—'

'No. I'm not going anywhere.' She grabbed the folded snuggle blanket from the back of the settee and wrapped it around her bust. Beneath it, she began removing her clothes. She knew she'd be asked for them. 'If you want to help me, pass me some more clothes. My wardrobe and drawers are in the first bedroom upstairs. Jeans and a jumper will do.'

The paramedic gave her a blank look. 'I must insist—'

'Look, you can help me by getting me some clothes or you can go, but I'm not going to any hospital. Please, look at me, I'm freezing now.'

The woman shook her head and stood. 'Okay.'

As the paramedic left, she rubbed her scabbing head and took a few uneasy steps. She'd be fine, she knew she'd be fine.

Jacob entered.

'I don't suppose you even got to Darrel Sanderson's house, did you?'

'No, guv. Come here and sit.' He led her back to the settee. She stared out of the window and watched as Briggs prepped Bernard and his forensics team.

'I'm fine. Right, get your notepad out. There are all my clothes, they need bagging up. My cat clawed him, I've trapped her in her basket. Get a vet to clip her claws. Grab your notepad and we'll go through what happened.'

Jacob sympathetically placed a hand on her arm and went to speak.

'Get your pen ready.' It was going to be a long evening. Her body had been through the wars but she wasn't going to make a fuss. No one was going to see the thoughts of her past trauma with Terry in her eyes as she spoke of her attack. She wasn't a victim. She was a witness. Never was she going to play at being victim.

CHAPTER SIXTY-FOUR

Thursday, 19 April 2018

Gina sat at Briggs's kitchen table, gazing at one of the spare department laptops. 'Stupid laptop,' she said as she pressed the same key over and over again. The letter E was sticky and the missing pixels on the screen made her want to throw it against the wall. As she repeatedly swore under her breath, his dog laid its head in her lap, staring with wide eyes that were pleading for fuss and biscuits. 'Morning, Jessie,' she said, patting the dog's head. The dog licked her hand and lay at her feet. Photos of Ellie and Melissa stared back at her from the table. Scooping them up, she placed them back in the folder and poured another coffee.

Briggs had stayed up until about 1 a.m. He'd offered to sleep on the sofa but she'd refused, sleeping on it herself. After waking about four with a stiff neck, she knew she needed to get back to her house and soon. Would she ever feel safe in her own home again? She made a note to call a security company, get a top of the range alarm fitted.

Hannah had been confused when Briggs took her to drop the cat off at hers late the previous evening. Maybe she'd call her later, fill her in on what was happening, give or take a few details. She'd miss out the part about the attack in her kitchen and would skip to thanking her for the clothes she'd given her at the hospital.

Or, maybe, she would tell Hannah that it was an attempted break in. She could do without her daughter making a fuss.

Flicking between screens, she tried to take in anything further that would help. What was she missing? There had to be a link somewhere. Selecting the Bruce Garrison file again, she re-read the information. He had a degree in accountancy and business – first class after going to university in London. He continued his studies in Chartered Accountancy and completed an MBA soon after. Her fingers began to quiver. He was in London at the same time as the attack on Lucia Ramos back in 1998. She waited as the laptop loaded the CCTV footage for that night. Her heartbeat quickened as she processed what she was seeing. After the third watch, she selected the CCTV footage from the Angel Arms and watched Ellie leaving the pub the previous Friday. The bus stop had been to the left. Why had she turned right? Dragging the cursor back, she began to sweat as she watched again. She checked the time before placing her phone to her ear, it was six thirty. 'Taxi, please. Yes, as quickly as you can.' She crept towards the door, coat in hand so as to not wake Briggs. He'd only try to stop her from following the lead and make her send someone else instead, but this was her lead and she was going to be there.

CHAPTER SIXTY-FIVE

The taxi rolled up in the car park, outside the maisonette that Jacob lived in. Gina passed the driver a ten-pound note and walked over to his front door. As he opened it, a tall brunette kissed him and left, rubbing her eyes as she headed down the path and got into a hatchback. 'You know how to ruin the best moments ever.'

'Amber, your Tinder date?'

He nodded. 'I got lucky and you know something, I think I really like her. How are you after last night?'

The woman pulled out of the parking space and blew him a kiss as she drove away.

'Better after a good night's sleep.' Gina knew she didn't look good. Jacob had been there the previous night. He knew the full extent of the attack. She'd just held back on how shaken and sore she was. After Jacob had taken her statement, Bernard had arrived and taken all the samples he'd needed from the scene, then he'd taken some photos of her injuries. She rubbed the friction burn on her neck.

'You could've fooled me. You haven't slept at all, have you? Did you stay at your daughter's?' She wasn't about to start discussing her evening at Briggs's with Jacob, even though there was no longer anything to hide.

'I need you to get your car keys and drive me to Bruce Garrison's. I'd drive myself but I'm not meant to and I want you with me. I have a bad feeling sitting in the pit of my stomach about him. This group of friends, their strange wives. Something's so off it's almost stagnant and I'm not waiting a minute longer to find out what.'

Rubbing his eyes, he left his front door ajar. She followed him in. 'What do we know?' He buttoned his shirt up as he scoffed a piece of toast.

'I was researching his educational background and he was in London at the time of the rape in 1998. I was watching the CCTV footage of the Angel Arms, last week, when Ellie was there. She was following a man out of the pub. I have a feeling she recognised him. I'm working on the theory that after going back there to confront her past, she may have come across her attacker or maybe she'd been following him. She'd need to make sure. Twenty-five years is a long time. I think she followed him home. His gait, the way he walks – I think he's Lucia Ramos's rapist, and that would make him my attacker. I need to see him for myself, to be sure. Samuel Avery identified that man in the pub as Bruce Garrison. We have to get to his now.' She snatched the cup from his hands and slammed it on the worktop. 'You can sit around drinking coffee later but right now, we need to be at his house before he goes to work. Come on.'

CHAPTER SIXTY-SIX

'Morning, sweetie,' the woman said as she opened the curtains to reveal blue skies.

Natalie tried to roll over but the binds halted her attempt. She'd had a strange night. Dreams of her wedding to Bruce had weaved their way through the nightmares. One of the dreams came back to her, as if struck by lightning. They were at their wedding but Bruce was marrying the woman who was keeping her trapped. Natalie was a singer at the wedding. She'd been watching them as the woman who was keeping her captive took her vows over the ethereal sounds of 'Ave Maria'. In her dream she'd been singing like an angel, then as the crescendo neared, her voice cracked. Everyone at the ceremony turned round and stared at her. The room was closing in, she couldn't breathe and she was toppling over. She pushed those thoughts to the back of her mind. It was just a dream – deep breaths.

She flinched as the cord drove into her wounded wrists. Thirsty, she needed water. The woman moved the gag aside and held a glass of water to her mouth. She swallowed as the woman gently poured. 'Where's Bruce? I need to speak to my husband.'

'He's busy right now, fixing everything.' The woman stroked her brow.

'I need to get out of this bed. Please tell him to come and untie me.'

'Look, you can help your husband by staying calm.'

She knew she wasn't going to win. The woman wasn't there to help her, she was there to help Bruce. 'Who are you?'

'You can call me Selina. I'm Rob's wife. You know Rob? Bruce's friend? He's asked me to help look after you. You haven't been yourself but you will be soon, I promise.'

She wrenched the binds. 'I just want to get out of this bed. Bruce!' she called. 'Bruce!' She could hear him pacing along the downstairs hallway. She knew he could hear her calls but he was choosing to ignore her. He wouldn't hurt her, he couldn't.

He thundered up the stairs, crashed through the door and pushed Selina out onto the landing, closing the door behind her. 'You ruined everything. Because of you, Ellie had to go. You did that, remember? You killed Ellie.'

Natalie's eyes filled with tears. She'd freed the woman and was letting her go. 'You're not pinning that one on me. I was trying to help her. You killed her. You took her to that park, you strangled her and you set fire to her body.'

'And this is why you're not going to see tomorrow. You just can't keep your mouth shut. If you hadn't let her go, we wouldn't be here now, and, you know what, she'd still be alive.'

'You raped her.'

'I didn't. She was lying. Back then, nothing like that happened. She was blackmailing me. She knew about Melissa. She was going to send us down.' Natalie could tell he was trying to cover a lie.

'Us?' Natalie waited for him to explain further. She knew Rob or Darrel weren't with her husband on the night of Melissa's murder as they were in the pub. Had it been another one of Bruce's friends?

'You ask too many questions. You've seen too much and, frankly, you've let me down. For your information, I did not rape that woman. She'd come on to me all evening back then. Right, confession time. That night, twenty-five years ago, when you were in London and I'd come back here to see my family and mates, I got drunk in the Angel Arms. Okay, I was weak and she was available. I gave her exactly what she wanted in the back of our car. I cheated on you, yes, but I didn't rape her. Since coming back to Cleevesford, she must have been following me. The woman was obsessed back then and she was still obsessed.'

'I don't believe you.' Tears fell down Natalie's face, wetting her hair and the pillow. 'You raped her and you killed her, and now you're going to kill me.'

Selina opened the door and crept back in. She stepped forward and held Natalie's hand. She spoke to her as if speaking to a young child who had just fallen over. 'It doesn't have to be this way. You can choose how this ends. You can tell the police your husband was playing cards at our house on the night of Ellie's murder. That's all you have to do. You should believe that he is telling you the truth. I know the truth, sweetie. That woman was trying to ruin what you and Bruce have. She was jealous. You're choosing to believe some deranged madwoman over the man you love.'

'Don't waste your time.' Bruce walked onto the landing and Natalie began to scream. 'Shut her up. There's someone coming. The damn coppers have been leaving me messages left, right and centre. It's them.'

'I can't,' Selina said as she stepped back.

He ran back into the room and tightened the binds, fixing Natalie in place. Selina grabbed an apron out of her bag and fed it over her neck, tying it up at her back. Natalie almost gagged as Bruce rammed a cloth in her mouth and re-tied the gag. 'Make a noise and I'll come straight up here, place that pillow over your face and I'll press until you turn blue. You know I mean it, don't you? Selina, just do what you were told to do.'

Tears filled Natalie's eyes and she nodded.

'Ready.' Selina kissed Natalie's head. They left, closing the door behind them. She could rock on the bed, build up some momentum. Bang the headboard against the wall. The gag wasn't too tight. She rubbed her head against the pillow, trying to loosen it, then she stopped. What if the person coming was a part of all this and Bruce was testing her? They'd kill her, but if it really was the police…

CHAPTER SIXTY-SEVEN

Jacob pulled the handbrake on. The trees that surrounded the bottom of the garden created an oppressive border, blocking the light from the sun that was just peering over a hill in the distance. Gina ran her fingers through her hair, trying to comb out the knots. If he was her attacker, she'd like to think there would be something about him she would recognise.

The large house stood proud at the end of the drive and the detached garage to the right-hand side looked like a mini version of the main house. She gazed along the top floor. The whole house looked like it needed some attention. The gutters were beginning to fill with moss and debris. Weeds grew between the block paving and the tangled grass needed a good cut. Daffodils randomly dotted the garden, offering hope to the unloved stretch of land.

'You've tried him at work, left messages on his phone and dropped notes through the door?'

'That's correct, guv. Had no responses at all. Robert Dixon's wife didn't contact us either after her shopping trip. These people seem to think we'll just go away.'

'That's one thing we never do.' Gina stepped out of the car. Her bruised thighs ached as she stretched, reminding her of the attacker pushing his knee through the gap in her legs as she resisted. She stared at the house and a shudder travelled through her body.

'Need a hand, guv?'

'No. I'm good.' She wasn't good though and Jacob could see it. She winced as her stiff joints fired into action. Blood began to pump around her body and adrenalin forced the discomfort to one side. She stepped up to the door and rang the bell.

They listened. Not a sound came from inside the house. She lifted the letterbox. 'Bruce Garrison. It's the police. DI Harte and DS Driscoll. Open up.' Banging on the door, she waited for a response.

Heels clipped a stone floor and echoed through the hallway. The old hardwood door unlocked and, from what Wyre had described, one of the Stepford Wives answered. Gina recognised the woman from the case notes. Petite features, perfectly pinned up hair. The cleanest lemon-coloured apron she'd ever seen in her life covering up a petite pair of boot-cut jeans and a crisp white jumper.

'How may I help you?' the woman asked as she held a duster in one hand and beamed the most false of smiles. 'Selina Dixon.'

Gina took a step forward into the hallway. 'Have we met?'

'You spoke with my colleague, DC Wyre. You were also meant to contact the station yesterday when you returned from your shopping trip. We spoke to your husband.'

'I am so sorry. I got back so late after seeing a friend and, well, I had to be here this morning, as you can see. You don't look so good, Detective.' The woman's smile was replaced with a show of false concern.

Gina ignored the statement. Her health was none of Mrs Dixon's business. 'What are you doing here?'

She held the duster up. 'Cleaning. I'm just helping the Garrisons out. They need help with their property. They've just moved in and my husband and Bruce are old friends.'

'Is this your line of business?' Gina pointed to the duster.

'I have no line of business. I'm just helping friends out.'

Gina walked along the hallway and poked her head through the kitchen door. 'How long have you and the Garrisons been friends?'

'May I ask why you're asking me all these questions?'

'Where are Mr and Mrs Garrison?' Jacob asked.

Gina stepped into the kitchen and walked over to the kitchen drawers and placed her hand on the one next to the sink unit.

'Do you have a warrant?' Bruce said. Without warning, he'd crept up on them. She dropped her hand and turned. He was about the right height to have committed her attack. His voice meant nothing as her attacker hadn't said a word.

'We need a witness interview from yourself. We were hoping that you'd come to the station and help us with our enquiries. We would need to know where you were on the night of Thursday the twelfth of April?'

Selina began wiping the surfaces with a cloth. Gina could tell there was no effort involved and the woman was trying hard to overhear anything she could.

'What business is it of yours?' Bruce Garrison asked.

'Well, let me see. A murder was committed that night and your name has come up as a potential witness.' Gina stared into his eyes hoping for some recognition. There was none. The man had been wearing a mask that covered his whole face. He'd worn coveralls, which removed his body shape. She knew her attacker was strong and that he was approximately six foot tall. Bruce Garrison fitted that part of the description.

'I gather you're not charging me with anything, otherwise you'd be taking me to the station.'

'Should I be charging you?' Gina remained still. He broke her stare and looked out of the kitchen window.

'I was with friends. You can check.'

'Which friends? I'd appreciate their names, please.' She already knew what his answer would be.

'Lee Munro and Ben Woodward. We were playing cards. You can check.'

Selina wiped the cooker over.

'Oh, we will, thank you. Where's Mrs Garrison?' Jacob asked as he made a couple of notes in his pad.

'She's not in.'

'We didn't ask if she was in. We asked where she is.' Gina stared at him, trying to weigh him up as she awaited his answer.

'At a friend's. She stayed with friends last night. Look, am I under arrest? I haven't done anything wrong. My mate's wife is here, helping me sort my new house out. My wife stayed with her friend last night. All of this has zilch to do with you.'

Gina walked around the kitchen and her hand rested, once again, on the kitchen drawer handle. She spotted a dent in the cupboard. Was it like that when they moved in or had it been caused in a fit of rage?

'Do you have a search warrant? I'd rather you leave my home, Detective. I have work to do and you are disrupting my day. I'm not saying any more except I was with friends on Thursday the twelfth. Either arrest me, produce a search warrant, or leave before I report you for harassment.'

Gina smiled. 'Thank you so much for your cooperation, it will be noted. Mrs Dixon, we look forward to you coming into the station to speak with us today. After all, the man your husband regularly sees has just lost his wife after she was brutally murdered. I'm sure you want to help as much as you can.'

The woman placed the cloth on the table and wiped her hands on her apron, scrunching up the material and revealing her jeans. 'I'll be there later this morning, Detective. Of course I want this matter to be dealt with. It's such a sad and shocking thing that happened.'

Gina's gaze followed the woman's hands with every wipe. Her heart began to pound. The woman in front of her was too much of a perfectionist not to notice what Gina had just noticed? Had Selina Dixon failed to notice the imperfection in her perfect world?

'It is. The woman was strangled in her own home and another woman has since been murdered. Cleevesford has certainly turned into a dangerous place these past few days.'

The woman nodded, grabbed her duster and left the room a little too quickly for Gina's liking. 'We'll be back, Mr Garrison.'

Gina's shoulder caught his solid arm as they nudged their way through the kitchen door. She flinched, wanting so badly to swear as pain jolted through her shoulder, all the way to her wrist. Her colleagues were right. She was in a state. As he followed them out towards the main door, she caught a smell coming from Bruce. His aftershave took her straight back to the night on Darrel Sanderson's lawn, where she was attacked. An image of her scrambling under the kitchen table as she avoided being throttled flashed through her mind. Her heart thudded against her chest and the knot in her stomach threatened to eject itself. Her hands jittered as she remembered grabbing him outside Darrel's house. That same smell had been all over her attacker. He opened the front door and an early morning breeze carried the scent away.

'Have a good day,' Bruce called as he slammed the door.

'Did you see what I saw?' Gina glanced back at the house. She held on to the car and closed her eyes. Blood pumped through her body, the drumming sound filling her ears. The smell of aftershave or deodorant that she'd inhaled in the hallway wouldn't leave her mind. Her knees buckled.

'Guv.' Jacob ran around the car and grabbed her arm.

She shook him off and stumbled towards the garage, peering through the little window. As she wiped the dust away, her phone rang. 'Answer that. It's O'Connor.' Jacob took the phone from her trembling hand. Gina wiped the window with her bandaged wrist, then pressed her face as close as she could to peer through.

'There is a black Audi saloon car registered to a Craig Garrison, Mr and Mrs Garrison's twenty-year-old son. It's registered to an address in North London. O'Connor's just confirmed it.'

'I'm looking at it now. I can also see a dent on the driver's side, just like our lorry driver described.' She turned and leaned against the garage door. 'I also recognised his cologne, the same smell as the man who attacked me twice. It's him. It has to be. He wasn't working alone. We know there are others. They're giving false alibis to protect each other. Melissa Sanderson, the night of her attack, they all thought they'd been so careful. Forensic suits, boot covers, no prints, just a measly bit of material that had caught on a rough shard of the wooden chair, tearing the twine of the suit and leaving behind a small shred of denim. Mrs Dixon hasn't noticed that her jeans have been snagged. The shade of denim we have in evidence matches that of her jeans – I should know, I spent ages staring at it last night. It was them.' They both turned and looked up at the house. 'Call for back up now and let's get every one of the friends brought in.'

CHAPTER SIXTY-EIGHT

The visitors were gone. She'd heard nothing but the muffled sound of voices from the bedroom. Natalie frantically rubbed the back of the gag on the pillow, eventually loosening it. The cord binding her slipped off. She spat the cloth out of her mouth and inhaled sharply. Sweat poured down her face as she continued tugging at the cord. She had to escape before they came back upstairs and drugged her again. She gazed around the room. There was a mirror in the one corner and the chair that Selina had been sitting in. She was about to shatter and break the world around her. She'd avoided any form of confrontation all her life but now, she was ready for it. Her life depended on her giving her escape attempt everything she had. As she tugged at her wrists, shaving off another layer of skin, she felt her blood begin to seep. The bind on her left wrist loosened and she yelped as her raw wrist slipped through the tiny gap, taking even more skin with it. She snatched her burning wrist to her chest, shaking blood all over the blanket.

Struggling one handed, she managed to loosen the other bind on her other wrist, until it fell to the floor. Lying on her back for so long had stiffened her bones. With both hands free, her bones crunched as she forced her rigid body forward and fumbled with the binds on her ankles. She was free. She flipped her legs onto the floor and they almost gave way. With each step, her muscles strengthened. As she neared the door, the voices got louder.

The woman spoke as they reached the top landing. 'Why are they still there? They can't find her in that room, gagged and tied to the bed. We can finish her off and dispose of the body as soon as they've left. It would be quick. It was part of the plan anyway. Just go in there, hold a pillow over her head and it will all be over. Between us, we can hide her for now. The story will be she went to a friend's for the night and never came home.'

'I've planned for this should it go totally wrong. I've always had a back-up plan in place, throughout my life. I have money and false ID. They'll never get to you, Rob or Darrel. I have enough money stashed away to last me a very long time. Rob is my oldest mate and you're a good woman.'

What the hell was her husband playing at? Not content with making her feel as though she'd lost her sanity, ruining her dreams, making her so scared that she'd been a prisoner in her own home – he was going to kill her. She closed her eyes as they both talked through their plans. She visualised her attack on them. Whatever she did, she would go at them with full force. She wanted to survive.

'Why aren't the cops going?' Selina asked.

The police were still there. They were around the front of the house, she was positioned at the back of the house. Now was her chance as they'd soon be gone. Sweat dripped down Natalie's forehead as she visualised running down the stairs – she wouldn't trip. Then she'd fling open the front door and run to the detectives for protection. As she imagined running out onto the drive, her chest began to prickle and sweat dampened her hair. Her heart rate sped up and she gasped for breath. No, this wasn't the time to get into a panic. She inhaled through her nose and exhaled through her mouth. It was time to take control of her life. Whether she won or lost the next stage of the battle, it didn't matter, because if she simply lay there, she was certainly going to die.

She grabbed the mirror and smashed it on the window ledge. The voices on the far end of the landing went silent. She now had something to stab with should they come close. She shoved a shard of mirror in her back pocket, grabbed the chair and crept towards the door.

'What was that?' Selina asked.

As Bruce barged through the door, she crashed the chair in the direction of his head as hard as she could. Pieces of wood shattered, flying in all directions. He went to stand up straight and she grabbed the back of the chair, which still remained intact, and struck him across the side of the head. The man she loved, had trusted, had married and had a son with, was nothing but a manipulator. He was one big lie. The man who'd caused all her illness and misery was now clutching his head. But he was still standing and as he looked at her she could see the rage in his eyes.

'Do something,' Selina said as she tried to push them both into the back bedroom. Natalie snatched the shard of glass from her back pocket and held it up to her two aggressors. Her husband didn't lose his strength for long, ever. He was fit and had the strength of an ox, but there was no way she was allowing him to finish her off and flee with his hidden stash, to start a new life. She plunged forward, stabbing the man in the side. Blood seeped from the wound, spilling all over the light grey carpet, spreading further outwards as he lost more blood. For a moment she saw the old Bruce, the man she'd met as a young woman when she'd been singing in a pub. She'd been so needy and gullible. He hadn't even been romantic or caring. She'd mistaken his sense of duty and his insistence to be the breadwinner as an act of love. Now she saw everything clearly. They'd been acts of control, chipping away at her confidence until she no longer felt like she had any value to the outside world. He'd played with her mind, twisting and distorting her perception of the world around her, until she believed his lies. She pulled the glass from his side and gripped it as she watched him struggle to his feet.

The woman kneeled beside him, getting flecks of crimson all over her lemon apron and crisp white jumper. 'You're not a killer,' she calmly said as she stood. 'Just think of the story we can tell the police now. Wife, already medicated and neurotic, stabs husband and attacks his friend. With you out of the picture, we can say exactly what we like.'

Selina grabbed a chair leg and held it up, roaring like a rabid animal as she brought it down on Natalie's head. Bruce stirred and grabbed his wife's ankle, bringing her crashing to the floor.

CHAPTER SIXTY-NINE

'Did you hear that? We have to go in,' Gina said as she ran to the front door. The hardwood door was fixed solidly. They ran around the back of the house and tried the back door, it was locked. She gazed through the glass, making sure there was no one in the way. Grabbing the spade that was leaning up against the wall, she smashed it through the door, shattering glass all over the back hallway. She heard shouting coming from upstairs.

'Get away from me. Let me go,' a woman shouted.

'Mrs Garrison,' Gina called as she nodded for Jacob to lead. Given her level of frailty, leading could be disastrous. She wanted them arrested and brought in, with no further injury to herself. She heard sirens in the background. Back up was on its way.

'Police,' Jacob called. As they crept up the stairs, all went quiet. Jacob flung open the bedroom doors, one by one, until he reached the final door. He pressed the handle and pushed but the door wouldn't budge. It had been wedged closed. Sweat began to trickle down the sides of his face.

Gina placed a hand on his arm and rested her ear against the door. She could hear a woman crying. 'Mrs Garrison, Natalie. Is that you?'

'No.' The woman's sobs filled the hallway. She recognised the voice of Selina Dixon. 'Bruce is dead. He's blocking the door and I think his wife is dead too. Get me out of here. Help me!'

'We're coming in.' Jacob leaned on the door, pushing the obstruction away. Blood sprayed the carpet as Bruce's body slumped forward. Selina Dixon was holding a shard of mirror and Mrs Garrison was lying still on the floor, with a stab wound to her stomach.

'He was going to kill his wife. He stabbed her, went for me and I—' Selina broke down. 'I could've been killed.'

'Mrs Dixon, Selina, throw the glass to the other side of the room. Let us help you.' The woman obliged and the glass landed safely, far enough away from her.

'It was self-defence—'

'Jacob, arrest Mrs Dixon while I check the other two.'

'What? They were trying to kill me!'

Jacob swiftly positioned himself between Mrs Dixon and the blade of glass. 'Selina Dixon, I'm arresting you on suspicion of murder. You do not have to say anything—'

As Jacob's words continued, Gina checked the pulses of the Garrisons. They were both still alive. The emergency services had pulled up and entered around the back of the house.

She stepped out of the room and Wyre ran up the stairs. 'We need the paramedics up here now. Bag Selina Dixon's jeans and give them directly to Bernard or Keith when they arrive.'

'On it, guv,' Wyre said as O'Connor caught up with her.

Two paramedics pushed Wyre and O'Connor out of the way as they entered and began treating the Garrisons.

Mrs Dixon's angry screams filled the house, and Gina could still hear her from the kitchen. 'I'm the victim here. Why are you arresting me? I want my husband. Call my solicitor now.'

Gina knew Bruce's DNA would match that of the London rapist and, in turn, evidence would show him to be her attacker. She was certain Ellie had come back to confront Bruce about an attack he made against her years ago, but that would be harder to prove now Ellie had been murdered. A search of the Garrison house and car would reveal traces of Ellie being present. And Gina was also certain that the denim sample they had in evidence would match that of Selina Dixon's jeans. A warrant would be applied for immediately to search Mrs Dixon's house. In the meantime, Bernard would be arriving with his crime scene investigation team. A flash of images went through her mind. The CCTV of the London rape, the CCTV outside the Angel Arms and her masked attacker on both occasions. Her legs weakened and her aches were getting worse. She was finally allowing herself to feel the pain she was in.

She wandered down the stairs, grabbed a tissue from her pocket to cover her free hand with and began rooting around in the kitchen. She wasn't even capable of putting her own gloves on. Bruce hadn't wanted her to be in the kitchen. She opened the cupboards and saw the cans of food lined up. They were just as Terry used to like cans lined up – labels facing forward, all beans in a row and tinned carrots in another row. It was clear to her that Terry didn't care about the beans or the carrots, or that they were in pretty little rows. She leaned forward and touched a tin of beans as she thought of Natalie and what she'd been through.

As she slid open the drawer by the sink, she spotted what they'd been looking for, blue cord on a spool, the same blue cord that had bound Melissa Sanderson and had been found at the scene of Ellie's burnt body. She leaned on the worktop and rubbed her aching shoulder before running her fingers over her reddened neck. It was also the same cord he'd tried to throttle her with. A few minutes longer, Gina knew she would have ended up just like Melissa Sanderson.

'Good result, guv,' Smith called through the door, holding a roll of police tape.

'It will be if we can finally get to the truth about everyone's involvement.' Who drove the getaway car from her attack? Was it Lee, Rob, Dan, Ben, Darrel or Selina? She was going to bring them all down for conspiracy at the very least. For now, she was going to interrogate the hell out of them until one of them broke.

CHAPTER SEVENTY

Selina Dixon had been in the interview room for the best part of an hour with her solicitor. Her husband, Robert, was being questioned under caution in the next room, and Bruce Garrison was conscious and being questioned in hospital.

So far Selina had been tight-lipped, repeating that she'd been acting in self-defence. Every resource had been focused on the case and every piece of evidence was being fast tracked. Bruce Garrison's DNA had been a match to that of the person who raped Lucia Ramos. He was, without any doubt, her attacker. The tyres on the Audi that belonged to Craig Garrison had been checked and they were illegal. The car had been impounded for further investigations. The tracks had matched those left at the scene of Ellie's murder. Traces of blood had been found on the dented car panel. Gina was certain they would match Ellie's samples.

Briggs walked down the corridor as Gina headed towards the incident room. 'You left without a word this morning. I could've helped you.'

'You'd have tried to stop me and sent someone else. I needed to be there.'

'You may be right on that note. You've been attacked twice in less than a week. You've gone through hell. I wouldn't be doing my job now, if didn't send you home.'

'Please. Just give me a while longer and I promise when we've done the interviews, I'll go home, I'll rest, I'll take a few days off, anything. But I need to be here. It's all coming together now.

We have them all on something. The only person I don't have is the getaway driver from my attack. You made me SIO and I want to be here to finish the job.'

'Okay. Just get it done and do it quick so we can all get some rest. Have you got someone to look after you at home?'

She smiled. 'Sir, look at me. I've been through the wars but you know what, I really am made of tough stuff. I don't need looking after. I'm going to collect my cat and then I'm going home.'

'You are stubborn, Gina. Oh, while I remember, you should call your daughter. She's been ringing the station. She tried you at home. I think she's worried about you.'

'I'll call her in a few minutes, tell her I'll collect the cat in a bit but for now, Jacob and I are off to the hospital. I need to speak to Natalie Garrison. I got a call saying she'd come round and wanted to speak to us before she goes into surgery.'

CHAPTER SEVENTY-ONE

Gina entered the trauma ward and spotted Natalie Garrison in a side room on her own. Smith was sitting outside, doing a crossword in a puzzle book. 'Is she awake?'

'She was a moment ago. A nurse went in and gave her a jug of water.'

The woman lay back on the crisp white pillow. As Gina and Jacob entered, she pressed a button to adjust the bed, letting go once she'd reached an upright position. The last time she had seen Mrs Garrison she had been covered in blood from her abdominal wound. 'Mrs Garrison. I'm DI Harte and this is DS Driscoll. Are you okay to talk?'

The woman nodded. Her wrists were bandaged and her bruises and cuts had been treated. 'I'm going into surgery soon but I needed to speak to someone. It was all my husband.' Her bottom lip quivered and she burst into tears.

'Go on.' Gina pulled the plastic chair close to the woman's bed and sat. Jacob stayed at the end of the bed and opened his notebook.

'The missing woman, Ellie, was in our garden. It was on the Saturday. She was watching us. My husband went out there and dragged her into our home. She was accusing him of raping her, twenty-five years ago. It was when I was carrying our daughter. I miscarried her before having Craig. I believe her – I believe my husband did those things.' The woman looked to the side and wiped her eyes. 'He kept her in the same room as he kept me. I tried to call you. He'd left your number and address on the kitchen table. DI Gina Harte was the name on the scrap of paper. That's you, isn't it?'

Gina's heart rate quickened. They'd researched her address. She remembered the files. Dan Timmons worked at the council. She made a note to obtain Dan's computer records at work and flashed it in Jacob's direction. She watched as he sent a message on his phone. The sooner they got his computer, the sooner they could cement the fact that he was very much involved in providing the information that led to her attack.

'I'm so sorry. I had to hang up on you when I called. He was on his way back and I don't know what he would've done to me.' Gina thought back to the night of the call. Her key *had* been hanging out of the lock. Somehow he'd got into her home. Had Bruce been intent on killing her that night? Was he in her house? Had his plans been scuppered by the phone call that his wife made in the middle of the night? If she'd been the victim that night, Ellie would probably have had enough time to escape. She shivered and stepped towards the other side of the room. The reality of everything was hitting hard. She wanted to cry, to scream, to yell, to hit something, anything – but she had a witness to question. She took a deep breath.

'I let her go but he came back as she was running away down the drive. He drove into her with our Craig's car. From nowhere he pulled out a length of cord then he strangled her to death. The poor woman. I was so scared, in shock. I haven't left the house properly in years. He was making me crazy, pretending that I'd lost things when he'd hidden them on purpose. I was so scared I'd lost my mind. I'm no longer petrified of what lies beyond though. Does that sound strange?'

Gina shook her head.

A fresh stream of tears meandered down the woman's cheeks. Her bottom lip quivered as she continued to speak. 'He made me go in the car with him and he forced me to take my sleeping pills. He left me in the car while he pulled the woman from the boot. I made myself sick but I think it was a bit late as the tablets had started working. As I staggered over the grassy bank at the park, the last thing I remember is that poor woman being set alight.'

Gina glanced at Jacob. 'What happened next?'

Natalie sobbed as she spoke. 'All I remember is being tied to the bed and then someone called Selina was watching me. I'd never met her before. She kept saying things like I wasn't a good wife – that my wedding vows meant nothing. That I could've been revered rather than reviled by them all. That I could have been one of them if only I'd been loyal to my husband. They were going to kill me after they killed you.'

'Me.' Gina swallowed.

'They blamed you for everything. I heard Bruce talking about Melissa's murder. He said Darrel had his child taken from him for no reason and it was under your instruction.'

No reason? Gina clenched her sprained wrist and almost cried out. There had been a huge reason. It appeared that Darrel had failed to mention the bruising all over his little girl's body. He'd probably failed to mention the state of his wife's body too. Darrel's child had been taken from him because the bruising and scars pointed to abuse.

'Ellie just got in the way but Bruce was fixated on you. I overheard him talking to Darrel on the phone, telling him that he owed him one. I had no idea how he was repaying what he owed but that was only yesterday.'

She thought back to Bruce earlier that day, lying on the bedroom carpet, bleeding. In her mind, she was back there checking his pulse. Instead of tending to him, preserving life, she was squeezing her fingers into his open flesh as his warm blood pumped out over her hands. She'd reach in deep and tug his intestines out of the gap before punching what was left, over and over again. She snapped back as she watched Jacob scribbling away.

Yesterday, Gina had been attacked and a driver had been waiting to take Bruce far away from the scene. 'What time was Bruce on the phone to Darrel?'

'I don't know, morning maybe. I was tied up. He kept forcing me to take my sleeping pills. I lost all sense of time. All I know is that it was yesterday and I think it was in the morning.' The woman wiped the tears from her damp face.

Natalie began to yawn and a nurse entered. 'I'm sorry but I think the patient needs to rest. Maybe you can come back after surgery.'

Gina nodded and left a card on the bedside table. 'When you're feeling better, we'll be bringing you in to make a formal statement. Here's my number should you remember anything else. Call me anytime.'

The woman smiled and looked at the card. For once in her life, Natalie might just have a good sleep in the knowledge that she was free.

When Terry had died, Gina finally started to live. She had no doubts that Natalie would remember what her dreams once were and she'd start living for herself. There would be many more questions and a huge court case, but people moved on and she hoped more than anything that Natalie would be able to.

As they left the ward and walked down the white corridor, Gina almost wanted to punch the air. The email she and Jacob were both reading on her phone had confirmed that the denim sample matched Selina's jeans but the woman was remaining silent when questioned. Bruce's condition had deteriorated and he was now unconscious but she knew that even in his absence from the world, his DNA matched that of the London rapist and that of her attacker. A search of Robert Dixon's house turned up a paperweight that matched the dimensions recorded during

Melissa Sanderson's autopsy. It could have been used by either Bruce or Selina to deliver the first blow to her head, the one that rendered her unable to fight back. The paperweight had been bagged as evidence. They'd also found a stash of red material in Mrs Dixon's sewing room and her handbag had contained a half-made mask at the Garrison's house. Her mind flashed back to the red mask that her attacker had worn. Mrs Dixon had been making their masks.

On first glance, the personal computers of Robert Dixon, Lee Munro, Ben Woodward, Daniel Timmons and Bruce Garrison were all being used to chat in private misogyny chat rooms. They mostly advised and discussed ways of keeping women under control and of actively fighting against the feminist movement. They'd already found such matter on Darrel Sanderson's computer. All this hatred towards women and Selina Dixon thought they'd revered her. She had been their finest accomplishment.

She scanned further down. Robert Dixon had ordered a batch of forensic suits and protective gloves on his tablet. The story was fast unravelling.

'Wow! That email was some reading. Let's hurry back,' Jacob said as he shoved his phone in his pocket.

CHAPTER SEVENTY-TWO

Gina described to Selina how each of the friends had been charged and arrested. The woman described as a Stepford Wife was now sitting in a police interview room repeatedly saying, 'No comment.' She'd been issued with a pair of oversized tracksuit bottoms and an old-but-clean T-shirt. Her hair was tied back with an elastic band and Gina could see the tension in her face. Underneath her smooth skin, she was clenching her teeth, trying really hard to maintain control of the situation and herself.

'Why did you do it, Mrs Dixon? There's no point remaining silent. We have forensic evidence that places you, beyond any doubt, at the scene of Melissa Sanderson's murder.' Gina leaned forward and looked her in the eye. Jacob remained by her side.

'Can I see my husband?' The woman tried to neaten her hair.

'No. There's no point lying any more. Why did you do it?' Gina slammed her good fist on the desk, making Mrs Dixon flinch. Selina paused and began picking out bits of dried blood that were stuck under her beautifully manicured nails. 'The way I see it, the truth is all you have left, Selina.'

'You wouldn't know truth if it hit you in the face. Look at you, thinking you know everything about life. It's the children who suffer when the woman devotes all her time to work or other selfish pursuits. Did your children suffer, Detective? Do they hate you? Or maybe you didn't have children, choosing not to fulfil your role to society. I don't think it's the latter as you have a photo of what appears to be your beautiful daughter on your bedside table. I can tell she's your daughter, she has your features.'

Gina felt her fist clench up as she stood and leaned over the desk and muttered. 'The key, leaning out of the lock. I would never have left it like that. Breaking and entering too!' Jacob gave her a glance as her neck and face reddened. She wanted to lean over further, grab Mrs Dixon by the hair and give her a slap. The deranged woman before her had been in her home while she was sleeping. Selina could see the rage in her face as she shifted her chair back. Taking a deep breath, Gina sat back down. 'Answer the question, Mrs Dixon. Why did you do it? There's nowhere to go, Selina. We have you at the scene.'

The woman's hands began to shake erratically. 'Melissa treated her husband with such contempt, having an affair, drinking all the time, swanning off in the day. I'd never do that and do you know why? I have self-respect and my husband respects me too.' The woman's voice quivered as she spoke. She wiped a tear away and stared straight ahead.

'Maybe you were jealous. She was trying to free herself while you were stuck in your servile marriage to Robert Dixon. Good little Selina does what she's told, even if that involves murder.'

Selina accidentally picked one of her nails. 'Look what you've made me do. It won't work, you know. You won't make me confess to a murder I haven't committed. I have nothing to tell. I've only ever done the right thing. I'm a homemaker, a good one. I love my husband and you know what – society is wrong. Society encourages unmarried women to get pregnant because they're so bloody promiscuous and places no value on the institution of marriage. Society leaves kids growing up in shit farms they call nurseries rather than at home with their mothers. You should be more worried about the decline of moral values than the loss of some stupid cheating alcoholic mother.'

'That mother you refer to was beaten over the head until she was almost unconscious. Dragged along a hallway, tied to a chair, then strangled while her little girl cried for her. We have you at the scene. Did you pull the cord that killed Melissa Sanderson?' The woman bit into one of her lovely nails and spat it on the floor. 'Did you strangle Mrs Sanderson? Was she one of those immoral women that you loathe so much?'

She removed her trembling hands from view and placed them in her lap. 'She deserved it. She wasn't a good wife, like me.' The woman began to crack.

'Like you?'

The woman began to rock on her seat. 'I'm a good wife. I take care of my husband and I stayed at home with my two when they were little. They are good people now, with good jobs and good marriages. We were young when we married and Rob worked hard. He achieved everything through his hard work. I've supported him and done everything right.'

'Are you sure you did everything right?' The woman didn't look up. 'Was Mrs Sanderson doing it wrong?'

'She was so wrong. So, so wrong. She never would've changed.'

'So you killed her?'

'Yes and I should've killed you too,' Selina shouted. Gina could see in Selina's eyes that she had run out of answers. The woman hesitated, then exhaled as she slumped and burst into tears. 'He said it was for the best. Rob always knew best. We had to do it, Bruce and me. I couldn't have handled her alone.'

'What did Bruce do?'

'Bruce hit her. She was going to leave Darrel, and Rob promised me that no one would get into trouble. He said it was about doing the right thing. I've betrayed him.' She broke down.

'How have you betrayed him?'

'You know.' She paused. 'I didn't feel my jeans rip. I didn't even see the tear.' She sobbed and lay on the table, banging on it, over and over again, with open palms.

'Why did you strangle Mrs Sanderson?' The room was silent except for Selina's sobs. Just say it, Gina thought. 'Why?'

'I did it for Rob. I wasn't meant to be a suspect. I'm a good wife, a good person. I'm a good woman, not like you,' she yelled.

Gina felt her face redden. 'Like me? Is that why Bruce Garrison tried to kill me in my home and Darrel Sanderson waited in the car, ready to drive him away from the scene? Was it because I was a bad woman?'

Jacob ran his fingers through his hair and gave her a look.

'You're so bad you can't even see it! You took Darrel's daughter from him.'

Gina wanted to shout and scream. She felt her fingers itching to hit something. Every pain she could feel, flashed through her body. Her joints ached; her shoulder and wrist were in agony because of what they'd done to her. 'And is that why Darrel agreed to drive the car, to help Bruce? He owed Bruce, didn't he? Rob would have been the middleman in organising everything. Was it time to cash in the favour? Did Darrel drive the car away from my house?'

'It was his duty, Inspector. Darrel owes a lot more than that to Bruce. As for my husband, he is a good man. You'll never understand duty, loyalty and respect like Rob does,' the woman spat.

Gina had worked her way up through the ranks and had fully understood duty, duty to keep the public safe; loyalty, she'd been loyal to the police, in her position and fully committed; and as for respect, the woman in front of her was spewing nothing but hatred. Full of hatred and blame aimed at other women who hadn't chosen to live their lives the only way she saw as the proper way.

That was all she needed. Her chair scraped on the floor and crashed onto its side as she stood. She left Jacob to finish off the interview. Briggs walked out of the viewing room. He'd watched everything that was being recorded. She almost stumbled. Her knees began to tremble and she held the wall as she steadied herself. 'I'm okay. We have them!' she said as she smiled. 'I can't believe that woman was in my house. Makes me sick!' It was over. She was safe to return home. Briggs held his arm out for Gina to grab and he walked her to her office.

'It's all over now and I should say, good job. The press have been on to us. In fact they're all outside the building, waiting for one of us to tell them something. I'll go out soon, just announce that we've made some arrests and that more details will follow shortly. How are you feeling?'

'Numb.' She stared at the wall behind him and struggled to contain her tears. It was now her time to recover, her time to work her way through the attacks and she needed a break. 'I know I only came back from a holiday a few days ago but I need a few days—'

'Granted. Say no more. You're in a bad way. I want you to keep your medical appointments, see the counsellor on Monday and put your feet up. Get some rest. I need you back here when you're fully refreshed.' As he left the room, a stream of tears fell down Gina's cheek as she realised how close to death she'd been. It was now over.

She wiped her face and headed towards the reception area and spotted James Phipps sitting on a plastic chair with his head in his hands. 'What are you doing here?'

'Them,' he pointed towards the car park at the journalists that were crowding the entrance. 'They're outside my flat, they've been to my workplace, they follow me everywhere, shouting across the street.'

'They'll be gone soon. We're just preparing a press release.'

'I'll wait here a while. At least I'm safe. Have you got him? Was it her husband?'

'I can't say anything as yet but I can tell you, you'll be able to go back home soon.'

'Home. What is home? The home I dreamed of had Melissa in it. She was going to be mine and now she's gone. There's nothing for me there. That's partly why I came back. I'm going back to London. I wanted to check in here just in case you'd all thought I'd gone on the run. I can't stay here, not after what happened.'

'You'll be called as a witness though. Make sure we have up-to-date details on record.'

'Too right I will. I want to see that bastard go down!'

She leaned in a little closer and noticed a swelling over Phipps's left eye. 'What happened? You been in a fight?'

'You could say that. Although he hit me too, Darrel, that is. I loved her you know. I was going to take her away, make her mine. I'd almost convinced her that leaving him for me would be the best move but she wanted to stay. Just a bit longer and I'd have had her. I just needed to work on her a bit longer, you know what I mean? She was a woman who needed a lot of convincing. I know her type well.'

Gina felt her cheeks burning up with his every word. To all the men in Melissa's life, she was nothing more than a prize to be fought over. He hadn't wanted to help her, he'd wanted to own her. 'Poor Melissa had no chance, not a hope in hell.' Before she started something she might regret, she left him sitting alone. It was too late for Melissa Sanderson now, too late for any help. Gina would have liked to have helped her but that was never to be. She pushed through the crowd of journalists, ignoring all their questions, flashes and boom poles. She was going to call a taxi, collect her cat and go home to have a hot bath.

EPILOGUE

Hannah had been called into work to cover a short notice absence. Gina knew she was last on the list of people to ask but all her daughter's friends had been unavailable and Hannah had been desperate. Gina would get to spend the morning on nanny and doggy day care duties. As she walked Rosie the spaniel over the fields at the back of her house, Gracie ran off into the meadow and pulled a daffodil from the earth.

She thought back to all that had happened over the past week. As per her promise to Briggs, she'd been to see the counsellor the previous day. She'd discussed the attacks and how they made her feel, but she hadn't mentioned Terry once. After confiding in Briggs about what she'd been through in the past, she felt a weight lift from within. She was finally sensing her past memories fading and she was ready to forgive herself for her involvement in his death. That was what she was working on privately, away from the counsellor's ears.

Birds sang in the trees and the April sunshine warmed her back. Gracie ran up to her. 'Nana. Flowers.' The little girl passed her a handful of long grass encasing the lonesome daffodil.

'Thank you, my lovely.'

The little girl chuckled and began running after Rosie. The black spaniel skipped along the field. Gina thought of Mia, the bruised toddler that had been taken from her abusive father. At least she was safe. Darrel's brother, Alan, had applied to be Mia's permanent carer along with his wife. The little girl had settled in nicely from what Devina in Children's Services had told her.

The rest of the group had been detained without bail until their hearings. There had been a mountain of evidence to catalogue and the gathering process was still going on. The Cleevesford Killer had been a group, two murderers and several accomplices, and the press had been permanently camping at the station since. They'd soon leave when another story made the Cleevesford Killer yesterday's news. This was by far the biggest case she'd ever worked on and in her mind the most complex.

She thought of Rebecca Greene. The woman had been broken knowing Ellie would never be going home. There would be a funeral and subsequent court cases. She hoped that one day Rebecca would heal and find happiness again but after speaking with her, Gina knew it would take a long time. She hoped that justice would be a good start and not just for Rebecca. Melissa's mother, Annabelle Hewson. She had been even more distraught once the truth had emerged. Gina had been to see her in person and had spent time speaking to the woman, explaining what had happened and telling Annabelle that Melissa wouldn't like to see her living the way she was. It had worked. Annabelle had arranged to visit her doctor and had poured her drink down the sink in front of Gina. She even contacted Alan Sanderson to arrange a visit between grandmother and granddaughter, taking the chance to bond.

Gina shook her wrist. Since the bandage had come off, she'd been feeling a little improvement every day. Her physical health was on the up, which is more than she could say about her mental health. Sleeping was still difficult. Her nightmares had become more violent but the counsellor assured her that it was because of the shock and trauma she'd been through. She knew the alarm system she'd had fitted was one of the best and she had a CCTV system that linked to her phone and laptop. Every hour of the day, she could see all round the front of her drive and all the way to the back of her garden.

Gracie chuckled and pointed as a light aircraft flew overhead, probably preparing to land at Long Marston Airfield just a few miles away. 'Plane,' she yelled as she continued to run, holding her hands in the air. She was chased by the little dog and they both weaved in and out of each other until Gracie tripped. The dog licked her hand and Gracie stroked the dog. Things were finally falling into place – for now.

A LETTER FROM CARLA

Dear Reader,

Thank you so much for reading *Her Final Hour*. I really hope you enjoyed the second instalment in the DI Gina Harte series, and I remain eternally grateful for the continued support of the crime reading community. If you did enjoy it, and want to keep up-to-date with all my latest releases, just sign up at the following link. Your email address will never be shared and you can unsubscribe at any time.

www.bookouture.com/carla-kovach

Whether you are a reader, a tweeter, a blogger, Facebooker or a reviewer, I thank you. Every little thing you do makes a big difference to my work getting out there for others to read and I remain grateful.

As a writer, this is where I hope you'll leave me a review. They not only help me, they help other readers.

Once again, thank you so much and I look forward to giving you DI Gina Harte, instalment three, very soon. In the meantime, I'm an avid social media user so please feel free to contact me on Twitter or through my Facebook page.

Thank you,
Carla Kovach

      CKovachAuthor
      CarlaKovachAuthor

ACKNOWLEDGEMENTS

First and foremost, I can't thank my editor, Helen Jenner, enough for all the work she's put into *Her Final Hour*. Her advice and suggestions make my stories shine and for that, I'm so grateful to her. I think, as a team, we work brilliantly together and I hope to remain working with her for a long time. Thank you, Helen.

Kim Nash and Noelle Holten, you both give so much when it comes to publicity and marketing. The hours you work are phenomenal and your enthusiasm is second to none. Thank you for all your support. At this point, I'd also like to give the other Bookouture authors a mention. Thank you for being so welcoming these past few months. The level of support that we give each other makes me want to shed a tear of happiness – I love being a part of the Bookouture team and you are like family.

Lynne Ward, Derek Coleman, Su Biela, Brooke Venables and Vanessa Morgan, you all give me so much useful feedback on my writing and ideas, and for that I'm grateful. I love that I have you all in my life and your input and support remains invaluable to me.

Insight into the real world of policing is what makes a story feel authentic. For this insight, I have to thank DS Bruce Irving. Our phone conversations and emails have all helped immensely to bring my fictional police department to life.

Last but not least, I have to thank Nigel Buckley, my husband. As always, he's there when I'm feeling the pressure, and he's also there when I'm on top of things and celebrating. Whatever the mood or situation, I always have in him my life and I'm grateful for that. Thank you Nigel for being you.

Printed in France by Amazon
Brétigny-sur-Orge, FR

11679352R00173